Books by Niki Livingston

Theia's Moons Series

The Chaos Awakened Saga

Novels

Novellas

Novelettes

TRANSFORMED CHAOS

The power of three healed the world, but transcendence requires a fourth

NIKI LIVINGSTON

Transformed Chaos

ISBN: 978-1-952537-09-7

Publisher: Unbound Wonders Press

Editor: Novel Nurse Editing

Cover Artist: Niki Ellis Designs

To connect: www.NikiLivingston.com

To Kylee.

The tornado raging within can take you places you never
even dreamed possible.

Embrace your passions.

My heart beats like the drumming of the ocean waves
against the earth.
An ebb and flow of dynamic courage and grit.
Isolated, but vast.
Poised with the unwavering vigor of a champion.
A sparkling blizzard that shatters iniquity.

CHAPTER ONE

Invasion

ALEX

Alex.

The voice calling my name was melodic in my thoughts, swirling around like a warm fog. It slowly dragged me away from the dark abyss that I wasn't sure I wanted to leave.

I drew in a deep, shaky breath. The ringing in my ears had quieted, but an endless drumming continued to beat ferociously against my skull. I pried open one eye, then the other. The sky had darkened. I blinked away the haze, but when I looked again, only a gray blur greeted me.

How long was I out?

I licked my lips and scrunched up my nose from the copper taste of blood. My hand shook as I raised it to my face and wiped my lips. The sticky, crimson residue smeared across my fingers. I squeezed my eyes shut, and using the back of my arm, I ran it across my nose, then used my fingers to clean away as much blood as I could without the help of a mirror. My breath stalled in my throat and I gasped several times, desperately aware of my depleted endurance and energy.

My eyes fluttered open again. I dropped my arm to my side and twisted my head, painfully aware of my bones creaking and my muscles screaming. Every movement was agonizing.

Kia Lynn was only a few feet away with most of her face pressed against the dirt. Slowly, I rolled and scooted to her using my elbows.

I pushed a lock of her hair out of her face and shook her shoulder. "Kia Lynn, wake up," I croaked, my throat instinctively clenching to ward off a cough.

I cleared my throat and tried to swallow the dry tickle, but it was relentless. I leaned away from my friend and coughed against the earth.

"Alex?" Kia Lynn whispered.

My teary gaze shot back at my friend, and I covered my mouth with the back of my hand. Her head hung as she pressed herself to her knees. She rubbed the palms of her hands against her eyes. After a few seconds, she opened them and blinked several times before focusing on my face.

"What happened?" she asked, shooting me a pained grimace. "My head feels like a boulder was dropped on it."

"Mine too," I muttered. My legs shook as I pulled my knees underneath me and sat up straight. "The last thing I remember was watching Rafael attack one of Lindon's people. Anything past that is like a black fog over my memories." I tapped my knuckles against my forehead. "Oh, and screaming. I remember that."

My gaze followed Kia Lynn's as she surveyed the others sprawled around us. Mom and Dad were several feet away. I crawled toward them as Mom lifted her head and looked around.

"Alex." Her raspy voice was barely a whisper. Her hands slid along the ground before she rose on her shaky legs.

Somehow, I climbed to my feet, and she curled me into her arms. Dad scooted to his knees and patted my leg. I glanced down, but his head hung low as he used his other hand to knead his temples. Mom's arms tightened around me, and I felt them quiver against my shoulders.

Mom whispered, "I think—"

Her arms fell away from me and she leaned to one side, losing the food in her stomach. It came out in waves and

Dad was up and by her side, holding her hair out of her face. I watched in silence, trying my best to wrap my mind around what had happened.

Whatever weapon Lindon and his people possessed, it could immobilize an entire village in seconds. Not to mention the aftereffects. Mom stayed hunched over with her hands pressed against her knees, while Dad rubbed her back. The sight of her trauma caused my anger to swell deep inside my core. Lindon had gone too far.

I turned to look at the rest of the people. Kia Lynn was helping Rafael to his feet. Blood was smeared across one side of his bald head. It looked like it was coming from his ear, but I could not tell from this distance.

My gaze drifted to Dax, who was leaning against the side of Dad's ship. His glazed eyes were struggling to focus on Malcolm and Covyn as they spoke to one another, but it did not look like he was bleeding, and neither were the other two.

Aly sat on the edge of the bay door with her head between her knees. Zoe Dawn's mum sat a few feet in front of Aly, staring at no one in particular, and she appeared to be unharmed. Many others were climbing to their feet or helping those who were worse off than themselves. Blood oozed from several of their ears, noses, and even eyes. It looked like a war zone.

Transformed Chaos

"Kia Lynn?" a man shouted frantically from the other side of the village center.

Kia Lynn whirled around, and when she caught sight of the older man, she flew by everyone else and only stopped when she was by his side.

"Papa, what's wrong?" she asked, touching his bloody cheek.

I limped toward them, but her father staggered to one side and then fell to his knees before I could reach them. Kia Lynn's weak muscles shook as she tried to keep him from falling forward completely. I hobbled faster. When I reached them, I curled my arm under his shoulder and helped her lift him to his feet.

"Let's take him into the ship," I said, pulling them in that direction.

The hysterical cries of the village people grew louder as Rafael pushed through the crowd and took Kia Lynn's father from us. I took the lead and made a path to Malcolm's ship, since Henry was in the medical station inside the other one. Mom and Dad were sitting just in the shadows of the bay door, watching the chaotic uproar with squinted eyes.

Dad rose when he noticed us and helped Rafael with the older man. We all followed them into the infirmary.

"Will he be okay?" Kia Lynn asked as they lifted her

father into the medical station.

"Yes, I believe so," Dad replied. He adjusted the pillow and then patted Kia Lynn's father on the arm. "Just close your eyes. When you wake, your healing should be complete."

Kia Lynn's father nodded. "The name is Gerome. You must be Alex's father."

"I am." Dad glanced at me, and a soft smile rose on his lips. "I most definitely am her father." He turned back toward Gerome. "We will take good care of you. I promise."

"I will stay with you, Papa," Kia Lynn said, stepping next to Dad.

Gerome smiled at his daughter, then closed his eyes as the glass shell enclosed him inside. Dad programmed the machine. His fingers shook, but he did not slow until the instructions were complete.

Mom's thumb trailed down my cheek. "Here. Better clean up, Alex."

I had forgotten about the blood. She handed me a wet towel from the nearby sink, and I covered my face with it.

"Jax. Adina. You need to come look at this," Eshah said.

I pulled the towel off my face after wiping the blood, dirt, and sweat. Eshah was standing in the doorway. Her expression was hard and almost unreadable, but I could see the slight hint of fear in her eyes.

"What is it?" Adina asked, following Eshah into the corridor.

"It would be better if I showed you." Eshah's gaze swept back to me, and she nodded for me to follow.

I squeezed Kia Lynn's arm, and she patted my hand. "Come back and fill me in when you can," she whispered, clearing her throat afterward.

"Of course," I said. I ran a fresh towel under the faucet and handed it to Kia Lynn. "There's a mirror over by the sink, if you want to clean up while you wait."

She took the towel and smiled, but I could see her thoughts were far from anything but her father.

I ducked out of the room and sprinted after Eshah. She was pointing at the sky, and as Rafael and my parents stepped outside, they tilted their heads to look up.

Mom grabbed Dad's arm and covered her mouth with her other hand. I skidded to a halt next to them and searched the sky. My heart dropped into my stomach.

A massive silver vessel spread out across the horizon, covering most of the visible sky from this valley. A shiver ran down my spine. I wrapped my arms over my chest, trying to ease the chill spreading across my body. It did not help.

"Who is it?" I asked, scanning the village center for Zoe Dawn. "Where is Zoe Dawn?"

Dad's gaze met mine, and I answered my question as a faint memory of her walking past me flitted through my mind. "They took her."

My blood ran cold. I don't know why it took me so long to realize the truth.

Mom reached over and smoothed back a lock of my hair. "We will find her."

Dax sprinted from the inside of the ship, and we all turned toward him. Right behind him was Aly and Covyn.

"Malcolm is speaking to his people in Zion. There are several small ships hovering not too far from them," Dax said breathlessly, focusing on Dad. He reached my side, and his hand instinctively found mine.

I squeezed it and shot him a tight smile. "Zoe Dawn is gone. Is there anyone else missing?"

Regret was written across Rafael's expression, and his gaze flitted briefly to meet mine before dropping toward the ground. "My aunt is tending to the wounded. I will find out what she knows, and if there is anyone not accounted for, I will let you know." He dragged his feet as he walked away.

I watched him leave. It looked like he held the weight of the world on his shoulders, and for the first time, I had empathy for him. These unknown northerners, who claimed to be Zoe Dawn's actual people, had infiltrated his village, and after finding out the Doyen had stolen her as a baby, he probably did not have a good footing on where he belonged in the world. I knew that shock well.

My gaze turned upward again. The silver vessel bothered me for many reasons, but most of all, I felt protective of this planet. Between preventing Mother Gaia from colliding with my previous dimension and stopping Tallisa from murdering Uncle Henry and leaving with the time machine, my weariness had overtaken my logic. But now, we had these unannounced visitors in the sky and a missing elemental—my friend. The psychological punches were not showing any signs of slowing down.

"Alex, are you listening?" Dad said, yanking me from my thoughts.

I focused on him, shuffling my feet in embarrassment. "Sorry." I shook my head. "I have a lot on my mind. What were you saying?"

If he was irritated with me, he hid it well. "I need to contact our ships in high orbit. We have to know what all nine of them are seeing up there and if there have been any calls from this vessel. While I do that, we need to set up a perimeter around the village. Can you help Eshah and Dax with that?"

9

I glanced at Dax, who was trying to suppress a proud smile. Dad had finally let him in to the circle of trust.

"Yes, I can help," I replied, even though I did not believe we could stop whoever was in those ships.

Dad shot past me with Mom in tow. Aly circled around the team and stood between Dax and me.

"What can I do?" she asked, looking at Eshah first, then turned to face me.

There was a look in her eyes that frazzled me. Fear, I thought. It wasn't surprising, but my gut told me it was more than that.

"Go with Alex," Eshah said. She waved at Covyn. "You can help me. Dax, gather as many people as you can to patrol the north end and arm them each with a weapon."

I holstered the firearm Eshah handed me, then tossed a bag of more weapons over my shoulder and set off for the village center in search of those who could help. Aly trotted after me.

"How do you want to do this?" Her voice trembled with   emotion.

I could feel her eyes on me, but my agitation kept my focus on the task at hand. "What's stopping them from flying right into the village? This will not help, but if it makes my parents happy, I will do as they ask."

She grabbed my arm and pulled me to a stop. "You and Kia Lynn can protect the village on your own. There is no need to involve these people."

"What do you want me to do?" I shrugged away her hold on me, and her arm fell to her side. "Throw water at the ship? We don't even know who it is up there, and that vessel is too big for me to fight alone."

I pressed my fist against my throbbing temple. My body still ached, and what I really wanted to do was snuggle into my bed and forget all about the troubles of the world. Instead, I continued toward the village center, hoping I would find some others who were willing to protect their people.

"Alex, I have seen a ship like this one before." Aly was beside me again. Her fingers held on tightly to my forearm. "Please listen."

My heart jumped into my throat. I whirled around, tearing her hold away, and threw up my arms. "Who are they, Aly? If you know so much, why are you here with me and not with Malcolm or my dad?"

"Because I think they have something to do with Tallisa," Aly whispered, her eyes darting back and forth, then focusing on my startled expression. "Right before Tallisa disappeared, maybe a day or two before the attack on this village, I saw a ship similar to this one leave our atmosphere."

"And this is when you decide to speak about it?" My question came out with a snarl. I was angry, but not with her.

"It vanished so fast, I thought I had imagined it." Aly's expression was growing more fearful by the second. "I was returning from a solo journey, so I did not know if I had hallucinated it or not, but when I neared the village, I heard a conversation between Tallisa and Tatum. They were arguing about someone else, and Tatum kept pointing at the sky. They have to be connected."

"We need to tell my dad," I replied. The realization that whoever was up in that ship might be helping Tallisa encircled me like a suffocating vice. I struggled to inhale a full breath. "What else—"

A blood-curdling scream filled the air. Every muscle in my body tensed as I scanned the area for the source of the noise. It abruptly cut off. Zoe Dawn's mum stepped out of their infirmary and looked around, using her blood-stained hands to push away the strands of hair covering her eyes. Her gaze fell on Aly and she hurried toward us.

A swarm of people scrambled frantically from the trees on the southern end of the village. A man was holding a woman in his arms, racing toward the infirmary.

"What happened?" I asked when one woman tore past

us.

"They are coming!" she yelled, not looking back at us.

I turned back as the frantic crowd sprinted past us and continued after the woman. Zoe Dawn's mum bolted toward Dad's ship.

She skidded to a halt, then whirled around and stared pointedly at me. "Where are your parents?"

"Inside the ship," I said, taking a shaky step toward her. My frazzled thoughts made it difficult to decide on the next best move.

Her gaze shifted to Aly. "You warned me. I am sorry I did not listen, sister." She turned back to look at me. "Please take me to your parents."

She held out her hand for mine, and as I reached for it, she lurched forward with a look of surprise etched in her features. Her eyes widened, and without a sound, she tumbled face first into the ground. A bright red circle formed between her shoulder blades, covering the charred remains of her shirt and skin.

The world slowed around me. I collapsed to the dirt and knelt beside her, and with Aly's help I turned her to her side. Her eyes had softened, but the life I had seen just moments before was gone. Aly shrieked, pulling her friend into her lap and cradling her close.

"No!" Aly cried as she buried her face in her friend's

dark hair.

I felt their eyes on me before I saw them. My knees scraped against small pebbles as I turned to look at the group of anaman marching out of the safety of the trees. I slowly rose, rubbing my fingers against my thumbs, willing the water to rise and encircle them. As streams of water bubbled into the air, the anaman attacker's leader focused on me, and her gaze locked onto my hands. She lifted her arm and pointed her weapon at my head.

"Water sorceress, do not force me to take your life as well," she hissed between clenched teeth.

CHAPTER TWO
Abduction

KIA LYNN

Screams tore through the corridor and brought me to my feet. These cries for help were much closer than the last one and continued to grow nearer.

I glanced at Papa and then back at the bright hallway. Terror had invaded my mind, and I was struggling to take in a full breath. I wanted to stay with Papa, but if my people needed me, I had to go to them. As I gasped out my exhale and decided to venture outside, Malcolm stormed past the door. His large fingers curled around the doorframe, and he popped his head inside the room.

"Stay here, Kia Lynn." His voice shook, and an unmistakable look of fear was etched in his expression.

I stepped toward him. "What if—"

"Just stay here," he replied, cutting me off. "Please."

He did not wait for me to reply, and his thundering

footfalls echoed toward the exit. I hurried to the doorway and looked after him. He bolted around the corner and disappeared. I turned to face Papa. Jax had said his healing would take hours, which from what Alex had explained about time, could mean the rest of the day. If something bad was happening outside, would he be safe in here? By not helping, would I be sending my people to their graves?

I ran my fingers down the glass shell. "Papa, what should I do?"

I stared at his sleeping face, memorizing the fine lines and wrinkles that had set into his expression from many seasons of working under the sun. He had been the one who held me up and kept me safe throughout the past nine full seasons. I had to protect him at all costs.

My legs shook slightly when I turned to face the door. Was I ready for another battle?

"No!" Alex's screams caused every muscle in my body to tense.

My hands shook in fear, but somehow I forced myself through the doorway. I jogged to the end of the corridor. As I stepped toward the exit, someone snickered behind me.

A woman's voice brought me to a dead stop. "Well, well, well. Lucky me. I did not think you would be so easy to find."

Transformed Chaos

My pulse quickened, and I slowly turned to face her. An anaman woman, much taller than Alex, stood just inside the shadows. Her gray skin glistened with sweat, and her anaman markings sparkled a nearly translucent white. Her clothing was dark, nearly black, embroidered with silver stitches around her neck and a two-headed snake-like animal on her chest.

She stepped fully into the light, and her hopeful expression melted into disappointment. "Who are you?" she asked, taking another step closer and raising her weapon at my chest.

I snapped my fingers, and a burst of wind knocked the woman to the side. Her weapon clattered to the floor, and each of her long limbs flailed before she hit the metal ground. I bolted through the bay door but came to a screeching halt when I was greeted by another weapon pointed at my head.

"Is this her?" the anaman male asked, looking over my shoulder.

"No," said the voice of the anaman woman who had greeted me in the ship.

Damn, she had recovered quickly. I threw a glance back at her. She was smoothing her short black hair as she stalked toward me. The left side of her head was shaved, and her locks of hair on her right side barely grazed her jawline. Everything about her screamed vicious warrior, from her rippling muscles in her shoulders and arms, to the sharp spikes protruding from the bottoms of her boots.

Her bright-green eyes seemed to sear me with her intense focus. They flickered dark, and the green disappeared, but when I blinked, the color had returned. I pressed my lips together. My pounding headache was not helping my mind see clearly.

"But they must be related," she said, standing next to me and wrapping her long fingers around my arm. "We will take her with and use her to coax that demon from the hole she is hiding in." Her gaze drifted sideways to me. "Pull that stunt again, and my kindness will vanish."

I swore my heart was going to explode from my chest. Who were these people, and why were they after Mama?

Alex stood not too far away, but she had her hands pinned behind her head, and another anaman held his weapon to her back. They had covered her fingers with iron gloves, which must be preventing her from connecting with her elemental powers. They knew enough about us to be prepared.

Adina was kneeling on the mossy ground not too far from Alex. Blood dripped down her cheek from somewhere hidden beneath her hair. Her eyelids fluttered and never fully opened, and her gaze did not focus on anything in particular. I could not see Jax or Malcolm. That was when I noticed Aly leaning against an old tree stump with a dark-haired woman cradled in her lap. I recognized those curls.

"Aly!" I screamed. I leapt forward, but the anaman held me back. "Who is that, Aly? Who are you holding?" I pulled again, but she only tightened her grip. "Tell me!"

Aly's tear-stained cheeks lifted, and all she could do was nod. My knees buckled underneath me, but I did not fall to the ground. The anaman woman held me up as I shrieked at the top of my lungs.

"No!" I screamed again. "Not her. Not Attica!" I set my feet firmly on the ground and straightened. My angry gaze shot back to the anaman woman. "I will kill you. Zoe Dawn will destroy you. Do you hear me?"

She yanked me closer to her. "Come and get me, peasant," she hissed between clenched teeth. "You have no one to blame but Tallisa."

My racing pulse seemed to stop entirely, and my breath came out short. "What?" I barely whispered the word. "What did you say?"

"Who is she to you?" the anaman woman asked. The edges of her lips twitched in amusement. "Your sister? Aunt?" She slapped her forehead. "I've got it. Your mother. That devil spawned a child." Her abrupt laugh came out like a lion's roar.

I pulled back, but she held me close.

"Did you hear that?" The anaman woman shoved me in the middle of her people. "Our devil procreated. Isn't this my lucky day? Take her to the ship with the other one. I am a big fan of family reunions."

A few snickered, but most glared at me. The nearest anaman male wrenched me forward, then jabbed me in the back with his weapon.

"Freydis, do you want them together or apart?" he asked the anaman woman.

She twirled a small dagger in her hand, examining me like I was an item to trade. "Keep them separate." The left side of her mouth twitched up in a sly smirk. "For now."

"Kia Lynn!" Alex cried.

I could not turn my head to look at her. The anaman man shoved me, and I nearly tripped over my own feet. I steadied myself and continued walking, eyeing the village people hiding among the trees and behind their homes as he marched me down the pathway.

"I will find you and my dad," Alex screamed.

Jax was their other prisoner. That would explain his absence. Alex was the bravest person I knew, and I had no doubt she would move mountains to free me and her father from her own people.

Transformed Chaos

Where neared the end of the path, several more anaman stood in silent formation near the tree's canopy. There was no way to their ship.

"Ret, we have her daughter," my captor said as he pressed his finger against the inside of his left wrist. "Initiate the tractor beam."

"Copy that, Wolf," a male voice responded.

A woman's voice flitted by my ear like the wind had brought it to me. *You do not live in anyone's shadows.*

I glanced every which way, but it was only me and the group of anaman warriors.

A bright light shot out of their ship, illuminating the ground where the anamans waited. Wolf hauled me toward it. His biceps pressed against the dark fabric, and his arms were probably bigger than my thighs. I knew fighting him would be useless, but I dug in my heels anyway. I was sick and tired of being forced to do something I did not want to do.

He whirled around to face me. "Don't test my patience, tiny human."

He leaned in close as if to show me how serious he really was. My heart leapt into my throat, but then I noticed he was not angry. I did not see the hatred in his expression that his companion had worn like a badge. His dark brown eyes were speckled with tiny flakes of green, and despite his massive body height and build, I suddenly felt comfortable with him. I stopped resisting and nodded.

"Thank you," he whispered before turning around and pulling me forward once again. We stepped into the light, and he wrapped his arms around me. "You may want to hold on to me."

My hands had barely found his waist when I felt a tug, and the ground dropped away. My heart fell to my stomach. We flew upward so quickly, I only caught a glimpse of my village I was leaving behind. I was not ready to be taken away again. Papa needed me. Rafael and I were just figuring out where we stood with one another. And now that Attica was dead, who would watch out for him?

A brightly lit room surrounded me, and I held my arm above my eyes to shield them. Wolf's arms fell to his side. Another anaman male stood waiting near the doorway.

"Where is Tallisa?" he asked, eyeing me with freezing disdain.

"She was not there, Ret," Wolf replied. He nodded sideways at me. "This is her daughter. Between Jax and her, Tallisa will not hide for long."

"My mother won't risk her life for me or my uncle," I muttered, remembering the last moment I saw Mama. She had chosen her own survival over mine. She ran away like a coward, leaving me to pick up the pieces of her onslaught.

Wolf and Ret stared at me with raised brows.

"Tallisa is as crooked as they come, but no anaman mother would ever abandon their child," Wolf said, shaking his head and throwing me a tight smile as if I had told him a joke.

I shrugged my shoulders. "You will be disappointed." My legs shook when I stepped down from the metal platform. "She is only half anaman, and there are many human mothers who have no heart." I glanced back at Wolf. "My mother is one of those."

Wolf's eyes narrowed, but he said nothing as we followed Ret into the corridor.

"She will stay on level eighteen, under the supervision of Trinity. No need to put her in the prison cell we have saved for Tallisa," Ret instructed, handing Wolf a small bag. "They will still want to interrogate and tag her. Everything should be in there for Trinity to complete that task."

Wolf took the bag. It looked like a tiny satchel next to his giant build, but he shouldered the strap and turned to look at me. "After you," he said, holding his arm out.

I rolled my eyes but took the steps down the corridor, anyway. It led to a window. I glanced at Wolf, unsure where he wanted me to go next. He pressed his hand against the wall next to the window, and it lit up like the ones on Alex's ship. Then it slid open and Wolf led me inside. Glass surrounded us.

"Level eighteen," he said as the glass slid back into place.

Through the other window a swarm of anamans walked below us, several stories down. It almost looked like the Black Mountain Festival, with shops and food booths for as far as I could see. In the middle of all of it stood dozens of trees and brush, with blossoms and colors of leaves I had never seen before.

Wolf's hand rested on my shoulder. "We have reached our floor."

"Why are so many of you here?" I asked, pressing my forehead against the glass and staring at the thousands of anamans. Their gray skin was dull, but some had purple-and-blue hues speckled across their features, while others possessed the white, blue, or even maroon swirls etched in their flesh. They were beautiful.

I heard Wolf draw in a long breath, then exhale loudly. "Our planet died. There are so many of us here because we are searching for a new home."

My heart burst inside my chest. Despite my circumstances, I still felt compassion toward these people.

Transformed Chaos

They were in it together. I turned to face Wolf. "And because of my mother, you are stopping here? Just for her?"

"That's a long story," he replied, grabbing my arm and hauling me into another corridor. "One I don't believe her daughter should hear. Just know your mother is a coward."

A weight settled over my heart. "Tell me something I don't know."

Wolf did not reply, but when I glanced back at him, he wore a pained expression that seemed to match the sorrow I felt inside. Mama's cruel actions had reached far and wide, which only hurt me more.

At the end of the hallway, a female anaman sat inside a glass-enclosed room. Her gray skin tone was darker than Wolf's, and the white swirls embroidering her flesh were much brighter than Alex's. A delighted smile blossomed across her face when she saw Wolf.

"Wolf! It is so good to see you," she said, rising from her chair and circling a table to exit the room. Her hand ran down his arm. "Did Freydis find her?" That was when she noticed me behind Wolf. Her smile melted into a frown. "Why hasn't she aged at all? Is this really her?"

"No, this is not her." Wolf jerked me in front of him and patted me on the shoulders. "This is her daughter. She will stay in your care for now. Orders from Ret."

"And does this daughter have a name?" the woman asked, eyeing me with a guarded look.

"Kia Lynn is my name," I replied, holding out my fist in greeting.

The woman stepped back. Her gaze fell to my feet, then swept back up to my head. "What does Ret want her to do?" She ignored my fist and instead glared at Wolf. "Why is she my responsibility?"

"We all know you are the best at accessing the past, Trinity," Wolf replied as he held up his hands in mock surrender. "I am just the messenger, but with this mission being Freydis's top priority, we will need Kia Lynn to help expose the others so we can find her mother. And you are the woman to make it happen."

I watched the vague exchange with growing irritation. Trinity's eyes narrowed more, but this time the look was directed at me. I returned her glare with one of my own.

"What are you two blathering about?" I asked, blurting the question before I could think it through. "My mother will not surrender in order to save my life, so get that through your thick heads now."

Trinity's expression brightened, and then she laughed. Her gaze shot to Wolf. "She's got that witch's sass. Too bad we aren't interested in saving her life either."

Wolf shoved me forward. "She's your problem now.

Prepare her for your interrogation, and no matter what it takes, dig those secrets out of her."

Terror clawed through my chest as I looked at Wolf, then back at Trinity. "She will not come for me. Don't you understand? You are wasting your time holding me prisoner. She will gladly let me die in her place."

"Ending her blood line would not be the worst thing that could happen." Trinity grabbed my arm and waved for Wolf to follow us. "Let's start right away. You will need to keep her in line until I have her subdued." She tapped my head. "We must find out what is hidden inside that skull of yours. If you really are that demon's child, then the devilry could have been passed along to you. And this time, we will not let her slip on by. I want to go home."

I gulped back my rising panic and wiped my one free, sweaty palm down the side of my trousers as she dragged me down the corridor. A door opened at the end, revealing a white room with a chair situated in the middle.

"Sit down," Trinity ordered.

She pointed at the chair as she pulled me inside the room. Wolf filed in behind us.

The door shut, and I glanced back at it in desperation, but she nudged me forward until I was standing next to the reclined seat. I turned and sank onto it, lying back against the cushion. She strapped my wrists in metal cuffs and snapped each of them shut, then lifted something cold to the sides of my head. It clasped on tight and I winced from the pressure.

"Now, child. Let's open you up and take a look around."

CHAPTER THREE
North Home

ZOE DAWN

"We are in the clear. They did not notice our ship," a voice echoed overhead.

My gaze shot up to the ceiling. Lindon reached over and patted me on the hand. I yanked it away and glared at him.

"The scary man in the ceiling won't hurt you. Promise."

I did not miss the sarcastic tone laced in his words.

"Shut it, keefie," I hissed back at him. I folded my arms over my chest. "Who was in that ship?" My shoulders and neck were tight with frustration and fear. Did I really abandon my family?

Lindon shot me a raised-brow look. "They are the anaman, but not the ones who reside on Earth."

"How do you know?" I twisted in my seat to see him

better by pulling my right knee onto the cushion and throwing my left leg over my right ankle.

He undid his restraints and rose from his chair. "I have traveled this entire planet hundreds of times. Those ships have not been seen for many years. They left nearly a decade ago. Their return is significant, but they will not be moving on with the elite." A smirk rose on his lips and he glanced my way as if I should understand his meaning.

We were seated in a smaller room away from the rest of his people. It was a quiet corner, more luxurious than what was on the other side of the door. On one end, there was a machine that delivered food and drinks, and the other had a large monitor like the ones on Malcolm's ship. Lindon stepped up to the empty wall in front of us and pressed his fingers against it. The wall disintegrated in front of my eyes, just in time to watch the black mountains disappear beyond the horizon.

"We will be there soon." He strolled over to the food contraption. "Would you like a quick bite to eat or a drink to calm your nerves?"

I undid my restraints and scooted forward in my chair. "My nerves are fine."

"Tell that to your clenched jaw and overly tense shoulders," he replied before turning away from me.

"You said the elementals are a myth," I said. His words

in my village came back to me, ringing like a warning bell in my head. "If they are just stories, why can I do this?"

I snapped my fingers, and a flame danced across the edges. He glanced over his shoulder and then returned to examining the options in front of him. My fire was unimpressive to him.

"I lied," he said, and tapped the glass. Seconds later, a silver cylindrical container slid out of the wall. He grabbed it and turned back to face me. "Are you sure you do not want a drink?"

"You lied?" My pulse drummed against my ribs. I smothered my tiny inferno with my other hand. Why was he being so cryptic?

He twisted off the top of his drink container and took a long drink. When his eyes met mine again, they were watering slightly. He dabbed at his lips and eyes with a white cloth he'd pulled from his pocket.

"Zoe Dawn, the elementals are all very much alive, and yes, you are one of them. Although, there is one who remains asleep and I am very curious about why that is." He sank back in his chair and stared out the window, his mind seeming miles away.

"Who's asleep?" I asked, squinting at his blank face.

He did not move, and his eyes glazed over. I scooted forward in my chair. Was he lost in a trance?

"Lindon." I waved my arms. "What did you mean when you said, there is one who remains asleep?"

His fingers tapped his armrest as if life had been breathed back into them. He blinked, then focused on the drink in his hand as he shook his head. "You are no more important just because you healed Mother Gaia." He peered over at me from the corner of his eyes.

"I never said I was," I grumbled, clenching my fists. Everything about him was odd, including how he communicated. "Who is still asleep? And why did you lie about the elementals?"

"Because those people do not need to know about the elementals. They do not have the right to access such a powerful ability. Fire is to be respected. Honored. They only want to exploit you." He took another sip of his drink, then turned to look at me. His pale-blue eyes swam with sadness. "It was my job to protect you, and I failed."

How nauseating. "It is my job to protect myself." I sprang from my chair and stood over him. He tilted his head to stare at me, unfazed by my quick movement. His calm demeanor told me he was not afraid of my wrath. "Those people are my family. More so than you will ever be. Kia Lynn connects with air, and Alex summons the floods of water. They were not exploiting me. Mother Gaia connects us. We are bond for life, and there is nothing you can do to break that."

He did not blink, and his stare did not falter from my eyes. "I do not have to break it. You will. It will not really matter since the connection is not complete."

His confidence was shattering my resolve. What did he know that I did not? I shook my head and turned away from him to rest my forehead against the glass that separated us from the outside. I was here to find out who I really was and how to stop the anaman fleet from destroying everything and everyone I knew and loved. Once I had my answers, nothing would stop me from returning.

The ship slowed. Not too far ahead, the land seemed to shift. I blinked to clear away the obvious haze, but the ground continued to move. It pulled away in a circular motion, revealing a dark hole. We hovered above it and then slowly lowered into it. I stepped back as the darkness folded over us.

"Where are we?" I asked, lowering to my seat and gripping the armrest. Sweat beaded on my forehead, and I swiped it away before looking at Lindon.

He smiled. "Home." He gulped down the last of his drink and rose gracefully to his feet. "Your parents will be waiting. Come." His long fingers reached for my hand.

I intertwined my fingers together and circled around

him. "Show me the way."

He traced over his kenaz rune, which remained exposed after showing it to me in my village. His eyes never left mine. "We will be coupled, Zoe Dawn. They promised you to me, and I will not allow your defiance, as my family expects an heir who possesses the flame. The Mother will show you the way."

My skin crawled from his possessive meaning. "Please, lead me to my parents." Ignoring him seemed like the only option at this point.

The door slid open, and I followed him into the corridor. When we reached the bay door, several others were filing out as well. The hole in the ground was filled with several other ships, some larger than the one we had been in, and others smaller. Once my eyes adjusted to the obscure lighting, I noticed several large tunnels leading away from this area.

This time, Lindon did not ask. He took my arm and clenched it, leading me through the throngs of people and toward a tunnel lit with a bright-blue light.

"Our people are the Sapphire Spirit Tribe, and our families rank above most others. You will learn quickly that we do not associate with those who are less than us." He halted and grabbed both of my arms. His fiery breath on my cheek was almost too much for me to handle. "We are betrothed because we are the elite. Your place in this world has been chosen by the Theian's themselves and you will be wise to listen to their guidance. Do not embarrass yourself."

I scrunched up my nose and yanked at my arms. He held me tighter.

"Do you understand me, Zoe Dawn?"

"I will burn you on this spot if you do not unhand me," I hissed in his ear. The temptation to start a blazing inferno pressed against my mind.

His arms fell to his sides, and he straightened. "We will need to work on your manners."

"Ahh!" I screamed in his face. "Just stay away from me." I rubbed the spots on my arms where he had squeezed. "Touch me again, and my heat will devour you whole."

His pale eyes stared at me, and I realized we were alone. The silence surrounded us in every direction. I glanced back at the ship. The area was now empty. Where had everyone gone? As I was turning back toward Lindon, a blonde girl crouched next to one of the smaller ships caught my eye. I squinted. She looked familiar. But before I could get a better look, he was dragging me into the blue-lighted tunnel.

I snapped my fingers, and Lindon's hand burst into

flames. He shrieked and flailed his arms, his confident expression melting into horror. I watched quietly as he bounced around on his feet, smacking the flames with his other hand until the fire was finally out.

"What did you do?" he screamed at me, staring at his reddening fingers. They were already swelling from the heat.

"I warned you, and you chose to not listen." I stomped past him, simmering with indignation. "At least I did not set your entire body on fire. You should thank me for that."

The tunnel widened as I walked farther, and up ahead, I noticed several larger, rounded doorways. Lindon passed by me, his long legs taking him one step for every three of mine. He did not bother to pay me any attention as he hurried to the end of the tunnel and hurried through the third doorway toward the left. I followed him and stopped on the other side of the threshold.

There was a lift at the end of another corridor. Lindon stood waiting for me with the doors open.

"Did you think we lived underground?" he asked when he saw my confused expression. "Our city is vast, spreading from the top of the hills above us to several hundred feet below. Then five times as wide. It was built centuries ago by our Theian ancestors and has protected us through all the catastrophes, both natural and man-made."

I needed to see it and did not think twice as I jogged into the lift.

"Level forty-four," Lindon said, cradling his reddened hand against his chest. The lift moved upward.

When the doors opened again, a lavish garden greeted me. Trees lined a stone walkway with an array of blossoms adorning the edges. As I stepped out of the lift, I looked up expecting to see the blue sky, but a white domed ceiling was above.

"How do these grow in here without the sun?" I asked, tracing my finger over a white rose petal.

Lindon pressed a button near the lift, and the ceiling became translucent, revealing a darkening sky. "It also opens, but we are careful to never reveal our location by doing it often. From the other side, it appears like a hillside of dirt and brush."

I stared in amazement. And these were my people, the ones who should have raised me. When Lindon nudged me forward, I did not even mind. I let him lead me through the vegetation toward another doorway. The door slid open when we approached, and an older man with a long gray beard stood on the other side.

His gaze traveled from my toes back to my face. "Is

this she?" He combed his beard with his fingers, watching me intensely with his pale-blue eyes. They were identical to Lindon's.

"Yes, this is Zoe Dawn. My betrothed mate," Lindon replied.

My infuriated gaze shot to him, and he backed away a few feet. I did not miss the change in his burnt hand. It already appeared to be healed, and any pain he had shown in his expression had disappeared.

"Do not mind my son's romantic gestures," the bearded man in the doorway said, picking up on my seething anger.

I returned my attention to him.

"You *were* promised to one another, but we are painfully aware that you were not raised with our beliefs and values. He has been told this is a delicate situation, and we will all understand if you need time." The older man held out his hand to me. "Come inside. Your family is eager to see you after all these years."

If that were so, why weren't they the ones greeting me at the door? I wanted to ask it out loud, but I held my tongue and grasped his hand. He led me inside a large entryway. Dark wood beams rose high above me, revealing a rounded staircase that continued farther than I could see from my viewpoint. The floor was dark as well, and it looked like the wood grain of the trees, but there was something off about it. Too shiny.

Lindon circled around us. His father and I followed him through the entryway and into an adjoining room filled with cushioned seating. A woman, much younger than Mum, rose gracefully from one of the chairs. Her mink-brown eyes matched mine, and I recognized many of my features in hers. My mother. It really was her. Her dark hair hung past her shoulders in loose spirals and shone like the Goddess herself had blessed it.

"Zoe Dawn, this woman would have been your mother if those greedy Doyen had not stolen you." Lindon's father held out his arm toward the woman. "Her name is Jamila."

Jamila stood quietly with a small smile on her lips. Her gentle expression seemed familiar, tugging at my mind like a long-lost memory I could not fully grasp. I studied her facial structure and the soft curve of her mouth. There was a comfort in seeing her, and for the first time I knew I was in the presence of my blood family.

I waited for her to speak, but she only stared back in reply. Just when I was about to speak up, another older man sauntered into the room with a wide grin plastered across his face. Gray hairs speckled the brown of his short beard and the top of his head. His golden irises met mine.

"Welcome, daughter," he boasted, walking past Jamila

and stopping in front of me.

My heart skipped a beat. His voice—it was a sound I had heard before. I squeezed my hands into fists, blinking back the dreams that had haunted my mind for as long as I could remember. I had once loved these two people.

The man reached for one of my hands and unraveled my fist in a familiar fashion. "You have changed little. Always one ready for a fight." His warm smile soothed my worries. "We have been waiting many years to see your face again. You must be exhausted from your travels." He waved me forward. "Please come. Sit down. We will have our cook prepare you anything you would like to eat."

I raised my brow at him as I sank onto a nearby chair, then glanced at Jamila, who was sitting again. She had not made a sound.

"You may call me Enoch or Father, whichever makes you comfortable," Enoch said as he sat on the edge of the chair next to me. He noticed me staring at Jamila. "Do not mind your mother. She is a woman of few words. This is a moment she has dreamed about for nineteen years."

"If she has dreamed about it, why does she not speak to me?" I asked, turning my attention to Enoch.

"Because her mate is loud enough for both of them," a man yelled from the next room.

Enoch's smile faltered for a fraction of a second, then

he burst into laughter. "Do not mind Koleton. He is not familiar with the Earthlings' way."

"What do you mean?" I drummed my fingers against my leg as my gaze swept across the four faces in the room with me. Their overly cheerful expressions made me uneasy.

A redheaded man poked his head through the large, rounded doorway, which led to what looked like an eating hall. Just slightly smaller.

"He means that I am not from this little planet of yours." Koleton winked at her, before ducking back out of sight.

I couldn't help but smile. I liked him. Something about the twinkle in his eyes drew me to him.

Then another person stepped into view from the eating hall, and a deep rage crashed over me, blinding me from all rational thought. I leapt to my feet, and without thinking, threw a ball of fire at Nikita's face.

Jamila moved so fast, I thought I was mistaken, until she reached for my fireball and held it in her hand as if it were a play ball. Her catlike reflexes caught me off guard as I stared wide-eyed at her. She turned to look at me and hurled the inferno back my way.

CHAPTER FOUR
The Painting

ALEX

Kia Lynn was gone. Just like they had done with Dad. I stared hopelessly at the massive vessel, unable to connect with my elemental powers because of the iron gloves. The light had beamed from the ship and pulled Kia Lynn inside. The same happened to me the first time Tallisa had brought me to my parents' ship. It was the day my life had completely changed.

I wiggled against the gloves and felt it slipping off my fingers. The female anaman named Freydis glanced my way, lifted her weapon, and pressed the trigger. The prick in my chest was followed by every muscle tensing so severely, my teeth ground against one another. An electrical current zapped through my nervous system. I collapsed to the ground, writhing from the pain that their weapon continued to deliver to every inch of my body.

Transformed Chaos

"She's not only a water sorceress. I swear she is the same girl in that painting." The woman's voice was close, but I only noticed blurred figures move past me. "Those northerners know something about her. Didn't the senators mention her ability to live forever?"

"She is not our concern," Freydis said abruptly. "We need to return home before it's too late."

"But the painting was dated over a century—"

"Are you questioning me?" Freydis said more than asked, with a slight snarl in her tone.

"No, Freydis," the woman replied, shuffling farther away from me. "I apologize for my disrespect."

I heard her footsteps recede as the two walked away from me. Everything hurt. The electrical current had dissipated, but I could not move, and it felt like someone had dropped a boulder on top of my chest. I wanted to cry out in pain, but my tongue stuck to the roof of my mouth, and my lips were numb.

They knew me from a painting. Was it possible I just looked like someone from the past, besides myself? It made little sense. I cannot remember a time when someone painted me. Why would they? I was a nobody, and the thought of living forever on this insane planet was the last thing I wanted.

The world grew quiet. I blinked several times, trying to

gain back some of my eyesight. My senses told me they we were alone, once again. I twisted my neck an inch but stopped when the strain on my muscles sent shock waves of agonizing pain down my spine.

"Alex," Uncle Henry whispered. His shadow loomed above me. "Alex, are you okay?" He pressed his fingers against my neck to check my pulse. "What happened out here?"

"Hen-hen," I said, stumbling over his name. My tongue was dry as a bone and still glued to the roof of my mouth.

"I'm right here," he replied, smoothing my hair out of my face. "Aly, what happened? You're the only one who isn't wounded."

I heard some rustling, but Aly didn't reply.

"Aly, I am so sorry." Uncle Henry's shadow left my view.

I tried to roll to my side. The pain was subsiding, but my muscles refused to cooperate. I threw my right arm over to my left side and somehow made it halfway onto my side. My eyes adjusted to the world around me, and finally Uncle Henry came into focus. He was kneeling over Attica.

He rose to his feet and lifted Attica into his arms. "I will place her in your infirmary for now. We need to help the wounded."

Transformed Chaos

Aly had remained unmoving while the rest of us lay in pain on the ground. A fury beat against my chest, pushing me to a seated position. I hung my head when a wave of pain rushed down to my fingertips. My mouth finally watered enough for my lips and tongue to move again, and I swallowed to wet my throat. Drawing in a long breath, I looked at Aly, who stared back with icy disdain.

"You could have stopped them," she snapped before punching the ground with her fist. She didn't flinch from the impact, but her eyes narrowed even more. Her anger matched mine. She shifted to her hands and knees, and her long hair hung in her face. Rising to her feet, she flipped her black locks over her shoulders and then she glared even harder. "Attica's death is on you. If you had struck them with an ice storm before they arrived, this would have never happened."

"St-stop placing the wor-rld's problems on my daughter," Mom muttered from a few feet away from me.

I scooted over to her, ignoring Aly. "Mom, are you okay?"

"I think so." Her hands trembled when she pushed herself into a seated position. "They're still here." She squinted at the sky.

A surge of energy wrapped itself around me. *Your power comes from within. Your will to produce the magic is all that is required,* Mother Gaia said in my head.

My mind raced, and I stared at my now-exposed fingers. Could I have stopped them from the beginning with just my thoughts? If these people knew so much about me, wouldn't they know if I could do it without skin-on-skin contact?

Stop doubting yourself. Another female voice floated around in my head.

I shot a glance behind me. The voice was not Mother Gaia, but I was sure it came from inside me. There was no one else around who the voice belonged to. I turned back to face the anaman ship. Who was she?

I rose to my feet with a shake of my head. My legs shook from sheer exhaustion, and the shocking sensation still reverberated in my muscles, but I ignored the weakness and focused on the fluid flowing in the ground below me. I inhaled a long breath, and when I released it, I drew water from the ground. It hung in the air like the bubbles I had blown as a child. My lips twitched from the happy memory, then I refocused and used only my mind to gather it above us.

I turned my attention to the ship. It was crawling away. I only had seconds to stop them. Pressing the liquid farther into the sky, I directed it at the ship and flung it with every ounce of my inner strength. It shot forward as if it were a raging river and struck the belly, then scattered like rain back to the ground.

Tears sprang to my eyes. It didn't even put a dent in the ship. All my hopes disintegrated with the water as I watched the vessel holding my sister and dad disappear.

"You are not strong enough anyway," Aly said with a trace of malice in her tone. "Why did Mother Gaia ever pick you?"

"Shut up, Aly," Mom snapped.

"You—"

"Alex! Adina!" Eshah yelled.

I turned and squinted at my family friend. She and Dax were holding Rafael up as they stumbled toward us, with Covyn trailing not too far behind. One side of Rafael's body appeared to be nearly useless, as Dax had him propped up almost entirely on that side. I wiped away my tears and raced by Mom and Aly.

"What happened?" I asked when I slid up to them. I lifted Rafael's chin with the tip of my fingers and made him look me in the eye.

"We found him like this," Dax replied. His eyes narrowed at the mess of people behind me. "What happened here?"

"Let's get him into the medical station and talk afterward," Eshah said, slightly breathless from Rafael's weight.

Uncle Henry stepped out of the infirmary and let out a long sigh when he noticed us gathered around Rafael. "Now what?" He slipped his arm around Rafael's waist and shooed Eshah away. "Will you help Adina and the others?"

Eshah circled around us and sprinted toward a dark-skinned man lying face down in the dirt. I squinted at him. It had to be Malcolm. My world crumbled even further inside my chest, unable to face another death. Attica had been more than enough for one day.

"They. Came. Out. Of. Nowhere," Rafael muttered between breathless gasps.

I glanced back at him. He didn't know about his aunt, and I did not have the strength to tell him. Uncle Henry gave me a slight nod, as if he were reading my mind. They stepped past me, taking Rafael to Dad's ship. He would be out long enough for us to make a plan.

My focus returned to Malcolm, who was now lying on his back. Eshah and Mom were checking his vitals. Mom met my gaze.

"He's alive, Alex," she said, waving me over to them.

The hammering in my head dissipated. Both Aly and I made it to Malcolm's side at the same time. Her eyes had softened, but I could feel the disdain radiating from her.

Transformed Chaos

Malcolm's eyes peeled open one at a time, and he stared up at all four of us. "What did I miss?" he asked, pressing his fist against the sides of his head and closing his eyes again. "I have a raging headache. What happened?"

I kneeled next to him and patted his chest. "We were attacked by a team of anamans. They were looking for Tallisa, and in her place they took Kia Lynn and my dad."

Malcolm popped his head up and looked around. Covyn was standing near us. The rest of the village people had left. There was no one else around but us and those who were in the ships.

"We need to go after them," Malcolm said, pushing himself to his knees. "Do you know which way they went?"

"I am already tracking Jax," Mom replied, holding up her hologram screen. "They are moving toward your area."

Malcolm was already walking toward his ship before Mom finished speaking. "Where is everyone? We can all take my ship and leave yours behind for now." He glanced over his shoulder at us. "Are you okay with that?"

"Yes, but Henry and Rafael are on our ship, along with a dozen of our people." Mom ran both of her hands through her dusty hair, pulling strands out by the roots when she snagged her fingers on a knot. She winced, but quickly refocused on the rest of us.

"Bring as many as you like. Henry can take your ship to your village to check on your people." Malcolm leapt onto the bay door and disappeared inside his ship.

Smeared dirt and blood covered Covyn's face, and when our eyes met, I noticed a stream of tears cutting through the grime. I'm sure I had a similar look. I held out my hand to her.

"We will find Zoe Dawn," I said as she grasped my hand. More tears burst from her eyes. I pulled her in close and wrapped my arms around her. "She will be fine. If anyone can take care of herself, it is Zoe Dawn."

"She is going to die when she finds out her mum is dead," Covyn whispered, weeping against my shoulder.

I nodded even though she could not see me. "I know." The thought of telling Zoe Dawn of her mum's death was tearing me up inside.

A few of Dad's guards raced past us and filed into Malcolm's ship. Mom's arms wrapped around me and Covyn.

"Uncle Henry and a few others will take the ship back to our town and wait for further instructions. Rafael can stay with them until then." She squeezed us tightly. "We have all our other grounded teams across the globe keeping an eye out for the ship. Someone will see them."

I pulled away and pointed at the sky. "What about the ships in high orbit?"

Her face fell. "We have been unable to contact them."

Terror bit me like a rabid dog, and every anaman marking on my body came to life as I felt the unmistakable itch underneath my clothes.

"We will keep trying on Malcolm's ship," Mom said, pushing me and Covyn toward the bay door. "Do not think the worst. There could be many reasons they are not answering."

"All nine of them?" I shrugged her grip off my back as we walked into the ship. "How do all nine of them go dark?"

"Because if they know there is a threat, going dark is protocol. They could have moved farther away to remain undetected." She pressed the button to close the bay door, then opened the communication module. "Malcolm, we are in."

The ship's engine ignited. I followed Mom and Covyn into the main cabin. Malcolm, Aly, Eshah, and several others were seated, preparing the ship for flight. I picked a seat close to the front so I could watch the outside.

Everything had happened so fast, and I was still digesting the result. My elemental powers could not stop a ship. I was much weaker than I realized, and now Attica was dead, and Aly hated me because of it. I should have listened to Aly.

Mom reached over and patted my hand. "She is mourning. Give her some time to come to terms with what has happened."

I peeked at Aly. Her expression was hard as a rock, and her eyes remained unblinking, staring straight ahead at the valley we were leaving. I did not agree with Mom. She didn't need more time. She believed I was the reason her best friend was dead, and if she was anything like the others I met in this dimension, she was already formulating a plan to wipe away my existence from their lives.

CHAPTER FIVE
Hidden Memories

KIA LYNN

The zap stung lightly inside my skull, but when the intensity increased, I squeezed my eyes shut to force away the agony searing like a hot poker in the center of my brain. A moan sputtered from my mouth, and I tightened my hold of the armrests with a grip so tight, I thought my fingers were going to tear through the fabric.

"Relax, Kia Lynn," Trinity said, resting her hand on my arm. "The more you fight this, the worse it will be. Think of a sunny place and then let it all go."

I pried open one eye. "What. Are. You. Trying. To. Do?" I asked between gritted teeth. The pain was nearly unbearable. The shock waves going through my head felt like thousands of little daggers stabbing my brain.

"You will see." Trinity adjusted something just out of my line of sight. She turned back toward me. "We will get there one way or another. It is your choice how comfortable it will be."

"Do you still need me here?" Wolf asked. He fiddled with his sheath as he stood over me.

"Yes. We might need *him*." Trinity turned her back toward me, blocking my view of Wolf. "She is just a child. Any information she has on that demon will probably be limited. He will have to be our next step."

Trinity faced me again and patted my hand. She stared down at me with a gentle expression as Wolf disappeared again. Was she having a sudden change of heart?

"Please, let me go," I whispered, struggling to find any other words. My breath came in short, and I coughed at Trinity's face. I could feel my face reddening.

"Do like me," Trinity replied, drawing in a long breath through her nose and then blowing it out slowly through her mouth. Her lavender eyes had a twinkle to them that irritated me even more. "It will relax you. I promise once you get there, you will wonder why you made this so difficult on yourself."

I was not the one who strapped me to this death machine; I snarled in my head. But I followed her lead and inhaled through my nose and exhaled through my mouth.

After several of those breaths, I noticed the pain in my head was subsiding and I could actually open my eyes all the way.

"There you go," Trinity said, smiling at me before turning back to a machine next to her. "Now, let's watch the show."

A light filtered from the gadget clamping my skull. I could see it just above my brow. It grew brighter and then an anaman hologram, like the one from Alex's arm, surrounded me. Except I was seeing my life. I squinted at the images. I must have been fifteen full seasons. Zoe Dawn and I were out in the forest. I gasped in horror. Trinity was extracting my memories from my mind.

A bitter taste filled my mouth. "How are you doing this?" I tried to crane my neck to see Trinity better, but the clamp held me still. My gaze darted all over the room, searching for a way to stop the hologram. "Please don't do this. These are private."

Trinity squeezed my shoulder. "Find a way to relax. You don't want those shocks to start again."

Her calm demeanor grated on my nerves. They were intruding on my memories, and I had no control over it. Unless…

"What do you need to see?" I asked. Maybe if I gave them the right memory, they would miss the ones I did not want to share.

"Did your mother ever take you north of your village?

Far north?" Trinity asked, leaning back slightly so I could see her better.

"Yes," I replied, thinking back to the day Mama showed me the anaman ship that had crashed.

The memory popped up in the hologram. I held my breath. It had been one of my most favorite days. I didn't want them to have it, but there were other memories I wanted to hide more. Mama's radiant smile greeted me first, and Wolf growled with disgust.

"I don't think I'm ready to see the woman again," he said, grumbling something else under his breath that I could not hear.

We were walking the ancient's path littered with crumbling buildings. When we came out of their shadows, I focused on the giant vessel far ahead. Mama laughed and turned to look at me again.

"Those monsters will never hurt us." She pointed at the ship, then wrapped her arm around my shoulders and hugged me tightly to her side. She had a bounce to her step. "I made sure of that. I will always keep you safe, Sugar Plum."

"Why do the anaman people hate us so much?" I asked Mama. The hologram was unnecessary to remember her facial expression when I said those words.

Her face fell briefly. It was a very rare moment when

Mama did not have a smile on her face, and for a tiny moment, she had lost her happiness. Now I understood why. She was an anaman, and so was I.

Her lips lifted back into a smile, and she bopped me on the nose. "No one hates you, my love. Not even the anaman."

"I thought you said your mother wouldn't save you," Wolf said, stepping into my view again. His forehead furrowed, and he folded his arms over his chest, waiting for an answer.

I pressed my lips together to stop my chin from trembling, but the tears streaming down my cheeks were unavoidable.

"Leave her be." Trinity pushed Wolf away. She reached over and wiped my tears for me. "I am sure those childhood memories are painful. Are you ready to proceed?"

"Yes," I replied, wanting this over with. My gaze drifted to Wolf. "My mother is not the same person she was on that day."

"Forgive me if I do not shed a tear for her." Wolf shook his head and walked far enough away I could not see him anymore. "She is a tyrant. She was then, and she is now. The day we try her for her crimes will be—"

The ship shuddered. I squeaked out a cry and every

muscle in my body tightened.

"What was that?" Trinity asked, grabbing hold of my chair.

"Ret, come in. What happened?" Wolf barked in his com as he came closer.

The surrounding walls shook again. Trinity whirled around to face Wolf, and I closed my eyes, so I did not have to see the shaking.

"We found another one of their establishments," Ret said. "It has a protective barrier around it. We are moving on for now. The one we need is to the north."

"Then why are we moving south?" Wolf asked.

"The senators ordered us to," Ret snapped in return. "Why are you questioning me? I outrank you."

"I told you he would start pulling that card," Wolf said to Trinity. He pressed on his com. "My apologies. Thank you for the information."

Ret did not reply, but the shaking subsided. Trinity turned back to her machine, and Wolf hovered over me. He searched my eyes for several moments before turning toward Trinity.

He nudged her with his knuckles. "How much longer will this take?"

"I have to be thorough. We don't want to miss the way in." Trinity didn't turn to look at him. She was focused on what was in front of her. "There. Let's proceed."

My memory returned to the hologram. We walked past the ship and slept under the stars that night. Mama showed me the constellations and the planet Venus, like she had done so many times before. It was what we did together. She knew so much about the world and the universe. Most everything I had learned had been from her.

The next morning, we continued until we could no longer see the ship behind us. Trinity asked me to move it forward, so I searched quickly through the next few days until she told me to stop. She pointed at a nearly hidden entryway on the side of a hill. It wasn't until this moment I even remembered that door.

Mama turned toward me. "I won't be long, my love. Will you stay next to this tree until I return?"

The fear had overtaken my mind, but I had nodded anyway. She kissed me on my forehead, then ran toward the door. A woman was waiting just inside the shadows.

My eyes widened. "Nikita," I whispered, realizing for the first time how long Mama had been working with that vile woman.

I watched as they disappeared into the darkness together.

"That's it!" Trinity exclaimed, bouncing on her toes as her gaze shot from me and over to Wolf. "Now, let's see if we can find out where Tallisa is hiding. Kia Lynn, let's see your memory of yesterday."

My blood ran cold, and a fresh terror gripped my heart. "Don't you have what you need?"

"Partly." Trinity clapped her hands together, and her smile widened. "We need to find out where your mother has been and who is helping her. Then we can deal with this otherworldly faction she's involved with."

I did not want her to see yesterday. The explosion. Zoe Dawn. Mama and her plan to destroy this universe. What would they do with the information?

My memory was fuzzy in the hologram as I fought it from showing, but the shocks stabbed me so hard in the head, I nearly lost consciousness.

"No!" I screamed, fighting away the memory. "You can't have it. Please, no!"

Wolf pointed his weapon at my head. "Do it now."

Trinity shoved him away. "She will be useless to us if she is dead. Pull it together, Wolf." Her hand rested on mine. "Kia Lynn, if you fight it for too long, you will damage your brain. How will you help your friends and family if you are a vegetable?"

I blinked at her. "A vegetable?"

"She means you won't be able to use your mind any longer," Wolf snapped. He holstered his weapon, but not before he shot me a look of disdain. "You will be nothing but a meat sack for the rest of your pathetic life."

"Not helping," Trinity hissed over her shoulder at him.

I relaxed and let the memory flow. Mama had not protected me. Why was I the one giving my life to keep her safe?

"There you go." Trinity stared at the hologram, and slowly, her smile faded. "Wait, go back. Who is this girl? The one who burst into a fireball?"

"She is my sister. My best friend." I gulped down a sob and balled my hands into tight fists. "We are connected as elementals. Connected to Mother Gaia."

Trinity's gaze shot down to meet mine. "The prophecy is true?"

"Yes. I am willing to just tell you what my mother did. There's no reason to pull those dreadful memories out again." I bent my knees and set my feet on the end of the reclined chair.

"She hurt you that badly?" Trinity asked. Her expression was soft, and I noticed a hint of compassion in her eyes.

"She wanted to use me to implode this universe with the one she came from," I replied. I hiccupped from forcing the sob down, and tears spilled from my eyes again. "Yes, she hurt me." My sobs were coming in waves now. It was embarrassing, but I could not stop now. "My mother, the one you saw in my memories, the one who called me her love, she chose her own life over mine. I was her ticket off this planet and out of this universe."

Even Wolf's face held a trace of sadness while I revealed the events of yesterday, from finding out Mama's true intentions for me, all the way to sealing the rip between the two universes. When I finished, they glanced at one another, then back at me.

"She really is a tyrant, sacrificing her own daughter for her selfish need to survive above all else. She has not changed. The woman you thought was loving was a façade. She never existed. We have only known the woman who will destroy everyone else so she can live," Trinity said, shaking her head as she undid my restraints. "Fetch the brother. It is time we find out what he knows."

Wolf left the room. When the restraints were off my wrists, I rubbed the sore spots and swung my feet over the edge to sit up straight.

"Now what?" I asked, watching Trinity work on a screen similar to the one in the cruisers.

Trinity stopped what she was doing and slowly turned to look at me. "Now, we continue to gather information. This isn't over for you, as much as I wish it could be. We have two goals, and the first one requires your mother being apprehended. The second…" She shook her head and focused back on the screen. "Let's just say we have a bone to pick with some very powerful people, and your mother is the key to removing their shields. Thanks to you, we have their location, but we cannot bypass their barrier. Yet."

"What do you need me for? Haven't I given you everything I know?" I stood and surveyed the entire room. There wasn't much to see, aside from the white walls.

"We are hoping she will come easily once she knows we have you," Trinity replied. Her fingers wrapped around my arm just as the door slid open. "And we need your uncle to be forthcoming as well."

I glanced at the doorway. Jax walked in with Wolf behind him. His wrists were shackled, and one of his eyes was sealed shut from swelling. A bright red-and-purple bruise ran from his eye down to his collarbone. His own people had tortured him.

His one good eye widened when he saw me. "Kia Lynn? No! She has nothing to do with this." He threw his shoulder back to hit Wolf's weapon out of his hand, but missed.

Wolf shoved him forward. "Get in the chair, Jax. I don't have the time or the patience to put up with your rhetoric."

"I mean it, Wolf," Jax said, whirling around to face the other large anaman. They were eye to eye. "Her mother has been gone from her life for nearly a decade. She knows nothing."

Wolf tapped his firearm against Jax's chest. "She knows plenty, and until we are finished with her, she remains here. Now, take a seat and make this easy on her."

I gulped, not wanting to know what Wolf's underlying meaning was. Jax glanced my way, then with a defeated expression sank to the chair.

"You will regret this, Wolf. We could have worked this out civilly." Jax reclined in the seat and held up his shackled hands.

"All civility went out the door when your sister got us stuck in this dimension. She is just lucky we found a team of anamans to take us in," Wolf replied, undoing the shackles and then restraining Jax to the chair. "We were on your side once upon a time. She is the one who broke that trust. Not to mention, you never came looking for us."

Trinity glanced at me and shrugged. "We just want to go home. If we had known there was a rip between the two universes, we would have left, and you would not be here right now. Those people in the north know how to send us back."

"All of you on this ship?" I asked, trying to keep up

with all the strange words. "None of you are from our universe?"

Wolf shook his head. "There are twenty-three of us remaining from our universe. We started with thirty-eight when we arrived with Tallisa through the wormhole she had discovered. One from our team is rumored to have remained with Tallisa, and thirteen have perished for one reason or another." His sorrowful expression held a story that pained him more than he wanted to reveal.

Trinity wrapped her long fingers around Wolf's arm. He glanced her way, but then shook his head as he refocused on me.

"We were fighting for the right to be equal whether we mate with a human or not." He pointed at Jax. "Your uncle was our leader, and your mother made promises of a better life if we followed her here. She lied."

"She lied to all of us." Jax lifted his head. "I didn't even know you had all come to this world, and when she returned alone, the only explanation is that you were deserters. I could not find you."

Wolf's gaze remained on me. "I am sorry you are the collateral damage here. It cannot be helped. I want to see my family again." He nodded at Trinity. "Let's get started. Freydis is waiting for results."

The clamp rose around Jax's head and encircled it

before gripping tightly. Jax winced but otherwise did not move. When Trinity initiated the machine, I could see the pain in Jax's tightened features. He was fighting it. He squeezed his eyes shut, and a groan bubbled from his lips.

"Jax, please," Trinity pleaded, her hand hovering just above his arm as if she were afraid to touch him. "It will only get worse if you do not let go."

"It's not happening, Trinity," he grumbled, prying one eye open to look at her. "I can't believe you—"

Wolf came up behind me and pressed his weapon against the side of my head. "I will end her life right here, Jax."

Both of Jax's eyes were open now. I trembled with rage. I had been nothing but a puppet to my mother, and now these people. The one person who had been kind toward me now faced an impossible decision. Give up all he knew or save me.

I shook my head slightly and snapped my fingers. A gush of wind hit all of us, throwing Trinity and Wolf off balance. Trinity collapsed to the ground, but Wolf's arm encircled my throat.

"Don't do it, Kia Lynn," he hissed in my ear as he squeezed my airway shut.

I sputtered and threw my elbows back and struck him in the sides. He didn't budge. With the little air I had in my lungs, I concentrated on the wind, circling it around us until the cyclone ripped away Jax's restraints. Wolf teetered to the side, and his grasp on me loosened just enough for me to slip away. I stomped on his foot and shoved him into my raging wind. He tumbled across the floor and smacked into the wall on the other side of the room.

I gasped for more air as I watched. Jax wrapped his arm around my waist and hauled me to the door. It opened when he punched the button, and we sprinted down the corridor. Turning the corner, we came to a screeching halt. Freydis and a team of her soldiers stood in our way, with their firearms pointed at us.

"I knew you would try to escape," Freydis said with a tiny smile twitching on her lips. "So predictable." She pulled her trigger, and a jolt of electricity sent me writhing to the floor.

CHAPTER SIX
Zeke

ZOE DAWN

I caught the flame with ease and snuffed it out, still staring in shock at my biological mother. Koleton had returned and was leaning against the wall while he chewed on whatever food he had in his hand. My gaze shot between him and Jamila, completely thrown off guard by the turn of events. The amused expression on his face was distracting, and I had to concentrate really hard on Jamila and Nikita in order to ignore him.

"Now you know who you inherited your magical fire from," Enoch said, wrapping his hand over my shoulder. He was now standing next to me. "It most certainly wasn't me. She is a woman of brilliant talent, that mother of yours."

Jamila stood protectively in front of Nikita, never uttering a word. Her defiance matched my own. I could see myself in her. Our wide, but strong hips were identical. The way she clenched her jaw reminded me of the times Kia Lynn had made fun of me when I was concentrating or just plain angry. And her hair. It was shiny and well-kept, but the color and fullness looked like it was my own.

"Why is she protecting that sadistic witch?" I asked between clenched teeth.

"Nikita?" Enoch laughed and clapped his hands together. "She is harmless. Although, she strayed from her orders slightly, but her penance was swift."

I turned my angry gaze to Enoch. "What are you talking about? She put me and Kia Lynn in danger. She and Tallisa planned to wipe out our entire world and escape to a new one." I jabbed my thumb back toward Nikita. "*She* is a horrible human being who needs more than a penance."

"We are aware of her actions." Enoch's smiling demeanor faded into a scowl. "You are in our home, and we have our rules. Nikita is not to be touched. Do you understand me?"

I ignored his question. "Did you know she pretended to be a member of the Black Mountain Doyen? Did you know she murdered two of them to scare the remaining two away? Did you—"

"Enough!" Enoch barked, interrupting me. He waved

his hand at Nikita. "Return to your room. We will discuss this later."

Nikita bowed her head in a polite response, then turned on her heel and disappeared into the other room.

Enoch turned toward me. "Sit down." He looked around the room at the other four. "All of you. Take a seat."

Koleton smirked at him, then shot me a soft smile. "Good luck, Lady Charm." He strolled back into the eating hall, and I heard something scrape against the floor. "If anyone needs me, you can find me in my favorite place on this ridiculously boring planet," he hollered so we could all hear.

A long sigh swept out of Enoch's mouth. I sank into my chair, not interested in upsetting these people any more than I already had. The answers I needed and help to save my family and friends. I would not receive that if I created a problem here.

Jamila, Lindon, and his father returned to their seats. Enoch looked around at everyone and then sank onto his chair. He crossed his left ankle over his right knee and then turned to face me.

"We are the reason Nikita was appointed a member of your Doyen. We arranged it. When she discovered your whereabouts, you were ten years old, and we did not want to rip you from your home." The lines etched between his eyes deepened as a sadness clouded his features. "It horrified us the way you lived, but you were happy. We did not want to take that from you."

"Nikita kept you safe for us," Jamila said. Her voice was delicate, like a bird's song.

My surprised gaze shot over to her.

She nodded with a slight tilt of her head. "Yes, I do speak, but only when I have something to say. Zoe Dawn, they stole you from your room. Not by Nikita, but another member of your Doyen. Those two are the ones who perished by Nikita's hand."

"What about her and Tallisa?" I asked, still looking at Jamila.

"Tallisa will not be an issue." Enoch was the one who spoke. "Nikita strayed from her path when she involved herself in that woman's issues. Her aim was to get you to the mating ceremony and make Lindon your only choice. That was it. From the day she became a Doyen until the day those people held their absurd mating ceremony."

I agreed with him on the absurd part, but I did not like the way he spoke about my people, as if they were the trash that needed to be burned away. I bit my lip to stop myself from responding the way I wanted. My goal had not changed.

"May I speak, your holiness?" Lindon asked, looking at Enoch.

Your holiness? Who were these people?

"Yes, Lindon. Please." Enoch raised his brows curiously.

"How long will it be until Zoe Dawn and I can be properly mated?" His gaze darted briefly over to me and then back to Enoch. He sat up even straighter in his chair, as if trying to make himself appear bigger.

I rolled my eyes.

"We will give my daughter time to acclimate to our world." Enoch reached over and grasped my hand. "First, her mother would like to know her better. Then, we will discuss wedding arrangements."

My heart quickened. They really believed I was their property.

"What if I refuse?" I asked, unable to stop myself. I regretted it the moment the words were out.

Enoch did not flinch. "You won't."

"Five steps forward, ten steps back for the Earthlings," Koleton said. He had returned to the doorway, holding another piece of food in his hands. "If Lady Charm does not want to marry the white elf, why are you forcing her to do so?"

I pressed my lips together to squash down a laugh. The

white elf. Fitting.

"You do not get an opinion, Koleton," Enoch snapped, rising to his feet. "Will you please make yourself scarce?"

"I would rather go on a stroll with your new guest," he replied, then finished his last bite and wiped his hands together to discard the crumbs onto the clean rug.

Jamila glared at him.

"I think she needs a break from all this… newness." He waved his hand around the room. "Zeke is taking a stroll through your gardens and shops. I think it would delight him to meet this Lady Charm."

"Zoe Dawn," I said, cocking my head with a playful smile rising on my lips. "The name is Zoe Dawn, but Lady Charm works as well."

"I knew you would like it." The corners of his eyes crinkled with his wide grin. He turned his smile toward the others, but the sparkle in his eyes disappeared. "We will return shortly, and you can continue this utterly boring conversation."

Lindon's father muttered something under his breath. Koleton gave the man an once-over, then stuck his tongue out at him. Enoch and Jamila were quiet. Whoever Zeke was, he had a hold on their tongues.

"I must insist on accompanying you." Lindon rose and pinned me with his eyes. "I will only be there to keep you safe from our brazen visitor."

Koleton burst with laughter as he strolled past all of them and held out his arm for me to take. "Be my guest, bean stalk, but I doubt Zoe Dawn cares for your protection."

I gladly hooked arms with the redheaded comedian and did not look back at the group as he led me back into the garden and into the lift. Lindon joined us and stood at the farthest corner, eyeing Koleton with clear contempt. I scrunched up my face in disgust.

"Completely agree," Koleton said when he saw my expression. "Do not be dismayed, Lady Charm. Our ghostly company will not deter the fun. And you will love Zeke. He is a ball of energy and is as mischievous as they come."

I smothered another laugh, but not before Lindon caught my wide grin. Koleton was most definitely one of my soulmates. Regardless of where he had come from, I wanted him to never return just so I could continue to enjoy his commentary.

The doors to the lift opened. We were back in the corridor from earlier. This time Koleton linked arms with me and waved me out the door. When we reached the wider tunnel, Koleton pulled me to the second corridor to our left. I could already hear the music. There was most definitely fun up ahead.

After a long stroll down the narrow passageway, it opened to a massive plaza. My gaze traveled the entire circular room, and I realized it was a dome. The outside was just beyond, with the moon and stars twinkling up above.

"Won't this place be seen by ships in the sky?" I asked, suddenly feeling exposed. We really needed to return to my village.

Koleton tugged me through a crowd of young girls giggling at a strange-looking person with bright purple hair and whiter skin than Lindon's. He was juggling some balls and when they would drop and hit his face, he would give them a sad look.

"No one can see us outside," Koleton finally replied. He wrapped his arm around my shoulder and drew me in close, then pointed at a red blinking light at the top of the dome. "That creates an illusion. You can see out, but from the other side it appears like a normal hillside. Rocks and all."

"This is amazing!" I exclaimed, pulling away and raising my arms up as I twirled in a circle. "What I would give to have this kind of security for my people."

"Maybe that could be arranged." Koleton sniffed the air. "Do you smell that? I think someone is baking their famous cinnamon rolls. We really should go eat one."

I laughed. "Do you ever stop eating?

"Not if I can help it." He grabbed my hand and led me through another crowd.

I glanced back to watch them, and my gaze landed on Lindon. He was still trailing behind us, his eyes fixated on my hand holding Koleton's. Was he jealous? Who did he think he was? I dropped Koleton's hand and whirled around.

"What is your problem, Lindon?" My tone rose an octave or two by the time I said his name.

He took a sudden step back, bumping into a woman with auburn hair. She whipped around to face Lindon, then her gaze shot to me and our eyes met. The color drained from her face.

The rage I had bottled inside for Nikita, exploded through my veins. It was like a poison infiltrating every inch of my body, just like when the void was overtaking my mind. Steam simmered from my flesh. I was losing my mind and control in the middle of the market.

Terror overtook Tallisa's expression, and she stumbled backward, then fell into the crowd behind her. Several people scattered, throwing startled glances back at me and Tallisa. Lindon held his hand out at Tallisa, then turned to me and did the same.

"Don't do anything foolish," he said. "We have—"

Koleton shifted in between me and Lindon. "Did they not tell you?" he asked, trying to pull my eyes from Kia Lynn's mother.

I pushed him to the side. "No, they failed to mention they were harboring a coward."

Lindon reached past Koleton and grabbed my arm. "We were going to tell you once you—"

"Shut your trap, Lindon," I hissed, yanking my arm free from his grasp. I turned all my anger toward him. "I told you not to touch me. Do you really want me to set your world on fire? Because I will, and this time you will not heal so quickly."

He held up his hands in surrender and backed away. Koleton waved at me to get my attention.

"Will you talk with me, Zoe Dawn?" A crimson flush was speckling across his cheeks, and the worry in his eyes slightly cooled the heat simmering just beneath my skin.

"Zoe Dawn, please let me explain," Tallisa said, her voice shaking in fear.

She should be afraid. I shook my head at Koleton and whirled around to face Tallisa. I glowered at her.

"Nothing you can say will redeem you!" I screamed at the frightened woman. "You were going to sacrifice my sister. Your daughter!" Spit flew from my mouth as I yelled louder. "She adored you. Worshipped you! All for what? So you could escape a world where everyone hates you?"

Tallisa cowered. The surrounding crowd had quieted, and more were gathering. Koleton and Lindon had disappeared, leaving me to finish what needed to be done. I circled Tallisa. She slowly straightened her posture, but her hands were visibly shaking. Her spirit was clearly broken. Seeing her up close for the first time since I was a child, I noticed how much she had changed. The fine lines had deepened at the corners of her eyes and across her forehead, and the brightness in her eyes had dimmed. Her youth and vigor had vanished, and in her place, stood a fractured woman.

"Is this what Kia Lynn would want?" Tallisa asked, squaring her shoulders at me.

"Do not say her name!" I screamed, balling my hands into fists. "You do not get to say her name ever again."

My hands burst into flames at the thought of it, and Tallisa recoiled, taking several steps backward. I did not wait for her to use the crowd as a shield. I released my fire, shooting it directly at her face, but she held up her hand and a burst of wind blew the inferno into a small tornado.

I jerked my fire back.

"Zoe Dawn, I am an elemental." Tallisa took one brave

step toward me, holding her hand out as a signal to cool down. Her meek efforts were not working. "I am not near as powerful as my daughter, but our connection is strong. I can still create the same magic on a much smaller scale. Tatum and Nikita were told it would be Kia Lynn pulling open the rip, but I never really intended for it to be her. It would always be me. If I had told them my actual plan, they would have never let me go through with it."

My stomach churned from the poisonous hate writhing through my guts. "Liar!" I shrieked, igniting another fireball and flinging it at her before she could blink.

A blue light encircled the fireball. It froze midair and rolled within the blue barrier, then flew high into the air and burst above everyone's heads. I stared in amazement as the flecks of light showered over us, extinguishing before they reached the crowd.

I whipped around in a circle and came face to face with Koleton and a younger man, maybe a few full seasons older than me. His sapphire eyes twinkled with amusement.

"Hello, Zoe Dawn," he said, holding out his hand. He grasped my right wrist and pointed at my limp hand. "You must do the same." He grinned. "I insist on teaching you my ways."

I shot Koleton a wide-eyed glance but grabbed the

younger man's wrist. Koleton shrugged happily, his wide smile never faltering. If he was that dedicated to this man, then I already knew he would be a friend.

My gaze returned to the sapphire-eyed man. "Who are you?"

His lips quirked up in a soft smile. "My name is Zeke, and I am so pleased to make your acquaintance, flame thrower."

CHAPTER SEVEN
Alone

ALEX

We hovered not too far from Zion. The barrier was holding strong and the small ships Tiordan and the others had seen earlier had vanished. From our viewpoint, the sanctuary appeared to be a forest of trees between two red cliffs with the moonlight shining brightly down upon it.

"When will you return?" Tiordan asked Malcolm. They were not used to having Malcolm missing for so long. Tiordan's gaze briefly met mine, and his worry did not go unnoticed. "The steam from the cave is increasing and—"

"Once the women and Jax are safe, I will return immediately," Malcolm said, interrupting him. His reassuring tone seemed to cool the seer's anxiety slightly.

Tiordan sighed, but the crinkles around his eyes softened. "We should do what we discussed and have the three elementals live here until the threats are fully eliminated."

Malcolm shot Adina a worried glance, but she only nodded in reply. It looked like she was considering the idea herself.

"Do we even know all the threats?" I asked, tired of having my life decided for me. "When we arrived here, Uncle Henry found absolutely no chaos between any of the inhabitants. It was as if we awakened a beast with our arrival. So, does anyone really know when we will be free of these enemies? We cannot live in your city forever."

"Tiordan, we will be in touch," Malcolm replied, ignoring everything I said.

Tiordan nodded, but he glanced my way one last time before signing off.

Malcolm turned to look at me. "These threats were here long before you arrived. They were waiting for Mother Gaia to awaken to make their move. We actually expected this." He ran his hand over the top of his head. "Just not this quickly."

"A warning would have been nice," Mom said, leaning forward in her chair. "We need to go. I think they have stopped near those new buildings we saw on our way to California this morning." She pointed at a red dot not too far from us.

Transformed Chaos

Was it really only earlier today when we stopped Tallisa from destroying this world? I shook my head at the thought. It felt like days had passed, not just hours. No wonder my eyes burned with exhaustion. I needed to sleep and so did everyone else.

Covyn tapped her toes impatiently against the floor. "Please, Malcolm. Can we go now? Zoe Dawn needs us too."

"Yes." He situated himself in his seat and tightened his restraints. Seconds later, we were shooting toward Las Vegas.

Dax patted my hand. He had sat to my right and Mom to my left. I turned to give him my full attention.

"We will find them," he said, leaning over the arm of my chair and planting a kiss on my lips.

I grabbed his face and pulled him closer, pressing my lips hard against his. I needed to remember this moment. All of him. His smell. His touch. The way he bit my bottom lip before breaking away from our kisses. His fingers ran through my hair as I deepened our kiss, forgetting the world around us. I just wanted to feel safe for a few moments.

When we broke away, he was blushing, but his lips were twitching with a satisfied smile. "My phantom sorceress," he whispered, running his thumb down my cheek. "You have most definitely put a spell on me."

I pressed my lips together and smiled. He was my reason for fighting and ending this battle once and for all.

I held out my pinky to him. "Pinky swear we will see this through together."

He looked quizzically at my pinky. "Not a problem, but what is a pinky swear?"

I hooked my pinky with his and held onto it. "This. It is binding. You and me, together until the end."

"Absolutely," he whispered and leaned in to sneak one more kiss.

We pulled apart and settled back in our seats. The ship was cruising over the outskirts of old Las Vegas and I could see the dark buildings up ahead, illuminated by a light streaming from the center where the pyramid stood.

"His signal disappeared," Mom said as we closed in on the buildings. "It was there a few minutes ago." She sat up straight, straining against her restraints.

I shifted closer to her and squinted at her hologram map. The red dot had vanished.

"Then they must be here." Malcolm's fingers flew across his screen. "I think someone is coming toward us." He squinted at the outside and then back at his screen. His nose flared, and pure terror washed over his features. "There are dozens of them flying straight for us. Anna

Rain, shields."

Anna Rain turned to her screen. "Done."

I heard the whiz of two ships fly over us, then another. It was quiet for a few seconds. Five more ships flew past us at record speed. We were outnumbered, and this ship did not move that fast. I gulped back the fear bubbling in my throat and closed my eyes, focusing on the sounds of the ships. It was hard to find them.

"We will have to return later, Adina," Malcolm said, interrupting my concentration.

My eyes snapped open. "Please, no. Not yet. Give me a chance to slow them down."

I focused again, pulling the water from the ground and aiming it at one of the ships. My ears perked up from the sound of an approaching vessel. I would strike it after it flew over us. I waited until it was flying overhead. The water shot like a bullet in front of us, striking the vessel with so much force it flew to the side and crashed like a rocket into the mountainside. The roar blew over us and Malcolm struggled to hold the ship steady.

"You might have just started our war," Malcolm muttered, throwing me a guarded look. "They weren't attacking us."

I shrank back in my chair, my heart sinking into my stomach. What had I done?

The ships circled around us and the first shot rocked the ship, but the shields held up. The second one knocked us forward. Malcolm eased the ship around the buildings to block them, but they were right on our tails. The next fired shots came one after another, and I noticed them striking a translucent barrier around their buildings.

I was so desperate to find Dad and Kia Lynn, I hadn't thought about the consequences. They hit us again and my fingers dug into the fabric of the armrests.

"The shields are down to twenty percent," Anna Rain shouted over the onslaught. "We have to leave now."

"I can't find a way out." Malcolm searched his screen. "They are everywhere."

The entire ship jolted, then convulsed. I thought my brain was going to break apart inside my skull. I grabbed the sides of my head and slammed my eyes shut.

"We are going down!" Malcolm shouted.

A loud buzzer sounded overhead, and I felt the momentum of our tailspin as we closed in on the ground. This was my last attempt to keep us from dying.

The water came easily. I sensed it burst from the dirt and encircle our ship. When we reached the ground, the ship slid across the land and came to a halt not too far from the three tall buildings.

The ships landed between us and the building, and

under the moonlight, many soldiers piled from the doors. We were screwed.

"Everyone needs to arm up." Malcolm leapt from his seat and raced down the corridor.

Anna Rain and Covyn were right behind him. Dax pushed me forward, then circled his arm around my waist when I did not budge and pulled me with him and Mom. Aly had disappeared before anyone else. I had given her another reason to end my life.

When we reached the weaponry storage room, Malcolm handed me two firearms. "There are several riders in the cargo area. Everyone grab one. Stay together and keep your lights off. We will hide in one of the ancient's buildings until morning."

I followed Dax down to the cargo bay and hopped on the back of his rider. He squeezed my knee.

"We are in this together, my phantom sorceress," he said reassuringly.

Mom climbed onto the rider next to us, and Covyn threw her leg over the back of the machine. They both glanced our way. I could see the blame in their eyes. If I had just not tried to be the hero, we would probably be back to Zion right now. Lived to fight another day. But instead, we were heading into the unknown with an enemy so powerful, they brought us down in only a matter of a few minutes.

The cargo door opened, and Anna Rain shot out into the dark, followed by several others. We went next, staying as close as we could to the rider in front of us. Mom and Covyn were right behind, with Malcolm taking up the rear. We cleared a small hill, circled around the buildings, and flew toward the nearest uncovered ancient structure.

As we were closing in on the first one, the person in front of us grunted and fell forward on his rider. It swerved to the left, and he tumbled into the weeds.

"They found us," I whispered in Dax's ear. "We need to make a run for it."

The others ahead of us kept going, oblivious to their fallen comrade, and we did not want to yell for them to come back. Malcolm pulled up next to the man and lifted him onto his lap, then he turned toward us and signaled to follow him. Mom and Covyn went first, and we took the rear this time.

I twisted around in my seat so I was facing backward. I pulled out my weapons and armed them, pointing them into the darkness. Someone out there was hunting us, and it was my fault. I squinted, then wiped away the film of exhaustion with the back of my wrist. Refocusing, my heart sank. Everything looked like a tree or a tumbleweed or a threat. I could not tell the difference.

Our rider jerked to the side. Dax reached back and held onto my hip. I heard another machine closing in on us. No, several machines.

"Can you go faster?" I asked, leaning backward so he could hear me better.

"I think we were hit. Maybe I was hit." He slurred his words. The rider decelerated even more, and Dax tilted to the side.

I twisted and held onto Dax's shirt, but the fabric ripped, and the world slowed as the rider flipped and I flew, then rolled in the dry dirt. I skidded to a painful halt. The rocks had torn through the side of my shirt. I bit down on my trembling lip and lifted my head slightly, scanning my surroundings. Dax lay several feet away with his face pressed into the dirt. The rider was on its side next to him.

I strained to hear the machines. They were closing in. I scooted toward Dax when a larger rider pulled up next to him. I shrank back into the shadows.

"Take him," a woman ordered, pointing down at Dax.

Another large rider stopped near Dax and the driver jumped off. "He needs medical attention." His voice was deep and burly.

"Take him in," the woman replied, adjusting herself on the hover bike's seat. "I will continue tracking the others.

We need them all. Esta's orders."

"Be mindful, Lala. They have water magic to protect them." He hauled Dax onto the hoverbike and shot off like a bullet.

Lala's gaze swept across the area. I held my breath. She squinted, but then looked past me. Her hoverbike took off as well, and I was left alone to find my way to the others. I rose slowly and twirled around in a circle, then slinked quietly toward the half-buried buildings of Las Vegas.

A shot rang out, then another. Several figures ran from the closest building, but they fell one after another. A hoverbike was parked unoccupied, only a few yards ahead of me. I leapt onto it and stared at the controls. It was similar to our riders, but the symbols were undecipherable. I just had to get it moving.

Mom screamed, and someone fired another one of our weapons. Then a silence fell over me. I gripped the handles and swore under my breath. It froze me to the seat, unsure what to do next.

I activated my com, even though Mom had warned me to stay dark. It was a chance I had to take. "Mom, are you there?" My voice was barely a whisper, but I did not dare to be louder. Silence greeted me. "Dad? Mom? Uncle Henry? Anyone?" No one answered. I could not tell if it was because my com was not working or if it was on their end, because turning on any light would alert the attackers to my presence.

A long sigh swept across my lips. I was all alone.

"This wasn't like the larger ship," a woman said from across the field.

I pressed against the cool steel, searching for the strangers. My gaze landed on two figures standing together, nearly half a footballs field's length away from me. They had stopped and one of them was pointing at Malcolm's ship.

"I agree. These people were in the wrong place at the wrong time. We should have been more careful when approaching them. Luckily, Esta was able to remove our pilot in time." This time it was a man who spoke.

"Does Esta really believe the large vessel was acting alone?" the woman asked.

"The two incidents appear to be unrelated, and the larger ship was last seen moving up the coastline. Why would the anaman send a smaller vessel without reinforcements?" the man asked, waving at the woman to follow him.

Kia Lynn and Dad were by the ocean. If I made it there, I could ask the water elementals to help me. They would know what to do. My fingers traced over the symbols etched into the hoverbike.

"We cannot be too careful." The woman pointed in the opposite direction they were headed. "I'm back that way."

"We are still missing one," the man replied. "I will meet you back at zone two after I find them."

It was now or never. I pressed the button that looked like it would be the ON ignition. The hoverbike vibrated to life underneath me. It was a quiet hum, and no lights came on. They used these bikes for stealth, which was exactly what I needed right now.

I twisted the handlebars and zoomed away from the approaching stranger, zigzagging around broken structures and fallen stone until I reached the outskirts of the old Las Vegas. I glanced back one last time. Everyone was gone, and I was on my own, but I would return for my family and friends—hopefully with the full force of the water elementals.

CHAPTER EIGHT
Unexpected Help

KIA LYNN

Drool dripped from the side of my mouth as my body spasms continued. Freydis stared down at me like I was a leech that needed to be squished. Jax must have been nearby, experiencing the same fate. I felt the rhythmic kick of someone's foot against my calf, and with my half-alert mind, I guessed it was him.

The light above dimmed, then brightened, and voices echoed from every angle. The faces above me blurred together into a demon who pointed his finger at my chest while his venomous laughter filled the surrounding space. His eyes were dark orbs, drawing me into their endless abyss.

I closed my eyes, and when I opened them again, the demon had vanished. I was lying in a room with more shadows than light. The quiet was unnerving and pounded against my ears louder than a beating drum.

A groan was all I could utter as I twisted my head to survey my surroundings. The walls looked dark gray in the little light filtering from a window on the far end of the room. Next to it was a closed door. Another window ran along the wall across from me, covering a large portion of it, but this one was dark on the other side.

I raised my head and scooted to the edge of the uncomfortable cot. My toes curled away from the freezing-icy floor, and blood rushed to my brain at the same time. I pressed my forehead against my knees until the swimming in my skull subsided.

"Rise and shine, sleeping beauty," a woman said.

I jumped to my bare feet and swung around, coming face-to-face with Freydis. My balance was unstable. I swayed to one side and then another, but somehow, I stood my ground. The female anaman had been standing behind me the entire time. I held out my fists in front of me. I was ready for her this time. She raised one brow, and the edges of her lips twitched with amusement.

"Calm down. We don't want a repeat of earlier." Freydis waved at the cot. "And take a seat." She pressed on her com, and I swore her eyes darkened like the black orbs I had seen from the floor, but when she focused on me again, they were their normal color. "Open the shutters and send in my men."

I melted down to the thin cushion and watched as the window lightened and several anaman stood on the other side. Jax was in the middle, bound and gagged. The desperation in his eyes seared into mine. This would not end well. When my door opened, I did not look. I was beginning to wonder if I would make it out of this ship alive.

A large machine with flashing lights and a long black cushion was wheeled in and set in front of me. Freydis yanked me to my feet.

"If you were just going to force me back up, why did you order me to sit?" I asked with clear malice in my tone.

She ignored me. Her fingers wrapped around the back of my neck, and she shoved me face-down on top of the hard cushion that sat atop their machine. Fear splintered my heart. Was this it? My ending? A loud noise echoed around me, and my body pressed harder against the cushion. I tried to push back on the tension, but I could not budge.

I screamed. "What are you doing?" It felt like a vice was clamping me down, but no one's hands were on me. Several strands of hair hung over my face, and I could not move them away. I peeked through them and stared up at Freydis. Her expression hardened even more.

"Jax, I will send shock waves through your niece's body until her heart stops. Then I will revive her and start all over again." She tapped her fingers against her chin. "Unless the drawings and specifications for your time machine are in my hands before that happens. Then with the northerners' assistance, they will ensure we return to the exact time we left, where I will hand you over to the human government." Freydis tapped her fingers against the hard surface next to my face. "And then the time machine will be mine."

"Ours, Freydis," one of the male anamans said. He was standing not too far from Freydis. "The time machine will be ours."

Her gaze drifted slowly to him, and I squinted at the dark fog swirling around the edges of her hair. I blinked to clear the hallucination away, but it was still there.

"Mine." Freydis jabbed the man in the chest. "Ours. What does it matter? Either way, we will have it."

He met her with silence, and I could not see his facial expression, but I wondered if he could see the same black smoke I was seeing. It was eerily familiar.

Freydis turned back toward the window. "Are you prepared to sacrifice your family, Jax?"

I could not see what Jax was doing, but if he gave them the time machine information, they could travel wherever and whenever they wanted. One of those machines had already caused more than enough damage. If there were more, chaos would never leave our world.

"Don't do it, Jax," I cried, trying to pull my head up.

There was a tickle on the bottom of my feet, then a wave of electricity shot up my legs, and my entire body seized. I clenched my jaw so hard, I was sure my teeth would break. Then the current cut off. I gasped in a breath.

"Give her something to bite down on," Freydis ordered.

One of the male anamans pushed a hard object against my lips. Tears spilled from my eyes, and I pressed my lips together. I did not want to do this. He pushed against my lips until it forced them open.

Freydis leaned in close to me, and sweat from her face dripped on my cheek. "Your resistance will only hurt you more." She was so close to my ear, her lips grazed them when she spoke.

I opened my mouth, weeping uncontrollably as the anaman shoved the object between my teeth. I sniffed loudly, trying to breathe between the object and through my stuffy nose.

"Again," Freydis ordered, standing up straight.

"No." I whimpered. My fingers trembled in fearful anticipation.

The shock exploded into my body, ripping up my legs and shooting straight for my head. The noise in my skull echoed violently. Reality seemed to slip away as the waves of electricity pounded against my muscles, jolting them to the point of sheer exhaustion.

It was quiet, but I wasn't sure it had ended. The pain vanished. I pried open my eyes and squinted at Freydis, who was whispering with another female soldier. They both glanced my way, then Freydis glared at the window behind me.

"Do it again," she barked.

I cried out, and the object in my mouth dropped to the floor, making a dinging noise that echoed back to my ears. Freydis held up her hand at the two men beside me, her eyes still focused on the window. After several painstaking, long moments, she gave the men a curt nod.

I slammed my eyes shut, waiting for the next wave of agony, but it never came. My arms became slack, no longer being held against the cushion. I forced my eyes open just as they lifted me from the torture machine.

My body was too exhausted to resist, and my head hung low as they set me on the cot. I rolled to my back and stared at the now-empty room on the other side of the glass. Jax had been taken away. He must have agreed to give them what they wanted. I couldn't think straight, and the walls waved at me like fabric in the wind. I gulped down the rising terror in my throat as numbness infused my body, and I welcomed the darkness.

<

"Kia Lynn." The woman's voice sounded so far away.

I curled my knees up to my chest. "Go away," I muttered, swatting her away from me.

"You need to wake up," she said, tugging at my arm. "Your uncle needs your help. *We* need your help."

"No," I muttered, turning away from the voice. "My body hurts. Leave me alone."

"Freydis is going to kill you and Jax."

My eyes popped open. I sat up straight, looking around the brightly lit room. The gray walls and window were still there. I turned my attention to Trinity, who was kneeling beside my cot.

"What did you say?" I asked, kneading my knuckles into my temples to soothe the raging headache in my skull.

"Something is wrong with Freydis," Trinity said. She slid her arm underneath me and hauled me to my feet. When I swayed, she steadied me with a soft smile. "I'm sorry for all the pain. I was following orders, but the direction Freydis is now taking us in does not work for me. No one was ever supposed to die."

"Where are my boots?" I stared down at my toes. If I was going to fight, I wanted my boots this time.

Trinity hurried to a few small doors at the far end of the room. She opened one, but it was empty. The second one had some pieces of fabric in it. The third and fourth were empty. Her gaze swept all around the room, then landed on the cot.

"Are those your boots?" She pointed behind me at the floor.

I turned awkwardly, trying to keep my balance. My boots were peeking out from underneath the cot.

"Yes." I smiled and sank back to the cot. When my boots were buckled, I turned my attention back to the female anaman. "Now what?"

"We have to break Jax out of his cell," Trinity replied, kneeling in front of me. She grabbed both my hands and held one to her cheek. "I know you are her daughter, and I probably could never forgive your mother, but you did not ask for this life. I am deeply sorry for the pain you have endured."

Her compassion moved me, but I was equally nervous to escape. I relaxed my jaw to give her a genuine smile. "I appreciate that, Trinity. Maybe later we will have the chance to talk more."

She nodded and climbed back to her feet. I followed her to the door. She glanced in either direction and then waved at me as she slinked into the corridor. We rounded the corner where Wolf stood waiting. His large stature nearly filled the entire hallway.

"Looks like you and I had the same idea," he said to Trinity. He switched his firearm into his other hand and turned to the side, allowing room for us to pass. "We have little time. Freydis has lost her mind, and at this rate, it won't be long before we are all on her hit list."

Trinity squeezed past him, and I followed right behind. I could feel Wolf's steady breath on my neck. He was so close, but I did not dare ask for more room. In fact, his close proximity was reassuring to my frantic mind.

"What will we tell the senators?" Trinity asked after we turned down another empty corridor. "Freydis promised we would only take one of the smaller ships once she retrieved Tallisa. I never knew about the time machine plans and her agreement with the senators."

"We tell them Freydis double-crossed them and we tried to stop her," Wolf muttered. The pain in his tone was deep. He was losing out on his chance to return home. "There is nothing more we can do, unless we kill her and take over the mission."

"I can help you with that," I whispered, still afraid someone would overhear us.

"How? Your wind ability?" Wolf chuckled and patted her shoulder. "Thanks, but no thanks. It is not strong enough to stop that woman."

"I just need space and my hands free," I replied, annoyed with his jabbing at my earlier weak attempt.

"Your mother's negotiation skills were far stronger than that absurd show we witnessed," Trinity replied, looking down the next corridor. "Jax is just at the end of this... wait." She held out her hand for us to stop. She lifted her finger to her lips and pointed down the hallway with her other hand.

Wolf pressed me against the wall and then stood in front of me. Trinity turned toward him and leaned her elbow against the wall as if they were in the middle of a deep conversation. I peeked to the side of Wolf's arm. Two male anamans walked by and waved at Wolf as they continued. No one moved until Trinity gave us a thumbs-up signal.

She tugged on my arm, and I crept behind her down the next corridor. There were more voices up ahead.

"We will never make it to Jax, let alone the docking area at this rate," Wolf grumbled. He opened a nearby door and shoved me inside.

It was a storage closet of some sort. Barely enough room for just me. Wolf shut the door, and it encased me in darkness. I pressed my ear against the door but only heard muffled tones. It sounded like arguing, then silence. I stepped back, thinking they would open the door again, but there was no movement.

My pulse beat ferociously in my ears and sweat trickled down my spine as I waited for them to return, but the other side of the door remained quiet. I slid to the ground, hugging my knees to my chest. Now what?

I scratched at my nose. Sitting in this dark nook was only going to drive me mad with worry. I sat up straight. I didn't need Wolf or Trinity. I would find Jax, and we would escape together. I climbed back to my feet and was grateful when the door opened with ease. I peeked out into the corridor. No one was there. Seconds later, I was racing down the hallway. Trinity had said Jax was at the end.

My wind was capable of breaking glass. I could use it to free Jax. It was the only plan I had, but if no one else was there, it was the only one we needed.

I slid to a halt at the end of the hallway and looked through the window of Jax's cell. He was lying on his cot with his eyes closed. Blood ran down his cheek from a wide gash they had not bothered to bandage.

Rubbing my fingers together, I summoned the wind and waited for it to build around me. My hair lifted around my face as my raging tornado grew in strength, beating against the walls and window. Jax's eyes popped open and he leapt to his feet, his gaze jerking back and forth until it fell on me. Our eyes met, and he noticed the wind thrashing against the glass between us. He grabbed the cot and tipped it to its side, then nodded at me before ducking behind his blockade.

I released the cyclone, and with ease it ripped through the window, scattering glass in every direction. I threw up my arms to protect my face from their sharp edges, but nothing hit me. My gaze followed the rushing wind, and I grinned from ear to ear as it carried the strewn glass away from me, leaving me unharmed.

Excitement surged within me as my arms fell to my sides. A smile teased the edges of my lips. Maybe I was, in fact, more powerful than I had realized.

CHAPTER NINE
Training

ZOE DAWN

Zeke threw his arm over my shoulders and pulled me away from the curious crowd. Resisting seemed unnecessary. Just like Koleton, he was intriguing. Different. We weaved in and out of different groups and entered a garden that led to the middle of the dome.

Lindon cursed behind us, and Koleton muttered something I could not hear to my promised mate. Zeke threw me a knowing smile before turning to look at the men behind us. Koleton was speaking in a hushed tone and pointing behind Lindon.

"He is right, Lindon," Zeke said, sauntering toward them and resting his hand on Lindon's forearm. "Zoe Dawn has not asked for your attention or protection. She is perfectly capable on her own."

Lindon opened his mouth to respond, but he took one

look at Zeke and closed it. He bowed his head slightly, then turned on his heel and disappeared into the market crowd. Zeke had an authority over these people I did not understand, but I intended on finding out.

"Now, where were we?" Zeke asked, holding out his arm for me to take.

Koleton joined us on Zeke's other side, and I linked arms with the handsome, sapphire-eyed man. His irises twinkled like the stars, and it was difficult to not get lost in them, but I pulled myself together and walked alongside him.

"Who are you?" I finally asked after a long silence.

The trees were lush and green, some rising higher than I could see from where I was standing. Zeke stopped underneath one and waved his hand. A stream of blue light spiraled from his hand and drifted over the flowers and various plants growing beneath the tree canopy.

"My people asked me to come and help rebuild so this world can shift to Her next level of evolution properly. I use my magic for creation." He pointed at the new blossoms opening their petals. "This garden grew by the touch of my hand."

I stared in wide-eyed wonder. "You can heal Mother Gaia as well?"

"I can do more than heal your planet," he replied,

waving at Koleton.

The redheaded man rolled his eyes but approached us willingly. "Why am I always your guinea pig?"

"Because you volunteered to accompany me and my sister here after I told Mother we would be fine on our own," Zeke replied. His chastising tone did not match the twinkle of amusement in his eyes.

Koleton held out his arms, obviously used to whatever Zeke was about to show me. "You know if I hadn't, she would have sent the beast, and he would have terrified these poor Earthlings."

Zeke laughed and pushed away one of his dark locks that fell in his face. "Apollo is a misunderstood soul. Stop picking on him."

"He likes it," Koleton replied, winking at me.

It was obvious from their bantering they were very fond of one another.

Zeke pulled out a dagger from the side of his trousers and, without warning, sliced Koleton's forearm. Koleton winced but did not move. I covered my mouth in horror as my gaze darted from one man to the other. Zeke's hand hovered just above the wound, and the same blue haze drifted from his palm and surrounded Koleton's arm. When Zeke lifted his hand, the cut had vanished.

"How did you do that?" I asked, unable to hide my

enthusiasm as I bounced on my toes.

"I was blessed by my parents." He shrugged, then chucked a ball of his blue energy into the air, catching it just after he tossed another one.

"He's a bit of a show-off," Koleton said, circling around the juggling show and stopping next to me.

"It is important to learn restraint, connect with your inner calm, and never allow another to control you, *especially* through your emotions." Zeke threw all five energy balls he had formed in the air at once, then flicked his wrist, and they burst into a shower of flower of petals. They fell to the ground and dissipated into a puff of smoke.

"Will you teach me?" I asked, completely enthralled with the ease he had with his mystical abilities. "I need to return to my village and help my family. An anaman ship arrived just before Lindon took me away from them and I must know if they are well."

"It would be an honor to show you how to master your skills and gifts," Zeke replied, bowing from his waist. "You are a descendant of the Theians and will be treated as such. As for your family, we will return tomorrow to check on their well-being. I will accompany you myself."

"What about the situation at the pyramid?" Koleton asked, plucking lint from the sleeve of his shirt.

"Esta contacted me again and said they had left after

we returned fire." Zeke removed his jacket and set it on a stone next to him. "They had other visitors shortly after, but we have detained those people, except for one. Once we assist our lovely Zoe Dawn, we will address that situation next. Will you please return to our quarters and relay this message to my sister?"

"As you wish, oh powerful one." Koleton brought his palms together in prayer hands and slightly bowed his head toward Zeke. "Is there anything else?"

"Well, now that you are offering…"

"I'm not," Koleton replied, softly punching Zeke on the back of the shoulder as he walked away. "Continue on without me. I will be fluffing up your pillow and drawing you a bath, Your Excellency." He waved goodbye, then skipped away like a child.

"Who is he to you?" I asked, watching his red hair bounce through the crowd. "He looks nothing like you, so I would assume he isn't blood family."

"He is like a father to me," Zeke replied, sinking to the ground and sitting cross-legged. "He is my mother's closest friend and companion and has dedicated his life to me and my sister. When my father was murdered, Koleton was with him and I think it makes him feel obligated in some way. Regardless, we are close." He waved for me to join him. "Let's start down here."

I joined him in a seated position, facing him. He closed his eyes, so I did the same.

"I sense a lot of pain and turmoil. Fear of losing your sisters. Your mum."

My eyes snapped open. His face was slightly scrunched, as if he was trying to pull out a thought.

"What are you doing?" My voice cracked.

"I am reading you." He opened his eyes and blew out his breath. "That was inconsiderate of me. I apologize. Let me explain."

I swallowed down my trepidation and nodded in reply.

"My mother has the ability to communicate telepathically, but only with those who possess the same gift. I received a version of her skill. I can read energy." He moved his hand around his face and body. "Your emotions emanate a message, and that is what I sense. It rolls off people like waves and, honestly, can sometimes be overwhelming."

"And you know my thoughts? Right now?"

"In a way, yes." He held out both his hands toward me and I took them. "I cannot hear your thoughts, but I can sense what you are thinking through the vibrations that surround you. Are you comfortable with me continuing?"

I drew in a deep breath, then nodded.

He closed his eyes once more. His forehead crinkled,

and I noticed his eyes twitching underneath his eyelids.

"You healed Earth." He paused and tilted his head to one side. "With your sisters and the spirit of Mother Gaia. She stepped in as the earth elemental. That makes sense, but She is not finished. Her evolution must transcend and requires the awakening of another."

Awakening of another, I thought. *That is what Lindon had said as well.*

He nodded, and a small smile deepened his dimples. "Now, I can see why you and I were brought together."

I did not understand his meaning or why he believed Mother Gaia was not finished, but I did not want to interrupt him.

He was quiet again, then he frowned. "Your hate for Tallisa runs deep. She hurt your best friend. I can understand how that would tear you up inside." His lips pursed and his grip tightened around my fingers. "She is Kia Lynn's test—her attachment to her mother's love and acceptance must…" His voice trailed off and he slowly opened his eyes.

"What do you mean?" I pulled my hands free from his grasp. "Tallisa is Kia Lynn's test?"

He stared thoughtfully at me.

I wiped at my cheeks. "Do I have something on my face?" I asked. My fingers trailed down to my chin.

"There is so much for you to learn and very little time if we are to leave in the morning." He rose to his feet and helped me to mine. "First, we need to address your red-passionate anger. This emotion usually stems from hurt, and the pain in your heart is fluid like lava. A dark entity was able to latch itself to your mind because you are more susceptible because of your deep rage. When we allow our emotions to control us, we leave the door wide open for others to do the same."

I nibbled on my bottom lip, embarrassed by my lack of self-control and at the same time amazed that he read me so well. "What do you suggest I do?"

"My mother had to learn this as well, so do not be ashamed. She is the most powerful Theian woman I know, and even she had to rewrite her reactions." He patted my hand and led me farther into the thick of trees.

It was quieter at the market, and more stars were coming into view. It must be late, but I was not tired, despite my lack of sleep. Being around Zeke was riveting.

He stopped at a small clearing and turned toward me. "My mother taught me the art of connecting to my inner knowing from a young age. It comes naturally for me because of her consistent teachings. You will feel strange at first, but trust me, when you reach the euphoria of soul unity, you will never want to be another way."

Transformed Chaos

"So you will not teach me some fighting skill that will help me be less emotional?" I asked, confusion furrowing my brow.

"Not entirely." He tapped his finger against my forehead. "The fight we are going to address is the one that is happening in here. Close your eyes."

I did as he instructed.

"Now, think of someone or a situation that infuriates you to the point you cannot think clearly," he said, wrapping his hands atop my shoulders. "I am your constant. In a way, I am standing in as your inner knowing and will squeeze your shoulders to remind you to take back your power. Do that by inhaling deeply, holding your breath for five seconds, and then releasing it slowly. Do you have something in mind to ignite your fury?"

"Oh, yes." My thoughts turned to Tallisa. She was nearby, and I wanted to burn her alive.

My skin simmered almost immediately, and a deep rage built in my gut when I remembered the sorrow in Kia Lynn's eyes. She was broken, her heart shattered. There was nothing I could do to soothe her pain away.

I felt my arms ignite into flames, but Zeke did not move away from the heat. He squeezed my shoulders.

I wanted Tallisa to experience the pain she had inflicted on Kia Lynn and Alex. Death was too kind. The thought of her suffering only fueled my fire, and I felt flames licking at my fingers.

Zeke squeezed my shoulders again. I drew in a deep breath and counted to five, then exhaled for another eight seconds. It gave me something to concentrate on, other than my thoughts.

"Do it again," he whispered.

I inhaled, counted, and slowly released my breath.

"And again."

He had me do it three more times and with each one my heart rate decreased and eventually my thoughts of murder faded.

"Now, focus on the core of your body, right beneath your sternum." He pressed his fist against my abdomen. "Right here. Imagine a white light spiraling in a circle. Your life force. The source of all your power. You have been given this gift to use as a light for this world. How do you want to show up?"

"In full control," I replied without hesitating. I knew what I wanted. It made perfect sense, but I would be the first to admit I was a hothead and struggled to contain the madness that writhed inside my mind.

"Good. Now do it again. Think of a situation, real or pretend, that would anger you to the point of losing control."

Transformed Chaos

I thought of Kia Lynn and Mum. I would die for either. Then there was Alex, my new sister whom I loved with all my heart. Covyn, my true soulmate. The woman who loved me unconditionally. If anything happened to her, I would torch the world.

My heart rammed against my chest as I visualized those four being hurt or worse. If any harm came to my family, I would destroy first, ask questions later. I felt a fireball burst from my palm. The flames crackled, urging me to make good on my thoughts.

Zeke's squeeze was barely noticeable. I wanted to listen to his guidance, but my deathly thoughts were intoxicating, and instead I leaned into the fire, envisioning the destruction in my mind as if it were happening right before my eyes. A dark fog blew into the vision. The tug of power surrounded me, and I relished the elated sensation as it swept over me like a warm blanket.

Another squeeze from Zeke brought me tumbling out of the reverie. He pinched harder. I winced, but it jolted me enough to return my focus to my core. I inhaled, pulling the air all the way down to my stomach. Five. Four. Three. Two. One. I released it. The flames still warmed my fingers. I drew in another long breath, then slowly counted again.

My breath blew across my lips, and I opened my eyes.

The fireball had been extinguished.

"I did it!" I exclaimed, throwing my arms around Zeke's neck.

He hugged me back. "I knew you could." His arms tightened around me, and he lifted me up and swung me around. "By the time we finish tonight, you will be a pro by morning."

I dropped my arms and stepped back. "All night?"

"If you want to master it, this is the time we have been given. Are you up for it?" He leaned against the tree behind him and crossed one ankle over the other. There is so much more I can teach you, including using your flame as a barrier of light. What do you say?"

Exhaustion was seeping into my mind and body, but my family needed me. I did not have time to sleep.

"Yes, I'm up for it. What about my parents?" I jabbed my thumb back toward the doorway to my new family's home. "Won't they want a say in what happens with me?"

He scrunched his face up, then laughed. "Their rules are old-fashioned and not the ways of the people of Theia's Moons. They want my help, then they can do this my way."

"I knew we would be friends the moment I laid eyes on you." I stood in front of him and bowed. A small smile danced across my lips. "I'm ready, oh mighty one."

CHAPTER TEN
Rogue Riders

ALEX

Driving through the California desert was not the same as it had been in 2025. Just like Las Vegas, most of the small towns and cities had been long forgotten and covered with hundreds of years of dirt, decay, and endless vines. It was almost pleasant with a twist of eerie, despite my circumstances. The air was not too hot, and the hoverbike moved better than any machine we had.

Then there was the face shield. It was unlike anything I had ever seen before. My hand swept right through it when I stopped, but while driving, it protected me from the bugs and wind and fully enclosed me inside the bike. I was able to activate a map onto it that was leading me toward the coast, and there was even a selection of instrumental music that was soothing to my worried heart.

By the time I made it to San Bernardino, exhaustion

had overwhelmed my mind, and I was struggling to keep my eyes focused on the incredibly confusing pathway. The roads were long gone, and the burnt remains of diesel trucks and cement structures were strewn in every direction. Most of them were covered in a green moss or weeds that had grown so high, they nearly blocked my way completely. It was messy, yet strangely beautiful.

I had found one blockade off one old exit that had allowed me enough room to hide the hoverbike and sleep for a couple of hours. Just enough time to give my mind and body a much-needed rest. Then I was back on the road before sunup.

I still could not reach Mom or Dad. I would contact Uncle Henry once I reached the coast, as I didn't need him trying to stop me from connecting with the water elementals.

Dawn was quickly approaching as I left the broken buildings of San Bernardino behind. From my limited viewpoint, it appeared as if the structures had not been as damaged or buried like the towns I'd already left behind, but their ghostly pasts were haunting from afar, and I had no intention of venturing closer.

As I came out of the valley, several flashing lights appeared on the screen. I slowed to look at them and noticed they were moving toward me at record speed. My heard drummed in my chest as I fumbled with my one remaining weapon. I glanced behind me, but I could not see anything threatening. Were they the vessels from the pyramid?

I faced forward and sped up. The obstructions in my way were lessening, but I still could not go as fast as I would like. I zigzagged around another diesel truck, and when I did, the pathway up ahead was mostly clear. I pressed the lever forward and increased my speed to the highest level. The hoverbike shot like a bullet, and the landscape zipped by too fast for even my comfort, but I kept going anyway.

The blinking lights were closing in on me. It had to be those vessels. They had probably tracked me through the hoverbike. It was the only explanation, unless they had been following me this entire way.

My hands shook, not only from being terrified but because my body was worn out from riding for so long with only a brief rest in between. Not to mention the traumatic day I had yesterday. This was getting old.

The sounds of their vehicles reached my ears. I took a chance and peeked at the sky behind me, but even with it being brighter out, there was nothing to see. That did not seem right. If the map was correct, they should be right behind me, but there was nothing except wisps of white clouds.

I heard them again, and in my left side mirror an object swerved into view. I gulped. It was another hoverbike. I bit down hard on my bottom lip. I had been wrong. They were on ground with me, and the worst part of all, they obviously knew how to maneuver these machines better than I did.

Within a few moments, they surrounded me. There had to be twenty or more of them. I glanced at the map, then at the hoverbike to my right. The occupant was wearing a helmet. They waved for me to pull over. I shook my head and leaned forward to cover myself better. I was too close to stop now.

The hoverbike shuddered underneath me, then the map disappeared, and the buttons flashed several times before extinguishing completely. I pressed the ON button, but it did not respond. Instead, it slowed to a stop, and the shield fizzled before vanishing completely. I was a sitting duck.

"Don't you fail me now," I muttered, frantically slapping the ON button several times. My gaze shot up to watch the growing crowd, then snapped back to the controls. I pushed every button and lever. The machine did not respond. "Damn it." I smacked the side of it and winced from the impact.

The bike gang circled me several times, then stopped

in formation around me. Two of them removed their helmets. I pointed my firearm at the man.

"Let me go!" I yelled, turning my firearm on the woman.

She held up her hands and smiled. "You passed through our territory, sweetheart. There's a toll required for safe passage."

These were not the people from the pyramid. Their leather outfits, dark and rugged, did not match the sleek uniforms the others had been wearing. Her light-brown hair was matted against the sides of her face, and her eyes were nearly the matching color. I glanced toward the man. His black hair was long and pulled back in a low ponytail. His deep-blue eyes pierced me with his intense stare.

"I have nothing to pay for passage," I replied. I wiped my sweaty palm down my pant leg. Then shifted my weapon to one hand and did the same with the other one.

The man cocked his head, lifting his brows at the firearm. "That weapon of yours might do."

I turned the object over in my hand, then held it out to him. "It's yours. Just let me pass through and you will never see me again."

He snickered. He leapt from his hoverbike, and his boots crunched loudly against the pebbles. His lips twitched with amusement as he sauntered toward me.

I held the weapon away from him. "Promise me you will let me continue on with no problems from your people."

He dove at me. We tumbled to the ground, and I struck my head against a sharp stone. A boot met my temple, and I felt the skin tear from my exposed lower back as I skidded closer to the other hoverbikes. The few clouds in the sky spun in a circle as I tried to blink away the pain radiating in my head.

The man leaned over me, holding my weapon in his hand. "This will go nicely with my collection. Thank you." He stood up straight. "Take her."

And this was the world I wanted to save, I thought venomously as someone lifted me and dropped me on another's lap. Their knees dug into my belly and ribs as I stared hopelessly at the ground, forcing myself not to vomit. Although, it would serve them right if they wore my stomach bile. The hoverbike accelerated, and I closed my eyes, too exhausted and in pain to do anything else.

The time is drawing near, a soft female voice said, floating in my mind.

Darkness surrounded me, and I welcomed it. Her voice echoed, and I wanted nothing more than to join her—wherever she was.

It seemed only a few seconds later when I was jolted

from my downward position and tossed to the ground. I grunted as it knocked the wind out of me, then I rolled to my side while rubbing the film from my eyes. I must have passed out. The sun had risen, and we were just outside a blackened building. I could not tell if it was from a fire or purposely painted that way. Either way, it appeared as a message to outsiders to stay away.

A pair of dark-brown boots paused in front of me. "Well, who do we have here?" a man asked.

I raised my hand to shield my eyes from the rising sun and stared at an older man with a cowboy hat on his head. His beady eyes stared back at me.

I scooted backward and sat up straight, ignoring the throbbing ache where the bike pirate had kicked me in the head. "My name is Alex," I replied, trying to sound more confident than I felt.

He reached his hand out toward me. "No need to grovel, my dear." He had a slight twang to his tone. "We know how to be civil in these parts."

I almost laughed. Civil, my ass.

I took his hand, and he helped me to my feet. Brushing off the dirt embedded in my palms and elbows, I took this chance to survey my surroundings. There were dozens of people, human and anaman, milling around and watching us from a distance. Some had leather jackets and steel-toed boots, while others wore cowboy hats and leather chaps just like in the Wild West. They looked to be reinventing the stories of old.

"See something interesting?" the man asked, stepping up next to me. His arm brushed against mine.

I licked my chapped lips and shot him a sideways look. He was invading my personal bubble. But then, what else was new these days?

"Just wondering where your goons have brought me." I did not try to hide my contempt.

"They like to play; that's all," he replied, pointing at my head. "The swelling will go down soon enough, and you will be back to normal before you know it."

"He attacked me, you old geezer," I hissed before I realized what I was saying. I slammed my eyes shut, cursing myself in my mind. "I just want to be allowed to continue on with no trouble. Is that too much to ask?" My voice shook with emotion, despite my trying to hide it. I pried open one eye. The man was smiling, so I resumed glaring at him.

"Of course that's too much to ask," he drawled, looking over my shoulder and snapping his fingers. "Toni here will take you to your cell. We can't have you wandering around our town, causing problems like you did yesterday."

Transformed Chaos

I felt a flush redden my cheeks. "What? How?" I did not know what to ask. He knew I had been in California. How was that possible?

"This is my territory, little lady." He held out a canteen of water. "Drink up. You will need to be hydrated for what is coming next."

Every inch of my body tensed from his words, but I was not reckless enough to turn away water. I gulped down as much as I could before he yanked it away from me. I wiped away the droplets of water from my chin.

"That's enough." He hitched the canteen on his belt and then grabbed my wrist and whirled me around, setting my hand in the grip of a wiry man with weather-beaten skin. His hand felt like old leather. "You cannot fool me. I know who is here and why. The little stunt your people pulled at the old amusement park shook us all to the core. We are a peaceful town, and those folks are under my protection. Do you hear me?"

Someone had recognized me. It was the only plausible explanation. My gaze darted around the growing crowd, searching for a familiar face. There weren't any.

The old man nodded at Toni. Without another word from either, he dragged me through the throngs of people. His grip squeezed firmly around my wrist and his fingernails dug into my skin. I yanked my arm, but he pulled back and I tumbled against him. He clutched my shoulder so tightly I had to bite back a scream.

"Don't do that again," he hissed. His face was mere centimeters from mine.

I pressed my lips together and nodded. He moved forward, hauling me into the black building. When he opened the door, the smell of ash filled my nose. This place had seen a fire recently. It was strange they would pick this as their home.

He pulled me further inside, and I noticed the black charred front lobby of the building. The fire had not extended past this space. A group of children raced through the hallway ahead of us but skidded to a halt when they saw us coming. The smallest child pointed at me and giggled, then turned on his heel and sprinted off with the rest of them behind him.

"How many of you live here?" I asked, trying to connect with him in any way possible.

Toni paid me no attention and continued dragging me through the winding corridors. The place was a labyrinth. We made so many turns that if there wasn't an old exit sign every so often, I could have sworn there was no ending. He was confusing me for a reason.

At the end of a dark, damp hallway, Toni threw open a door and shoved me inside. It was even darker in the room, and I jumped when the door slammed, encasing me in blackness. I blinked several times, and a sliver of light from a covered window at the far end caught my eye. I hurried toward it but stopped short when a figure rose in the room's corner.

I shrank back, covering my mouth to smother my scream.

"Why'd they throw you in here?" the woman asked, leaning against the wall behind her and crossing her arms over her chest. "You don't look like the other ones."

"I have no idea who you're talking about," I replied with a shaky voice. I pressed the palms of my hands against my chest to calm my racing heart.

The woman struck a match against the wall. She brought it to her mouth, where a rolled cigarette was hanging, and lit the end. The smoke quickly drifted through the room, making me cough. I waved it away from me and backed all the way to the door.

She pulled back the cover from the window and peeked outside. "They bring me the ones who need to be forgiven." Her gaze turned back to me, and I could see her silver eyes and white threads swirling in her cheeks. She was part anaman, like me. "Would you like to confess your sins?"

"Are you serious?" I ran my fingers through my hair,

scanning the entire room for an escape route. The room was devoid of all furniture, aside for two wooden chairs and a table on the other end. There wasn't even another window. "I have nothing to say to—"

She moved like a cat and was beside me before I had a moment to react. Her fingers wrapped in my hair, and she yanked my head back. "Liar!" she screamed, hauling me to the table. She slammed my cheek against the wood surface.

I shrieked in pain. It was my wounded side. A searing ache shot down my shoulder and into my hand. I bit back another cry, trying to ignore the fire devouring my nerves.

Her fingers remained entangled in my hair as she leaned down to me. "You will confess, or you will die." The cigarette hung from her bottom lip and the smoke blew in my face.

I coughed. My hand worked its way up to her shoulder, and I pushed against her. She did not budge. "Why are you doing this?" I asked, reaching farther up to unravel my hair from her grip. "I just want to save my family. Please!"

She ignored my cries. Instead, she shoved me into a chair and stormed away. "If he wants your confession, then you must have hurt someone. You must have caused death among our people." She turned toward me like a tiger eyeing her prey. "Confess now, and your penance will be swift. Continue denying what we already know, and your suffering will be long and grueling." She pounced and struck me on the other side of my face with her long nails.

I pushed her back and wiped at my cheek. There was blood on my hand. "You are mad!" I screamed, leaping from my chair and stalking toward her. She held her ground but did not touch me. "My father has done nothing but try to create peace between the anamans and humans. He brought me here to have a safe and happy life, but at every turn, there is someone else threatening to rip that from me."

The laugh that burst from her lips sounded like an evil witch cackle. She pointed at me, then slapped her knee and turned back to face the window. I watched in shock as she collapsed to the ground just under the streaming light.

"You are a murderer," she said, her fit of laughter ceasing immediately. "And they will burn you alive for it."

I stared at her. She closed her eyes, and a soft snore rumbled through her nose. She really was a madwoman.

With her guarding the window, my only way out was through the door. I reached into my boot and pulled out the small dagger I had hidden in on the side. I tiptoed to the door and jiggled the knob. It was one of those bathroom locks, with the hole for the bobby pin on our side. I had picked enough of those. They obviously did not think anyone would make it out of this room alive.

I glanced at the sleeping woman. My death still might be a possibility if I did not escape soon.

In my other boot, I had stored a small pocketknife that had a pin as one of its options. It was a good thing they didn't search me very well. Several tense moments later, the lock clicked, and the door creaked open an inch. My gaze snapped to the woman, whose eyes popped open.

A sneer rose on her lips. "Where do you think you're going?" she asked, rising slowly to her feet.

I yanked open the door the rest of the way and sprinted down the hallway, levitating some of the way and running the rest. I turned down several other corridors before noticing an exit sign up ahead. I barreled toward it and aimed for the door, smashing my shoulder against it.

I groaned from the impact and grabbed my aching arm.

My gaze shot to the hinges. No wonder. I had to pull to open it, not to mention it was as solidly built as they came.

The woman raced past the corridor and I heard her feet squeak against the hard floor as she skidded to a halt. I didn't wait for her to return as I sprinted through the doorway and into the sunshine. There were people scattered in every direction, so I just ran into the thick of them without looking back. I pushed past the surprised strangers and raced down an old, broken road.

"She's escaping!" the woman screamed.

I threw a look over my shoulder and saw her pointing at me. A hand grabbed me. I whipped around with my little dagger and sliced the man across his cheek. He wailed in pain and thankfully dropped my arm. I tore down another road, determined to lose them in the maze of buildings.

As I sprinted down a nearly deserted road, a foot shot out from nowhere and caught my leg. I flew forward and face planted into the dirt, then slid several feet. Someone yanked me up. A drip of water hit my outstretched hand. My mind froze for a split-second, then I collected and dumped the water in the air on top of the man's head. He jumped in surprise and leapt away from me.

I tumbled forward but caught myself from falling again, then whirled around to face the crowd gathering at the other end of the block. A few snarled at me. I smiled in response.

With a flick of my wrist, a wave of water burst through the ground and froze in midair, blocking anyone from passing through. I could see the mad-as-a-hatter woman on the other side, pounding on the ice. I waved, then dropped all my fingers except the middle one and raised my hand so she could see it. Then I was off again.

CHAPTER ELEVEN
Escape

KIA LYNN

Jax's head popped out from the gaping hole. He beamed with pride. "Way to go, Kia Lynn." His hands found my trembling shoulders, and he wrapped me in a bone-crushing embrace. "How about you and I make a break for it?"

I nodded against his chest. "Best plan ever."

He leaned back and shot me a wide smile, then ruffled my hair. "With that power behind us, no one can stop us." He winked at me before folding my hand in his. His gaze drifted down to the other end of the hallway. "You wouldn't happen to know the way out?"

I had not thought that far ahead. My lips lifted in a smirk, and I shrugged. "You were lucky I found you. I was hoping you would know where to go next."

"We will figure it out together." He squeezed my hand

and tugged me forward, leading me to the other end of the hallway.

Our boots scrunched against the glass, and a petty part of me was happy I had left Freydis with a mess. Of course, she probably would have her minions clean it up for her.

"How did you escape your room?" Jax asked, his voice barely a whisper. He glanced down the next hallway and pulled me around the corner before looking back at me for an answer.

"Trinity," I whispered, a small tug of remorse reminded me that the woman had never returned. I really hope nothing had happened to her. "She told me Freydis has a new agenda that she cannot support. Same with Wolf. They were both with me, but then Wolf had stuffed me in a closet to keep me out of sight. I heard arguing, but I'm not sure if it was between Trinity and Wolf or someone new. Whatever happened, they left, and I had no choice but to find you on my own."

"They are all good people." There was a thick tone of regret in Jax's voice. "Even Freydis. Especially Freydis. Your mother led them here, unbeknownst to me, and then she abandoned them. I do not fault them in their anger toward me, but I'm infuriated they involved you."

He was quiet again when we stopped at another break in the corridor. Jax peeked around the corner and squinted his eyes. The fine lines in his forehead crinkled when his brow furrowed. He pointed.

"I think that is the way to their cargo if I read that sign correctly."

I stepped around him and looked. A sign at the end of the hallway was lit with a purple hue. I could not read what it said. "Might as well go for it." I turned to face Jax. "We have little choice at this point."

"Hold it!" a man yelled.

Jax whipped around to look the way we came. I followed suit. Two anaman soldiers were barreling toward us. Jax took my hand again and yanked me toward the purple sign. The ones in pursuit turned the corner not too far after us. I lifted my hand and rubbed my fingers together, invoking the winds to rage. The air thickened almost immediately, and moments later, I heard the groans of the two behind us as they tumbled backward.

I can do this.

The door with the sign needed a handprint to open. Jax punched the wall and cursed under his breath. He kicked the door, then barreled at it and threw all his weight against it. It barely groaned from the impact.

I grabbed his forearm. "Step aside. Let me have a go."

He nodded, panting as he moved out of my way.

I pressed my fingers together hard, then had an idea to

rub my hands together instead. My palms kissed, and I focused on the air as friction built between my hands. A gust of wind blew around me, building in strength with each passing moment.

"Kia Lynn," Trinity yelled over my storm. "Let me open it. Save your wind for when you really will need it."

My hands fell to my sides as I turned to see Trinity and Wolf standing with Jax. I breathed a sigh of relief at the sight. Trinity squeezed my arm when she slid by me. Her hand lit up the screen next to the door, and it slid open with ease.

We raced through the opening and barreled down the staircase with Trinity leading the way. Wolf took up the rear, and Jax stayed close to me. Five flights down, and Trinity opened the final door. She stepped over the threshold and jerked back when something sliced through the side of her left thigh. She threw a pained expression back at us before collapsing.

Jax dragged me away from the opening, and Wolf pulled Trinity back inside.

"I'm so sorry, Jax," Trinity muttered as Wolf pressed his hand against her wound. Her sleepy gaze turned my way. "And you, Kia Lynn. We were wrong."

Jax nudged Wolf away, covering Trinity's hip with fabric he had torn from his shirt. He wrapped it tightly.

"I've got this. Keep them away from here."

My hand found Trinity's as Wolf moved away. I squeezed it. "You will be okay, Trinity. I will find a way to get you to a ship."

The blood had already soaked through Jax's fabric, but Trinity swung herself into a seated position, then leaned against the wall behind her.

"We will do this together," she replied, holding out her hands. "Damn, that hurts. Help me up, child. We have work to do."

"The same, courageous and reckless Trinity," Jax said, helping me pull Trinity to her feet.

She leaned against him for support and shot him a weak smile. "I have gotten soft. Our people of old were much kinder."

Wolf beckoned at me to come closer. "They are closing in," he hissed. His jaw was set tight, and his fingers tightened over his weapon.

"I will push them back," I said, falling to my knees and scooting to the doorway.

I peeked around the frame. I counted eight anamans coming from our left. The right was clear, but I was sure more were on their way. I checked to the left again and noticed a few figures farther away. Freydis stood in the middle, holding a weapon against her hip. She did not need me any longer—not alive, at least. If she wanted to cause Mama any pain, it would be to throw my body out at the last moment for dramatic effect. I already could see it unfolding in my mind. It would be the last jab before Freydis left.

"The ships are all being covered by Freydis's troops," Wolf whispered, leaning closer to me. "If you can push them out of the way, Jax can get Trinity inside and then you can follow."

I nodded, rubbing my hands together. I pinpointed a spot in front of the approaching warriors, pulling the air into a whirlwind to block their path. It built quickly, and the eight scrambled backward, climbing over one another as gusts of wind tore over pieces of equipment, shooting loose pieces in various directions.

Freydis ran toward the cyclone. I motioned for Jax and Trinity to go, directing the winds to turn full steam on the female anaman. The duo squeezed passed me and hurried toward the nearest ship. Wolf stood beside me with his firearm trained on Freydis.

He grunted and stumbled into me, knocking my concentration off the approaching woman. I glanced behind us and saw one anaman hiding behind a vehicle. Wolf was holding his arm but had turned to face the one who had shot him. He fired and then the entire room awakened with the sound of anaman weapons shooting at us.

I ducked behind a cement beam and concentrated on my dying whirlwind. It had lost its momentum, and Freydis slipped by it. My gaze fell on her growing shadow, sneaking toward my hiding spot. I focused on the spot around the corner and hit her with everything I had. Her figure spun by me with a surprised look flashing across her expression.

She shot at me, but the dart embedded itself in the cement near my shoulder. I plucked it out and hurled it across the floor. She was intent on zapping me again, this time until I no longer moved. Her body was flung out of the cyclone, and Wolf turned his firearm toward her, then fired at her startled face.

He missed her face but grazed the side of her neck. A black fog oozed from the wound and twirled above her head. She winced. Her hand folded over the slash and she rose to her feet as if nothing had happened. The darkness seeped back into her skin and her eyes flickered black. Her free hand rose, and she pointed at me once again.

The dark void had found its new vessel. Now I understood why it was determined to take ownership of the time travel machine. Its destruction would spread across the universe.

Transformed Chaos

"Go!" I yelled at Wolf.

He did not argue and flew by me, racing toward the ship Jax had taken Trinity to. I pushed my wind against Freydis and built another behind me, forcing the others to run for cover. Freydis pressed against my assault and inched toward us.

From behind Freydis, a figure swung out of the shadows, knocking her companion out with a large hammer. Jax swung at Freydis, but she ducked and turned on him. He shifted to the side and swung again. This time, it connected with her shoulder and threw her across the floor.

He raced after her, dragged her to her feet, and knocked her firearm from her grasp. The remainder of her team trained their weapons on him. With a flick of my wrist, my cyclone sent them all flying so far away, none of them stood again.

"We need to confine her," Jax yelled, pulling Freydis toward another ship.

I surrounded both in a wall of wind, careful to keep the torrent away from their bodies, only using it to keep her from escaping. Her eyes darkened and turned black as night. It could not leave Freydis's body. They needed to die together. Jax's eyes turned toward me, and I saw the same realization in his expression. We had to find a way to eliminate the entity that had possessed his old friend's mind.

"Tell them to go without us," Jax shouted over the raging wind. "This is on me."

I nodded and sprinted toward the other ship. Wolf stood just inside the shadows of the bay door.

I skidded to a halt. "We are right behind you. Take Trinity to safety."

He glanced over my shoulder at Jax, who was fighting his way to another open ship. Then Wolf's gaze shot in the other direction. "There are more coming, and I can't leave my people."

My gaze followed his. An entire fleet of anaman warriors were inching their way toward us. "You should convince them to hold their fire, then lead this ship away. Jax and I will finish this with Freydis."

His expression fell, and the grief of what was about to happen melted across his expression, but he nodded and waved me away. "May the Goddess be forever by your side, Kia Lynn. I hope we meet again under much better circumstances."

I brought my palms together and bowed slightly at him in response, then tore off in the direction of the ship Jax was hauling Freydis onto. My cyclone had died down somewhat, and Freydis was recovering from Jax's hammer strike. He threw her inside the ship, and I pushed her the rest of the way with my wind.

Jax opened the door to the cargo hold, and my raging wind folded over the angry woman and lifted her into the metal-encased space. Jax pressed a red button, and all the doors below closed and sealed shut. Then the door in front of us did the same. He flipped a switch and locked all the doors from the outside.

I heard Freydis scream. Jax shut the bay door and raced for the control room. I stayed put, holding onto a handle as the ship lifted from the ground and zoomed out of the massive anaman vessel.

I slipped to the ground and cradled my face in my hands. We had to kill her. It was the only way. Whatever entity had bound itself to her, needed to be returned to the void, and the only way to do that was to fly straight into it.

"I've already contacted Henry," Jax said, interrupting my thoughts. He knew what we had to do as well. "He will open the rip enough for me to take it inside the darkness."

"You?" I shook my head. "We are doing this together."

"No, we aren't." He sank to the ground in front of me and took both of my hands. "You have a full life to live. I had my time to be here. I may have failed your mother, but I will not do the same to you. I will not allow you to sacrifice your life when you have so much to give this world."

A sob rose in my throat, and I shook my head again before burying my head against his chest. "I can't lose another person. Alex will never forgive me, and we both need you."

"That's not true." His hands curled around the sides of my head, and he tilted my face to look up at him. "You don't need anyone. Alex does not need anyone either. But together, you three will keep this world from collapsing. The world needs *you*."

Tears spilled from my eyes, but I wiped them away, furious at the turn of events. "We can find another way," I snapped, pushing his comforting arms away from me. "Don't you dare leave me."

He sighed and swung his legs out to climb to his feet. "You have to go, Kia Lynn. We don't have time to argue about this." He reached down and hauled me up.

I threw my arms around his waist and clung onto him. "What will I tell her?"

He choked on a sob and held me tightly against his chest. "Tell her I did this for her. For all of you. And that she will always be the best thing I ever did in this life." His arms fell to his sides, and he pushed me toward the bay door. "Tell her I love her more than life itself."

I glanced at the bay door, then back at him. "How will

I make it to the ground?"

A small, grief-stricken smile rose on his lips. "The air will guide you down. Don't you realize, Kia Lynn? You command the air. All of it. Never, ever, shrink yourself down to make anyone else comfortable. You do not need anyone's permission to rise in your power." He leaned down and planted a kiss on my forehead. Then he did it again. "The second one is for Alex. Please love her through the pain I'm about to cause."

With those words lingering in the air, he turned on his heel and stepped through the doorway. He sealed the door from the inside. The bay doors creaked as they opened. I turned back to face them, and as the wind gusted in from outside, I allowed it to fold me in its arms, drawing me from the safety of the ship.

CHAPTER TWELVE
Shattered Heart

ZOE DAWN

Every inch of my body ached. When Zeke said we were going to work on my mind, he had mentioned nothing about running, jumping, or spinning. And these were not lessons on fighting but an entire list of ways to avoid it altogether, and most of them included dodging another person's throws without fully igniting my fire.

The orange-and-yellow energy flowed along my skin like a warm blanket. Zeke grinned, and I wanted to jump up and down for joy. It created a barrier between me and any weapon, including the one Lindon had used on the people in my village. Zeke even mentioned that eventually I would learn how to create a shield around other people as well. It was a gift very few possessed, and my connection to another star system had given me an advantage.

Transformed Chaos

"My mother has a purple light that has protected more lives than I could ever count," he said when my smiling gaze met his. "She is my hero, the reason I am who I am today."

"You really do admire her," I said, twirling the energy around my body and expanding it a few inches from my skin.

"Very much so." His smile widened, and he pointed at my progress. "You will have this ability mastered before we leave in a few hours."

"I could protect them all." I beamed with pride. I never thought this possible, at least not in this lifetime. Only in my dreams was this world filled with magic and endless energy. "What is next?"

I heard footsteps on the path, moving toward the small grove of trees we had been hiding in. Zeke rolled his eyes, seeming to be aware of who was approaching. I turned to wait for them.

Jamila and Koleton stepped into view. Koleton threw Zeke a look of apology as Jamila slowed her pace. Her gaze swept from me, over to Zeke, then back to me.

"Daughter, I hear that you will leave at dawn." She reached out her hands toward me, and I took them in mine. "I would have liked more time with you."

"Your silence earlier would speak otherwise," I

replied, not sure how to take this woman. Her lack of excitement at seeing her long-lost daughter told me she was not really interested in having me return.

Jamila dismissed Koleton and Zeke with a wave of her hand.

Zeke obliged, and Koleton followed him. Neither of them looked at me before leaving. I stared after them, wishing they had stayed.

"Zeke's power over our community does not mean he rules with an iron thumb," she said, her voice pulling my gaze back to hers. "He is not our ruler, but our guide. We follow him and his family because we hold a connection to them as our people. That is all. Do not mistake our quiet response yesterday for an agreement between us and Koleton. We do it for Zeke."

I yanked my hands away. "I do not know what that means, but if you are implying that I am your property and you only allowed me to leave with Koleton because of Zeke, then you are the one who is mistaken."

Jamila sighed and clicked her tongue, just like I would do. I glared at her, but she ignored the look.

"We are not saying you are our property," she replied after a few quiet moments. "But we ask that you stay and fulfill your obligations to your people."

"You are not my people," I snapped, throwing my arms

out wide in exasperation. "I do not want to be Lindon's mate. I am not interested in men. Do you not understand? My heart belongs to another woman and I will return to her. Mark my words."

My outburst did not faze Jamila. She stared at me until I finished.

"How will you produce an heir with another woman?"

Her question bit my heart. I never intended on having children. Jamila must have read my answer in my expression as this time a sadness clouded her features.

"You are our only chance for our bloodline to continue." Jamila fiddled with a large ring on her thumb. "You were my only child who did not die before birth."

Her words tugged at my heart, but I was equally infuriated. "Is this why you came for me? For an heir?" I stabbed my fingers into my curls and turned away from her, unable to look her in her eyes any longer. "You could have come for me at any time, but you waited until you needed something from me. I am only a means to an end for you."

Jamila's fingers, heavy with stoned rings, snaked over my shoulder. I tried to shake them off, but she held tight. "That is not what I am saying. We had hopes—high hopes—but we told you the truth earlier. We did not want to break you away from the only world you knew." She turned me toward her. The look on her face had softened, and so did my emotions. "I will support you in whatever decision you make. I will not allow those men to mold you into what I am, a subservient woman to them all. You deserve better."

She reached her hand up and ran her thumb down my cheek, then turned my face and planted a kiss on the side of my forehead. Without another word, she walked away.

Her quiet demeanor was a mask. She was a woman who had bowed to men her entire life, and within a few moments, she decided her daughter deserved better than that life. A deep gratitude swelled in my heart for the mother I had never had the chance to know.

"Wait," I said, against my better judgement.

Her shoulders tensed, but she turned back with a soft smile.

I swallowed back the rising heartache from never having the opportunity to know this woman. "Who is Nikita to you? Why do you protect her after all the horrible things she has done?"

"She is my cousin and the only blood family I have, aside from you." Jamila entwined her fingers and rested her hands against her belly. "Her relationship with Tallisa is toxic and will be dealt with once we move beyond this state of being. Tallisa will not be joining us."

I scrunched up my forehead with confusion. "What do you mean?"

Jamila drew in a long breath, then smiled once again. "It is wonderful you have Zeke to guide you. When our final transition is complete, you and I will finally be able to know one another. Until then, I send you off with all the blessings of my heart. Farewell, daughter."

I watched her go, unable to find my voice after her last words.

Koleton returned to the grove after Jamila disappeared, with a bag in one hand. Zeke was not with him.

"We will be leaving soon." Koleton hurried to my side and wrapped his free arm around my shoulders. "Are you okay?" His eyes searched my face for answers, as I did not reply right away.

I drew in a long breath and turned my attention toward him, patting his hand that hung over my shoulder. "I think I will be fine. This place would have been my home. She would have been my mother. My life would have been completely different if I had grown up here, and I am so glad I didn't."

"It's not all bad. Maybe someday you can visit Theia and her moons. There is an entire universe of opportunities and exploration for you." He pulled away from me and gathered Zeke's jacket from a nearby rock.

"I think I will stay on my own little planet for a while." I felt Mother Gaia's pull, a heartbeat in rhythm with mine. Alex and Kia Lynn needed me. This world was under our protection, and we needed to take it more seriously.

Koleton just smiled. "I brought you nourishment." He opened his bag, and the smell of cinnamon filled the air. He pulled out a circular piece of bread with cinnamon swirled within its folds. "These are my favorite. I knew you would need something to fill your belly after a night with Zeke.

I took the gooey bread and inhaled its scent before biting off a large piece. The cinnamon was only a portion of the delicious taste that invaded my senses. My lips widened into a satisfied grin and Koleton nodded in recognition.

"Exactly how I feel about those as well," he said, holding out his hand for me to take.

We walked down the pathway toward the shops, while I enjoyed the delicacy. Zeke and I had been training all night long, and the market was opening again. The buzz of life met our ears as we neared the opening. Zeke was with Jamila. He kissed her cheek, and she turned and left.

I licked each of my fingers as we approached Zeke from behind.

He turned, and his gaze met mine. A bright smile

blossomed across his face. "We have her blessing. Are you ready to return to your people?"

"More than ever."

Koleton tossed Zeke his jacket. We entered the market together, and before I knew it, we had arrived at the holding area for their ships. The blonde girl I had seen yesterday was standing next to a tall anaman man. They both turned our way and my heart dropped.

Tatum and Beatle.

"Why are they here?" My voice shook. A deep loathing swirled inside my gut, and I had to focus my concentration on my breathing. Zeke's guidance was helping, but I worried I would not be strong enough in worse circumstances.

Zeke's brows lifted in question. "Are they a problem for you? I need Tatum, and Beatle will not stay here without him."

"Tatum is Tallisa's goon. He tried to abduct my sister for Tallisa's selfish need to destroy our world."

"I think Tatum is misunderstood." Zeke nodded his head at my hands.

I stared at the glow of my fire, ready to explode. Closing my eyes, I pulled my powers back to my core and then allowed it to dissipate through my body. Using that one little trick Zeke had taught me had been more euphoric than anything else I had experienced. It sent waves of elation crashing over my nerves, calming them to a point of complete joy. This time was no different. I did not need to use that energy yet.

I opened my eyes and refocused on the two in front of me. "We will learn to get along. For now."

Zeke just smiled, and Koleton patted my hand before we all piled into their ship.

This vessel differed from the one I had been in with Lindon. It was silver on the outside and blended into the background like all the others, but they filled the inside with color. That was when I remembered the name of my family's tribe. The Sapphire Spirit Tribe.

Once we took our seats, I turned toward Zeke. "They named their tribe after you, didn't they?"

He pursed his lips and fidgeted with his restraints so he could see me better. "Yes." His sapphire eyes twinkled with amusement. "I have been around a lot longer than it appears."

My eyes widened. "How old are you?"

"He's an old man," Koleton said from the captain's chair.

Tatum and Beatle were situated across the room, but they were paying attention to our conversation. I think everyone was curious.

Zeke laughed and settled against the back of his chair, crossing one leg over another. "I am not as old as my companion, but yes, I have been alive for forty-eight Earth years."

I sat up straight and pulled against my safety belt. "What? That is impossible. Your face is as young as mine."

Koleton raised his hand. "Nothing is impossible," he said in a deep voice.

"How old are you?" I asked, directing my question at Koleton.

"I am closing in on eighty years." Koleton eased the ship through the now-open entryway above us. I watched as it closed underneath us, then we zoomed away. "I have been with Zeke since his birth. We are close. Forty-eight years close."

I collapsed against my chair, astounded by the revelation. Never in my wildest dreams would I have thought this man sitting next to me was that old. I was a baby compared to him, but his young appearance would disagree.

"Why are you even here?" I asked after a long silence.

"I have family here," Zeke replied, scratching the short stubble on his chin. "My grandparents live here full-time and will probably die on this planet. My aunt wanted a connection between our civilizations, and since my mom cannot leave right now, we thought it best if my sister and I made the journey. We are helping restore your planet to Her full beauty, but apparently, She already had three girls chosen for that job. Now, you need the fourth to finish what you started."

"We already completed…" The black mountains rose into view and excitement sparked inside me. My hands tapped the armrests. I was eager to see Kia Lynn and Alex again.

As we neared my village, I noticed the anaman ship had left. I stared down at the mess left behind. Several structures had been burned to the ground and there were no signs of life for as far as I could see. My elation dropped into despair.

"They aren't here," I said, turning to look at Zeke. "We need to go to Alex's village."

"Where is that?" Koleton asked. He shifted in his seat, and his concerned gaze landed on me.

I jabbed my thumb over my shoulder. "Back the way we came. Not too far, though. It lies just outside the old city." They had to be there. I traced the kenaz rune, then folded my hands into one another to stop their shaking.

He nodded, and the ship rose from my village, spinning around to face north. I could already see the outline of

Alex's protective fencing. I pointed at it.

"Right there. You can't miss it."

Koleton steered the ship toward Alex's village and set it down next to her parents' vessel. When we walked outside, Henry and Eshah greeted us. Aly was right behind them. I raced past the first two and threw myself into Aly's arms.

She smoothed down my hair and held me tighter than she ever had before. "I thought you were gone for good this time," she whispered in my ear, her voice thick with emotion.

"Are these the ones who took you away?" Eshah asked, pointing her weapon at Koleton. Her gaze traveled up and down the silver ship behind us.

I ripped myself away from Aly and knocked Eshah's firearm out of her grasp. It clattered against the rocks and skidded away from us. "These people took me away from the ones who abducted me. Where is Mum? Kia Lynn?"

No one spoke, and I felt the temperature drop around me. I could not tell if it was just me or if a breeze had swept in a chill. I turned in a circle, staring at each sullen expression.

"What happened? Where is everyone?" I asked. My gaze landed on Aly. "Tell me, Aly. What happened to our village?"

"They murdered her, Zoe Dawn," Aly whispered. Her hand shot up and covered her mouth as a sob burst from her lips and tears spilled down her cheeks. "I tried to warn her. I asked Alex to use her water to stop them, but she didn't listen."

"Do not blame Alex," Henry snapped, circling around Eshah and standing next to me. "Zoe Dawn, it was too late. We could not save her."

"Save who?" I screamed the question. A crimson flush spread across my cheeks and my fire simmered just beneath my skin. I did not know if I could control it this time.

I slammed my eyes shut and focused on the flames nipping at my flesh. I forced them back to my core, but the euphoria did not spread like it had several times before. My muscles trembled with a deep fury, and I peeled my eyes open to stare at everyone surrounding me.

"Tell me," I hissed between clenched teeth.

Aly gulped, but she stepped closer and took my shaking hands. "Attica. Your mum. She did not survive."

The world around me fell away. My knees buckled, and I collapsed to the ground, pulling my knees into my chest. With trembling arms, I wrapped them around my legs to stop the endless quiver that had overtaken my body. I muffled my screams against my knees, then tilted my chin

Transformed Chaos

up to the morning sky and pleaded to Goddess it was not true. The grief ripped through me, crushing my spirit, my heart, and my mind. I could not hold back any longer. The pain spiraled and my entire body burst into a ball of fire.

CHAPTER THIRTEEN
Sacrifice

ALEX

My abductors had taken me into the thick of Los Angeles. Just like Anaheim, they had cleared away most debris and several of the stable buildings were being occupied. Their numbers were vast, and now I had created an enemy out of them. I could not understand why they had chosen this area to live when the world had much better land.

It also surprised me California was still above water, considering the shift in the climate. The air was much drier, and the trees were sparse on the outskirts of the city. Brittle weeds crowded around every structure, reminding me of the ugly drive through southern Wyoming back in my old time period.

I had levitated for nearly an hour before my exhaustion set me back on my feet, but at least it put enough distance between me and that rogue community. When I had heard them, I could easily hide. They could not find my footprints in the dust, which had forced them to look for me elsewhere.

My focus was on reaching the ocean, so I walked away from the sun until it rose above me. As it fell in front of me and beat unforgivingly against my face and neck, I prayed I was doing the right thing. The water elementals were my last hope. I had no way back to Mom or the others, and the ship that had taken Dad and Kia Lynn was nowhere to be seen.

When my gaze fell on the waves of the ocean water, my heart nearly burst from my chest. Elation buoyed my spirits, and I picked up my pace. I fixated on the horizon and the crumbling buildings around me blurred. Finally, I was here again.

I pressed off the ground to levitate, but my toes skidded against the dirt, and I tumbled forward, sprawling to the ground in a heap of sweat and tears. The sandy shore was mere inches away. I reached out for it and pulled myself to my hands and knees, then crawled onto the warm beach.

"I'm here!" I cried, kneeling at the edge of the sand.

The water was still so far away. I noticed several structures nearly submerged in the advancing waters, but most others near the ocean had been destroyed from hundreds of years of decay. Piles of bricks lay mixed within the sand, along with other remnants of the once steady buildings.

I wiped my dirty hand across my face and then rubbed my eyes, trying to wake my senses. It did not help. A heavy film blurred my eyesight, but I hauled myself to my feet, anyway. My hands quivered as they pressed against my knees, and I heaved in and out several long breaths.

Somehow, I moved my feet. I shuffled them through the sand, kicking it up and creating a dust cloud around me. I paid it no attention. My tunnel vision was taking me to the water.

When my toes felt the cool ocean wash over them, I smiled and breathed a sigh of relief. My muscles relaxed, and I waded into the waves, relishing in its arms as they enfolded around me. My mind suddenly filled with frantic and panicked whispers. Something was wrong. I drew in a deep breath and collapsed into the water.

There was only darkness in every direction. The murkiness made it difficult to tell if my eyes were open or shut, but my lungs were already screaming for air. I swam in the direction I thought was upward, grateful when my face was above water again. I gasped in a few breaths, then dove under again to search for the same elementals who had come to me not even two days earlier.

Transformed Chaos

Once again, darkness surrounded me. It was as if the ocean was devoid of life. I pulled back and swam to the surface again.

Something tugged on my leg. I jerked away and tried to see what it was, but the cloudy water was not revealing its secrets. My muscles cried in exhaustion, so I turned to face the shore. It was farther away than I thought possible. I had only been in for a few minutes. A nagging feeling swirled around in my stomach, and I whipped around to make sure I was alone.

There was no one there, which made me even more uneasy. I felt a presence, and it was not the same one I had experienced earlier. There was a darkness surrounding it. A sinister spirit or energy.

As I swam back around to face the shore, something grazed across my hip. I threw myself forward and kicked my legs to get away from whatever was circling me.

Alex hurry, a voice whispered.

I glanced back to find the source of the voice, but just like before, no one was there. I swam harder. The shore seemed to move farther away from me, and my exhaustion was making it hard to keep going, but I pushed forward regardless, ignoring the pain radiating up my sides.

You must swim faster, the voice whispered again. This time, I knew it was in my head. Was I losing my mind? It sounded so clear, like someone was right next to my ear.

Something knocked into my legs, then again. The third strike nearly whirled me around in a circle. I dove back toward the shore. It was close.

It wants you most of all, Alex. The voice was nearly screaming now. *Do not let it in. You have to save us from—*

The voice stopped when my feet touched the sand beneath me. I pushed through the water, glancing over my shoulder several times, before I collapsed on the wet sand just outside the reach of the next wave. It crashed mere inches away from me and it looked like massive hands reaching in my direction. I scooted farther up the beach, gasping in one deep breath after another.

Where were the water elementals? And was that the same dark void that Zoe Dawn had experienced?

I was not about to stick around and find out, but my body hurt more than ever now, and my mind was hazy with exhaustion. I crawled toward a large tree that had probably been planted over a thousand years before. Its burly branches spread far and wide, and I sensed the safety underneath its canopy. I just needed to close my eyes for a minute.

My knees and palms were scraped up from the gritty sand, and there were three welts down my legs. When I reached the base of the tree, I curled my legs into my chest and laid my head on my arm. I could not think. I did not want to move. My eyelids were so heavy, I could not fight it any longer. When I woke, I would find my water elementals and save them all.

<

Our moment to unite is drawing near. The melodic female voice swirled like a thick fog inside my dreams.

I was back in Zion, staring at the pool of water inside Mother Gaia's cavern. A woman with green markings stood in the middle of the water, waving for me to join her. She looked familiar, but I could not remember how I knew her. My toes grazed the edges of the pool, and the tiny waves sparkled brightly as they moved toward the woman.

Return to where it all began. We will transcend together. She spoke, but her lips did not move. *I am waiting for you.*

The ocean waves greeted me when I woke. The sun was blistering on my face, and I reached up to wipe the beads of perspiration from my forehead. My other arm was numb, so I shook it out, trying to recall where I was and what day it was. I pried open my eyes and squinted at the setting sun.

My memories from earlier came crashing back to me. The rogue gang, the insane woman, my exhaustion and lack of food and water, along with the darkness in the ocean water. Not to mention the fact my family and friends were all captured by two entirely different enemies.

And that voice. Who was she?

I rolled to my other side and screamed, scrambling backward several feet.

A young girl stood a few feet away, dripping wet and staring hard at me. Then her image wavered and dissipated into a fog. The wind carried it away, leaving droplets of rain on the sand where she had stood.

I jumped to my feet and whirled around in a circle, searching for anyone else. Off in the distance, a lone figure stood just on the edge of the water, looking out at the ocean. I scrambled behind the trunk of the tree and then peeked around it, watching the woman's hair flow like the raindrops. She had to be an elemental. I sprinted toward her.

"Wait!" I yelled as her image faded as well. She looked back at me just as she disappeared completely. "No! What is going on?" I fell to my knees and covered my eyes with my hands. "I don't understand. Where are you all going? What is in the water?"

Transformed Chaos

"Save us," a voice whispered along a breeze as it swept across my cheek.

"From what? Where?" I didn't know where to start. How was I going to save the water elementals and my loved ones?

"It is aware of your powers and is using us to find a way to invade your mind. Two is better than one." The voice was clearer now.

I slowly dropped my arms and tilted my head upward. A nearly translucent woman stood a few feet away. Her long white hair hung past her waist, and her crystal-blue eyes shone like two gems. I recognized her from yesterday morning's encounter with the water elementals. My brief detour from our group to connect with the ocean had given me the advantage on Tallisa's plan to use Kia Lynn to implode this universe. The face before me now was one I had seen within the flow of the water when I had bonded with the elementals.

I rose to my shaky legs. "What is it?"

"The void. A fragmented piece of it, at least." She frowned, and her image waved with the wind. "Please hurry. We are stuck in transition and will disappear completely if it is not extracted from our connection to Mother Gaia." The woman faded even more, but I noticed her pointing at me. "The answer is in you."

A breeze swept her away, and I was alone again. The sun was dipping low on the horizon, and I had nowhere to go for the night. I had failed, and now I would fail the elementals. She had said the answer was in me, but I had no idea what that meant. I drifted silently toward the small structures that still stood nearby. I imagined their stability was lacking, but I had been surprised many times already. Maybe this would be another one of those moments.

The chill in the air was already biting at my arms, and a train of goosebumps swept down my spine. I hugged myself, but that did not help.

When I reached the first home, I noticed the front steps broken and scattered across the dirt. The door hung from the top rusty hinge and something or someone had blown all the windows out. A disaster probably waited for me inside, and I did not need one more problem on my very achy shoulders.

As I turned toward the next home, I noticed the clouds shifting strangely off in the distance. I squinted, trying to see it better with the fading light. A dark object moved into view. My heart leapt in my throat. It was the anaman ship that had taken Kia Lynn and Dad. My feet were moving before I could think about it. I raced down the broken cement, leaping over mounds of dirt, clumps of tar, and shattered debris of homes.

Transformed Chaos

I reached up and activated my com again. "Uncle Henry, are you there?"

It was quiet on the other end. Defeat roared through my mind. My body was still so tired, and the ship was moving in the opposite direction. There was no one around who could help me. I really was alone.

"No!" I screamed at myself. "You are not giving up." I pushed harder and finally levitated from a surge of energy radiating from my core. I flew forward twice as fast, closing in on the slowly moving ship. I pressed on my com again. "Uncle Henry, I need you. I really need you. Please answer me."

"Alex, is that you?" Dad's voice shook through the connection.

I slowed, and my feet touched the ground again. "Dad!" I exclaimed, stopping completely and collapsing to my knees. "I see the ship. I'm coming for you."

"Alex, listen," Dad said sharply. "I need you to pay very close attention to what I'm about to say."

"Yes, Dad," I whispered. The pit of my stomach fell. I knew he was in trouble.

"Tell Dax that he is to love you harder than ever before. Tell him he has my blessing, even though I know don't need it. You picked yourself a fine young man, my sweet Alex." His voice shook with emotion. "I am so proud of you."

"Dad—"

"Alex, your mother will need you," he said, interjecting before I could continue. "Stay close until she is done mourning and please keep her head above water. Tell her I will love her forever and always."

My hands fell to my sides and a flood of tears burst from my eyes. "No. Dad. No." My voice was barely a whisper, but I knew he could hear me. "Please, don't leave me."

"Alex, you are the best thing I have done in my life." He hiccupped, and I heard faint screaming on his end. "I am doing this so you won't have to worry about your future. I am protecting the world we have come to love. The darkness needs to be returned to the void."

My ears perked up at the mention of the darkness. "But that demon has subverted the ocean waters. You don't have it."

"Yes, I do," he replied, and I could imagine the fine lines around his face deepening the way they did every time he became serious. "I have the portion that will matter. Once it is back where it belongs, the rest will fizzle away."

"How do you know that?" I asked, crying loudly and not caring if I drew anyone's attention my way. "What if it doesn't work?" I felt like I was drowning in the depths of a sorrow I could not escape. There was not enough air to fill my lungs.

"Trust me, my love." His voice sounded farther away, as if he had moved away from his com. "I have to go now. I love you more than life itself. Shine your light, Alex. Shine it for everyone to see, and don't you back down for anyone. You deserve it all."

"Dad, I love you," I cried into my hands. "I'm so happy that you brought me back to you and gave me this new life. I love you so much."

"I will watch over you from the stars." His voice was fading, and I rose to my feet to get a better connection. "Love you forever, baby."

"Dad?" I raced down to the ocean and searched the sky. "Dad, are you there?" I screamed the words at the empty air.

Nothing but silence filled my ears.

It felt like my heart stopped, and I fell to my knees again, weeping uncontrollably.

My fingers dug into the sand. I desperately needed my connection to Mother Gaia. I had to know Dad would be okay—that we would all survive this.

An explosion ripped through the atmosphere. I looked upward and gasped in a startled breath as a wave of energy rushed toward me. I could see it coming—feel its power. When it washed over me, it threw me to my back and knocked the wind out of me.

I gulped for air and angrily slapped my hands down on the sand. My grief shattered like glass inside me and I screamed as I pressed my palms into my eyes, trying to drown out the image of the gray smoke trails spreading across the night sky.

He was gone. Dad. My hero, gone in a blink of an eye.

CHAPTER FOURTEEN

Trust

KIA LYNN

The wind held me firmly, even after the wave from the explosion plummeted back to Earth. From up here, I could see the old towns, some of them crumbling from the shock wave. Others shook but held strong. It was as if I was flying, except I was not comfortable letting loose and diving into my flight. I rode the wind downward, jumping from one air pocket to the next and stopping only once more to take in the quiet beauty around me.

The sun was down, but its rays still beamed up from the horizon. Someone was down by the ocean. Alex. Even being so far away, I knew it was her. She was crying for me and Zoe Dawn.

My attention turned back to the heavens. Jax had given his life for this world. The darkness had been forced back into the void, and somehow, I had to break the news to

Alex. Dread washed over me as I lowered myself to the sand. My feet touched lightly, and I hurried toward my sister.

A dark haze drifted just above the water. It twisted and pulled as if something was preventing it from moving. Alex was staring at it, her back toward me.

"Alex!" I cried as I drew nearer.

She whipped around and bounded to her feet. When she reached me, she threw herself into my arms, and I had to step back to hold myself steady. I rubbed her back as she wept against the top of my shoulder. Her fingers dug into my skin, and her sobs came in waves.

"He's gone." Her wet cheek pressed against mine. "My dad is dead. That void. That horrible, awful darkness forced his hand." She quivered under my embrace, and I squeezed her tighter.

"I'm sorry, Alex." I was grateful I did not have to break the news, but my heart hurt for her. "I wish I could have stopped him. I tried, but he insisted he had to do it."

She pulled away. "You were still with him?"

"We escaped together." I wrapped her hand in mine, and we turned toward the ocean. "The leader, Freydis, was the one who had been overtaken by the darkness. It was messing with her mind, and even her own people could no longer follow her. Two other anamans helped your dad and I escape, but we took Freydis with us. I promise, I tried to talk him out of it. I did not—"

A light shone on the edge of the water, and the dark haze lifted higher. More lights brightened in front of us, almost like silhouettes of people. The haze gathered, swirling higher into the sky. I glimpsed at Alex and noticed her closed eyes. Had she even been listening to me?

I looked back at the haze. It was drifting toward the stars, but then it clumped together and shot like an arrow so far above, I could no longer see it. I let go of Alex's hand and turned in a full circle, searching the stars for the dark fog, but it had vanished. My gaze dropped back to the growing number of lights.

Alex was walking toward them. When she reached them, they surrounded her, and together they walked into the ocean.

"Alex, where are you going?" I shouted, rushing after her and holding out my hand as if it would stop her.

She did not turn back, but continued in until the waters submerged her. My shoulders slumped forward. I promised Jax I would be here for her, and instead, I let her disappear into the water. Would she return? I do not think I would, if I had a choice to be with those who knew and understood me.

Tears swam in my eyes as I sank to the ground, feeling more alone than ever. I crossed my legs and let the tears flow, weeping into my hands for all we had lost. First Attica, now Jax. And who knows how many others had lost their lives.

Wet hands touched my legs, and I jumped back. Alex was kneeling in front of me.

"Where did you go?" I glared at her, not furious but scared out of my mind.

"We need to contact Uncle Henry," she said, climbing to her feet.

I did the same and glanced over her shoulder at the ocean. All the glowing figures had disappeared. "What did they tell you?"

"They will support us in whatever we need. You say the anaman threat should be over, then it is time to return to the pyramid and save my mom and the others." She swept her thumb down her right wrist. "We need a ride and backup."

Just as she finished speaking, a small ship shot over the water, startling both of us. It circled back around and landed near us on the beach. The bay door opened, and Wolf waved at us.

"There's our ride." I tugged Alex toward the ship. "He is the one who saved me on the ship."

"He is also the one who took you to the ship in the first place." Alex pulled away from me and stared at Wolf with thinly veiled contempt. "I don't trust him. He was the one who abducted you."

"I know and I do trust him," I retorted, grabbing at her hands.

She swatted me away. "Stop it, Kia Lynn. What if this is a trick? We can call Uncle Henry instead."

Wolf was walking toward us. "We saw you land here, Kia Lynn. With Jax and the ship gone, we hoped we could give you a lift home."

"See," I whispered, nudging her forward with my shoulder.

Wolf squinted at Alex as he drew nearer. He skidded to a halt. "Aren't you that woman in the painting?"

"What painting?" I asked, looking between Wolf and Alex.

"How do I know you? Other than back at your village." He did not answer my question but continued to examine Alex. His eyes widened in recognition. "No. Tell me it is not true."

"Wolf," I snapped. I was growing impatient. "What are you going on about?"

"She's his daughter, isn't she?" He pointed at Alex. "And Adina's daughter."

For the first time since I had met Wolf, his resolve shattered, and he wiped at his watery eyes as if sand had blown in them.

"Yes, Adina is my mother," Alex replied for me. "Jax is my father. The one who just sacrificed himself to save you. That is my father."

"I didn't know he retrieved you from the past." Wolf shook his head and collapsed to his knees. His face softened. "Your mom was pregnant with you the last time I was with them, and I heard from Tallisa they had hidden you away in another time period. All that they did to protect you…" He shook his head and refocused on Alex. "I know you don't know me, but I was one of your father's guards for many years. He was a close friend of mine."

"You must have hated him something fierce to have taken him away from me," Alex said, her voice shaking with indignation. "Now, he is gone forever."

"Then I will spend the rest of my life making up for it," he whispered, bowing his head in shame.

"We must go, Alex. Please." I tugged at her arm. "I must know if Rafael is okay. And Zoe Dawn."

She glanced my way, then nodded. "Okay, you win. We will go with them, but I still do not trust them."

Wolf rose to his feet, and we followed behind him, hand in hand. Alex gave the ocean one last look before stepping onto the ship. When we were all seated, Wolf lifted our vessel into the air and we shot across the ocean toward their larger ship.

"I thought you were taking us home." I leaned forward in my seat.

"I am, but in order to stop them from coming after you, I need to show the senators you have anaman blood in your veins. It takes only a few moments and then we will be on our way." Wolf glanced over his shoulder at us. "I promise. This way they will not see you as a threat but an ally."

"Where are your senators?" Alex asked, undoing her restraints and stepping up to Wolf.

He steered the ship into the cargo bay and set it down. "There are five other ships like this one stationed in orbit around one of Jupiter's moons. They are there."

"Will they be returning to Earth?" She blocked him from leaving his chair. "What are their intentions?"

"Alex, I won't let anyone come after you." He rose from his chair and stepped forward. She moved enough for him to slip by. "This is how we stop them. They are not like the anaman of our time. The only fear they have is another alien civilization who call themselves the Sapphire Spirit Tribe. Their descendants come from a much more powerful star system, and their technology and supernatural abilities far surpass our own."

Alex did not flinch, but I knew she was thinking the same as me. That was the same tribe Lindon had claimed Zoe Dawn belonged to.

"We don't want any part of your engagements with this other civilization," Alex said, following right behind Wolf. "Once we take this test, we are to be taken home, and the anamans will leave us alone from here on out. Am I clear?"

"Crystal." He led us out of the ship.

Trinity was waiting. She waved us over and led us through a door. Two flights up, there was another door with two other female anamans ready to draw our blood. We sat in the two chairs and I noticed Alex's right foot wiggling uncontrollably. I reached over and grabbed her hand again.

"We will be fine," I said, trying to reassure her.

They stuck her first, then me. It was over soon after, and Wolf was leading us back to his ship. When we stepped into the cargo hold, five anaman in full combat gear stood waiting. They pointed their weapons at Wolf and Trinity.

"What are you doing?" Trinity asked, holding up her hands. "The senators only asked for blood to be drawn."

"They changed their minds," one of them said through

the small slit in their helmet. "We still need to unlock the barrier that hides the northerners and that one,"—he pointed at Alex—"is required to accomplish that."

"Who gave you these orders?" Wolf asked. His fingers curled around his firearm.

"The senators will interrogate the women themselves." The anaman jabbed his weapon at Wolf's. "Leave it there, Wolf. Your quarrel is with our leaders, not us."

"The senators are not here," Wolf replied.

The masked anaman sighed. "They are—"

Alex snarled, and a bead of sweat rolled down the side of her face. "Enough. They do not get to change their minds."

One of the anamans turned their weapon on her and released its dart. Alex flicked her wrist, and a bubble of water entrapped the dart. It froze and dropped to the ground, shattering to pieces across the floor. The anaman sputtered, ripping at his helmet as ice formed around it. Another gasped for air and collapsed to the ground. The other three stepped back, then frantically grabbed at their helmets as well.

The entire ship quivered. My gaze swept across the cargo area and landed on the slit windows at the far end. Hundreds of glowing figures clung to the outside. The vessel shook again, and a blaring sound echoed through the room. A red light flashed above just as the ship slightly tipped.

I skidded across the floor, but Alex grabbed my arm and pulled me close to her.

"Use your wind, Kia Lynn," she yelled over the noise. "We will remind them who we are."

I didn't have a team of air elementals to help. It was just me, but I knew I could be fierce on my own. I rubbed my hands together, and the air gathered around us, pulling both of us into its arms. Alex grabbed my hand and smiled.

"You don't need to do that." She tapped her finger against her forehead. "Just think it."

I had not noticed her using her hands or fingers as much as she had done in the past. Was it really that simple? I focused on the cyclone just as the ship tipped in the other direction. Several pieces of equipment slid toward us. I threw a wave of wind at Trinity and Wolf and scooped them up, then directed them back to the ship we had used earlier.

We all rode on the wave and met at the bay door. Alex dropped to her feet, and the shaking ended. She turned to look at the mess we were leaving behind.

The five anamans rose to their feet, and once again started toward us.

Alex sighed and planted her hands on her hips. "If you

ever try to abduct me or any of my family and friends, I will destroy your ship with you inside. Do you understand?" Alex's voice carried over the sirens.

One anaman lifted his weapon toward her, but another slammed it back down and elbowed the keefie in his side.

"We will relay your message," the anaman said, waving his people away from the ship.

Alex turned toward Wolf. "You promised me a ride home. Once you have delivered us there, you may return to your ship."

Wolf raised his brows but did not argue. The bay door closed, and we were off with the wind soon after.

Alex activated her com. "Uncle Henry, are you there?"

"Alex!" Adina cried over the com.

"Mom, where are you?" Alex asked, scooting to the edge of her seat. She bit at her nails as she waited for the answer.

It was quiet for several long moments, then Adina breathed a sigh of relief. "I haven't left. We are still at the pyramid."

"I am coming for you." Alex jumped up from her chair and stood next to Wolf. "We need to go south again. To Las Vegas."

"Where is that?" he asked, scanning over his map on the screen in front of him.

She tapped her finger on the screen. "Here. We need to go right here."

"We can't," he replied, gripping his armrests as the coloring in his face drained to a pale white. "They will destroy this ship. We do not have the technology to match theirs."

"I am well aware of this. Get me close." Alex pressed on her com. "Mom, why can you reach me now? I have been trying to contact you since they took you."

It was quiet again, and it looked like Alex was holding her breath.

"They know who you are, Alex," Adina finally replied. "There is too much information to explain without you being here in person. They will not fire on you. When you arrive, land the ship on the outside of their shield. They will send someone out to retrieve you."

"And how do I know this is really my mother?" Alex asked. The trusting, naïve girl was long gone.

"It's me, Alex." Adina's voice was barely a whisper. "I felt him leave. Your father. That was the explosion, wasn't it?"

Alex's chin quivered, and she bit down on her lip to stop it. "Yes, Mom. He saved us."

Adina's sobs echoed through Alex's com.

After several long moments, Adina blew out a breath.

When she spoke, her voice quivered uncontrollably. "I will be here waiting, my love. We will get through this together."

"You heard her." Alex turned to look at Wolf. Her fingers shook as she wiped away her tears. "They are waiting for us."

Wolf nodded, but I did not miss the fear in his eyes. As he turned the ship back the way we had come, a bright light exploded not too far in front of us. It reverberated over us, causing the entire ship to quake from the impact.

"Trinity, activate the shields," Wolf yelled, his concentration staying on the outside world. "Back to your seat, Alex."

She did not argue and strapped in before another shot smashed into the ground just ahead of us. The shock waves knocked us backward, and Wolf frantically tried to gain control of the ship. We spun in a few circles, stopping only to see the anaman ship in front of us.

"I guess they did not heed your warning," Trinity said, white knuckling her armrests.

She and Wolf exchanged a look.

"What is it?" I asked, pressing my back against my chair. My fingers shook in my lap, and I clenched them into a fist, desperately trying to calm my nerves. This was not the time to lose my mind.

"Do you really think it is her they want?" Wolf asked, shaking his head and then throwing a look at Alex. He gulped and turned back toward Trinity. "That's Jax's daughter."

"It was her all along." Trinity scratched at her head, her nerves apparently frazzled as well. "They weren't after Tallisa. That was Freydis's mission, not theirs. It all makes sense now."

"What makes sense?" Alex screamed at them.

We were at a stalemate with the anaman ship, and Wolf knew it. He stared straight ahead.

"We were alerted when your people arrived," Trinity replied to Alex. She piled her dark hair on top of her head and pinned it there, refocusing on the screen in front of her. "The senators informed us your parents were here. They told Freydis we could all return to our time as long as they received the specifications for the time machine first."

"That's what they told us anyway," Wolf said, turning his seat to face us. "I should have seen it. You see, Alex, you exist in this dimension as well. Many have seen your painting, but recently, it disappeared. Why is that? Why is everyone so curious about you?"

Alex glanced from one to the other, waiting for them to respond. "I. Do. Not. Know." She enunciated each word. "Are you going to tell me? For hell's sake, it is just a painting. It does not mean anything."

"I have two guesses," Wolf said, ignoring her last statement. His hand ran over the top of his bald head. "Either someone else slipped through with you from our universe besides Tallisa and is feeding the senators a story of your heightened abilities, or—"

"Or," Trinity said, interrupting Wolf. "There are others in this world who know something about you that the rest of us don't. I suspect it has something to do with your past and those illuminated markings on your skin." She bit her lip and pointed at her own markings. "Mine don't glow like yours, and I have never seen patterns like yours before. You are something more. A warning. A beacon of hope. Whatever you are to our senators, they will stop at nothing until you are theirs."

CHAPTER FIFTEEN

Independence

ZOE DAWN

You are nearly ready. The voice was close, but it floated in and out of the darkness like a faraway raging wind. *The time is drawing near.*

I woke to a pounding headache. I pressed my hands to my temples and kneaded them as I focused on opening my eyes. The woman's words still reverberated in my mind. What was drawing near?

"She was not ready," Aly said harshly. Someone smacked their fist against a piece of furniture.

I jolted upright and looked around the room. Landscaped paintings decorated the walls. They were much better than the ancient ones Kia Lynn and I had found over the years. Across from where I sat, Rafael was sleeping in a seated position with his head leaning back on a cushion.

Transformed Chaos

I twisted on the couch and saw Aly, Zeke, Henry, and Koleton talking around a table. Aly's face was red, and the dark circles under her eyes revealed her exhaustion.

"How long have I been out?" I asked, rising to my feet and noticing it was dark outside. I had missed the entire day.

The group turned toward me, and Aly jumped up from her seat. "Come up here, Zoe Dawn." Her gaze swept over to Rafael, who must have awakened. "You too, Rafael. We need to talk."

"What was I not ready for?" I asked Aly as I passed by her and sank onto a chair next to Zeke.

"She thinks you are too inexperienced to learn the full extent of your powers," Zeke replied, taking my hand within his and planting a kiss on my knuckles. "I am so glad you are awake. Your mother's passing was a trigger I did not expect. I wish I could have prevented that pain for you."

Mum. My heart broke all over again. Tears welled in my eyes, but I nodded in response.

"How did Malcolm not know that Zoe Dawn belonged to your tribe?" Aly asked, changing the subject. "All of this seems wrong. The only one he did not know of was Alex, and that is because she does not belong here."

"What do you mean?" Zeke asked, sitting up straight

in his chair and turning to see Aly better.

"She is not from this time," I whispered, wishing nothing more than to have my two sisters here with me. "But she belongs here. She is one of us."

"How did she arrive here?" Koleton joined the conversation, stroking his long beard.

I sighed and threw a look at Henry. If he did not want to divulge the information, I wouldn't be doing it either. His gaze dropped to his hands, but he nodded at me, giving me permission to continue.

"Henry built a time machine and brought their people here." I watched Koleton and Zeke carefully. Henry and Alex were my family. I did not need additional turmoil brought upon any of us because of this disclosure.

Zeke slowly nodded. "Interesting." He turned toward Koleton, and they exchanged a look only the two of them understood. "That would explain the increase of life here on Earth when we arrived." He leaned forward and placed his elbows on the table to see Henry better. "Were your people spread out across the globe?"

"Yes. We did not want to flood our presence in just one area. Our goal was to unite with the local communities and help them rebuild now that the civilizations were growing again." Henry stood and walked to a cupboard. Inside were piles of enormous books. He ran his finger along their spines and then pulled one out. He flipped through the pages until he found what he was looking for, then set it on the table. "You claim your civilization resides up north. We did not see it. These are our scans of the world."

Zeke barely glanced at it. "You wouldn't have found it. We have a protection barrier over all our communities. The anaman technology will find none of them."

Rafael waved his hand in the air. "Does anyone know where Kia Lynn disappeared to? What about Malcolm? Anyone else? That is what I really would like to know."

"I agree." I rose from my chair, pushing it out harder than I had planned. It skidded across the rock flooring. "We can discuss who saw what—and whose technology is better—later. I want to find my sisters."

"Henry?" Aly turned to look at the one person we knew could find them.

"I haven't been able to reach them by com. Jax has been the only one who has made contact, and he said Kia Lynn was safe at that time." He laced his fingers together and rested his hands on top of his head as he paced the floor next to the back windows of Alex's house. "We might be able to contact the others from the ship. But they went dark when they arrived to those buildings, and I've lost all tracking to their whereabouts."

Zeke jolted upright and then shot out of his chair.

"What buildings?"

We all turned to look at him. Koleton rose slowly from his seat and pressed his palms into the table as he leaned forward, eyeing us with a guarded expression. We had hit a nerve.

"The dark ones with the pyramid in the middle," I replied, touching Zeke lightly on the arm. "Do you know of them?"

"Why didn't you just say so?" Zeke asked, his jovial tone returning. "Those are my buildings." He closed his eyes, wrapping his hand around the back of the chair to hold him steady. "You are correct. Your people are at our facility down south."

"Alex? Kia Lynn, too?" I asked, excitement bubbling in my stomach. They were safe.

"I don't know the names of who is there, but I sense their connection to you." He smiled at me, and his sapphire eyes sparkled once more. "Let's go find out."

"Are you serious?" Aly snarled, hauling me away from Zeke. "Have you lost your mind, Zoe Dawn?"

"Why are you so angry?" I ripped my arm from her grip, and she scraped her nails down the tender flesh of my forearm. I glared at her.

"They took you from us." She jabbed her finger in Zeke's direction. "Their weapons are highly sophisticated, and they easily subdued our entire village in a matter of seconds. Why are you not angry?"

"Zeke and Koleton were not there," I replied, shocked by Aly's demeanor. A rage I had never witnessed from Mum's best friend had replaced her usual calm. "They have been nothing but kind to me since I met them. If it weren't for them, I would not be here right now. It is your turn to cool down, Aly." Her quickly narrowing eyes showed she knew I was referencing the moment she had abducted me in Malcolm's ship and told me to cool down. She had forgotten so easily.

"But they brought that monster with them." Aly waved her arm toward the window.

I glanced at the window, unsure what she meant. My gaze shot around the room. Tatum and Beatle were not here. Tatum had to be Aly's monster.

I shook my head. "They have their reasons, and right now, I just want to make sure Alex and Kia Lynn are safe." Tatum was my monster as well, but I was not about to start a war in Alex's eating room.

"Someone has been trying to reach me." Henry scratched his head and activated his com. "I wonder why I did not hear it."

"Because you were all too busy bickering away like a bunch of children." My blood was boiling, but I held my flame at bay like Zeke had taught me. I did not need a repeat of this morning.

"Uncle Henry, are you there?" Alex's frantic voice filled the room.

Henry's jaw clenched, and Rafael pressed his hands against the sides of his head.

"There is more," Henry whispered.

"Uncle Henry, I need you. I really need you. Please answer me."

Tears sprang to my eyes. She was in trouble, and no one had heard her. "We have to go." I snapped my fingers. "Now, please."

Zeke nodded and followed Koleton from the house. The rest of us filed out one by one and raced for the ship. Henry deactivated their electrical fence, then turned it back on when we were all on the other side.

Henry, Rafael, and Aly sprinted inside Jax's ship, and Zeke and Koleton disappeared into theirs. I stood outside both, not sure who I wanted to be with, then chose the ship that gave me the most advantage. Zeke knew more about this world than the rest of us did, and I trusted him.

"Can we speak with the others?" I asked after entering the bridge.

"I will send them a request to connect." Koleton looked surprised when he saw me, but his startled expression melted into pure delight. "So glad to see you here, Zoe Dawn."

I smiled and sat in the chair next to Zeke.

"Can I tell you something about your mum?" he asked, whispering the question so no one else could hear.

"Yes, of course." I leaned in close to him, hugging the armrest against my abdomen.

"She was thinking of you when she died. Her last thought was of your safety." He turned his face so I could see him head-on, and I noticed the sorrow in his eyes. "Losing a parent is difficult, and I cannot imagine the heartbreak you must be experiencing right now, but I am here for you. I hope we will always be friends."

"How do you know what my mum was thinking?" I asked, not fully understanding his abilities.

He stretched his neck to one side and then the other, rolling his shoulders afterward. "It is a gift. Sometimes a curse, but I try to use it for good. Especially in moments like this."

"So, you can—"

"We are connected to your friend's ship," Koleton said, interrupting our conversation. He glanced our way. "Are you prepared for them to see you with us, Lady Charm?"

"It will only be Aly who will be upset." I pressed my lips together and nodded.

"Hold on to your knickers. If you thought the battle in the house was explosive, wait for the next scene." He flipped a switch, and Henry, Rafael, and Aly appeared on the screen on the window. "Hello, new friends. Are you ready to follow us?"

"Yes," Henry said while working on his own screen. He did not even look up.

Aly glared at me. "I can see you have chosen your side."

I rolled my eyes and clicked my tongue in annoyance. "Just stop, Aly. We are on the same side."

She pointed at Tatum, who was still sitting in the same seat I had last seen him in. I wondered if he had ever left it. Maybe that was his punishment, being glued to his chair. Serves him right. I laughed out loud at the thought and did not hear what Aly said.

"Say that again, Aly. My mind, that is clearly not mature enough to think for myself, was mulling over something funny, and I missed whatever you are griping about this time."

She folded her arms over her chest and fell back against her chair. Her lips pursed, and the scowl on her face only deepened the two lines between her eyes. She did not get to decide my life for me.

"Now who is clearly not the mature one?" Sarcasm

laced my tone. "Do not forget your place, Aly. I decide if I am ready, not you."

I felt the ship shift, and the ground dropped away from us. Henry followed us. The black mountains were ominous under the night's sky. There was not enough light tonight and viewing the darkness reminded me of my life before all the "save the world" begun. I missed it. It was not perfect, but at least I felt safe. My heart ached to have the simple times again.

"Esta is hailing us," Koleton said, turning off our connection to Henry's ship.

"Answer it," Zeke replied, leaning forward in his chair. He had unclasped his chest safety belt.

A blonde woman with nearly black irises flashed on the screen. "Zeke, are you on your way?"

"Yes, we should be there soon. Is everything okay?"

"The woman in the painting, the one we purchased from the anamans, she is alive. Did you know this?" she asked accusingly, settling her hands on her hips.

He crossed his ankle over his knee. "I had heard, but I did not have any proof. Why?"

"The anaman believe she is some kind of god or a Theian descendent who holds the key to eternal life. Now that she has incarnated right before their eyes, I don't know how to convince them otherwise." Esta raked her hand through her hair and turned to face Koleton. "Did you know anything?"

"I'm just here for the food, my lady," he said jokingly. When she did not laugh, he shrugged his shoulders. "We are all on the same team. Where is this painted lady?"

"She is near to our base, but she is traveling with two anamans. They have somehow convinced her to trust them. I believe they will use her to reach us in the north and not deliver her here like they promised. The anaman are convinced we will be able to free them from the promise of death." Esta waved at someone we could not see.

Adina stepped into view. She saw me, and her eyes widened.

"Zoe Dawn, are you okay? I have been worried sick about you." Adina brought her prayer hands to her lips.

"I am well, Adina. Are they taking good care of you?" I asked, suddenly uncertain about Zeke and Koleton with the cryptic conversation I was hearing.

"Yes, we are fine. Covyn is here. I will let her know you are well. She has been distraught, pacing the floors like a caged animal." Adina chuckled, but her amusement did not reach her eyes.

"What's wrong?" I undid my restraints and stepped closer. "Something is wrong. I know it."

Transformed Chaos

Adina pressed her lips together and turned away from me. "Alex is in trouble. I don't know why there is a painting of her, but the anaman fleet is convinced she is their ticket into these people's establishment. If the anaman can take control, they believe they will possess the secret to living forever."

Esta sputtered out a sarcastic laugh. "We don't live forever. Just a really long time that has no secret behind it. I wish I could get that through their thick, stubborn skulls."

"What else is wrong?" I asked, not fully convinced that Alex was the only reason for the sorrow in Adina's eyes.

"Jax." Adina's lower lip quivered, and she pressed her palm against it, gulping back a sob. "Jax is gone."

Zeke reached up instinctively and grabbed my elbow. "Take a deep breath, Zoe Dawn."

I sucked in a lungful of air, then blew it out slowly. The pain in my heart only doubled in size. Mum... and now Jax. I was parentless, and Alex was one down. It tore me up inside to think about it, but I needed to know how. "Tell me what happened."

"I'm not sure exactly." Adina shook her head and squared her shoulders to keep herself steady. "But we will find out, and when you arrive, we will talk more. First, we need you to go to the ship Alex is in and rescue her. Can you do that?"

"No problem," Koleton replied, flashing Adina one of his charming smiles. "We are on this. Do you want to tell Henry or should I?" I could tell he was eager to shake the trio in the other ship. They had obviously not left the best impression on my newest friend.

"I will. Thank you." She looked at me and blew out a quick breath. "See you soon."

They disconnected, and Koleton turned us toward our new destination, paying no attention to the ship behind us. I could feel the tension rising, not only between us and the anaman fleet that had taken Jax and Kia Lynn—the one now attacking Alex—but between the people I loved and the new ones I wanted to love.

It was a battle I was not prepared to fight, nor did I want to, but in my mind, I could see the dark clouds hanging over us. They threatened to unleash a war this planet most likely would not recover from, and neither would we.

CHAPTER SIXTEEN
Attack

ALEX

The thought of someone else from my parents' time slipping through the wormhole sent waves of terror washing over me like ice-cold water. That had to be the explanation. The other one was absurd. I stared at Trinity and Wolf, unable to reply.

Kia Lynn reached over and squeezed my arm. "Are you okay, Alex?"

I turned to look at her. Every inch of my body was locked up in fright. Who was after me? "But why do your senators want *me*?" I could finally spit out my question. "Why now?"

One button in front of Wolf beeped loudly. He twisted back around. "We are being hailed." He sighed. "I have to answer, or they might fire again."

"Then do it." I gripped the armrests tighter, and my

foot wiggled against the base of the chair. My nerves were shot.

Wolf accepted the call. The face of an unfamiliar anaman appeared on the screen. His hands were behind his back, and his straight as an arrow stature made me squirm even more in my seat.

"Wolf and Trinity, if you do not return to the ship, you will be captured and executed for treason." His gaze shot to me and Kia Lynn. "Bring the women with you. The senate is not done with them."

"What do they want with us?" I asked, crossing one knee over the other and trying my hardest to not lose my mind.

"It is not my place to ask questions." He turned back to face Wolf. "And neither is it yours. Return now. Do not forget all the senators and these people have done for us since we were abandoned here." He quieted and stared pointedly at Wolf. When he did not receive a reply, his eyes narrowed. "You have five minutes."

The connection ended, and Wolf fell back against his chair. "That's it. Everything we've built over these years is ruined. Just like that." He snapped his finger.

"Let Kia Lynn out the bay door." I unbuckled my restraints and motioned for Kia Lynn to follow me. "She can use her wind to guide her to the ground. How far away are we from the location I showed you?"

"Not too far," he replied, shaking his head as if he was going to disagree with me. "They will hang us for sure if we do not return with both of you."

"Then I call my mom, and the people you are so frightened about can come pick us up." I activated my com again. "Mom, we need your help."

Wolf jumped out of his seat and stomped toward me. "Don't do that, Alex. Not yet." He grabbed my wrist and twisted it behind me.

"Don't touch her!" Kia Lynn yelled.

She leapt at him, and from the corner of my eye, I saw her clawing at his back. The wind howled around us, and it nearly knocked him to his knees, but he held on tightly to me and I yelped out when my arm was bent the wrong way. The wind died down quickly, and Wolf reached behind him and hauled Kia Lynn off his back.

"A little help, Trinity," he snarled at the female anaman, who was watching intently from her seat.

Her arms folded over her chest, and her raised brows spoke volumes. She was not interested in getting involved in our scuffle.

"Did you really think subduing them with force would work out well for you, Wolf? Have you not learned anything in your old age?" she asked and blew out an exasperated breath. "I, for one, am tired of living under the rule of the anaman. If I can't return home, then I want to live on Earth and have a proper life. I vote to call their people."

"Mom, can you hear me?" I yelled, even when Wolf tightened his hold on me again. My com was still on, so she had probably heard the entire exchange.

"Yes, they are already on their way," Mom replied. "Is that you, Wolf? Did you really put your hands on my daughter?"

"Don't start with me, Adina." A growl rumbled up his throat, and he pushed me forward, letting go of my arm. "Survival of the fittest. Isn't that how you and Jax lived? Isn't that why I have been stuck in this dimension for nearly twenty years?"

A deep rage thundered through me, and I whirled around to face Wolf. "You said you would not let anyone come after me." My tone was so dark, I even startled myself, but I was not about to stop now. I stretched my fingers out wide and then clenched them into fists. "You promised to make up for losing my father." I whipped around to face Kia Lynn. "I told you I did not trust him, but you were convinced he would keep us safe."

"I know," she said, holding out her hand to me. "I'm sorry, Alex. I should have never trusted him."

Transformed Chaos

Trinity rose from her chair and strode toward me. "I will get you to your mother. She was my friend, and I choose her, you, and this planet over a life of battle. I have your back."

My temper cooled slightly. "Thank you, Trinity. How will we make it to the other ship?"

"If Wolf wants this life, we dock the ship, toss him out, and then shoot our way back out." Trinity shrugged. "It will take them by surprise and by the time they recover, we will be long gone. They would not dare to follow us to the pyramid."

"Sounds like a solid plan. I'm in. Mom, we will be ready for backup here soon."

"They will be there. I love you, Alex," Mom said, her voice slightly cracking.

"See you soon. I love you more." I switched off my com and turned toward Trinity.

Wolf threw his arms in the air. "For the love of all that is holy, I made you a promise, and I intend on keeping it!" he shouted, stopping everyone in their tracks. He pointed at my com. "I knew your mother was listening, which meant everyone else was as well. You use anaman technology. Duh. If you had given me two seconds to think before you reacted, we could have talked this through. Instead, I had to play the game to win it." He jumped back into the captain's chair. "Take your seats, ladies."

I hurried to mine, taken aback by the realization of how long the anaman fleet must have been listening in on our conversations. Why had we not taken extra precautions? Was that why Uncle Henry could not answer my calls?

Kia Lynn reached over and grabbed my hand. "He had me fooled as well. Just grateful he is still on our team."

"Me too," I replied, staring out the window. "Wolf, what are you going to do?"

"Exactly what my brilliant sidekick suggested, leaving out the part where you dump me out." He threw Trinity a darted look as he eased the ship toward the anaman vessel.

"Sidekick, huh?" Trinity shook her head. "Just like a man to take the hero position."

Wolf just smiled as he guided them to just inside the cargo hold. "Let's give it all we got."

Both he and Trinity opened fire on the crew inside the anaman vessel, knocking down personnel and destroying the other ships and equipment. I was gripping the armrests so tightly, my knuckles were aching, but I could not let go. My breath shook with each exhale, and after several minutes of watching the carnage unfold in front of me, I was gasping for air.

"Stop!" I cried, throwing out my hand. "Just stop. Please!" I could not take it any longer. These people were dying for a cause they did not understand.

"It is too late to back out now!" Wolf yelled over the gunfire. "If we do, we will be the dead ones."

"Then go!" I screamed, covering my eyes with my hands. "We can make a run for it."

Wolf and Trinity both paused at the same time, so I peeked at them through my fingers. They were both glancing my way.

"We have started a war we cannot run away from," Trinity said, her calm demeanor never faltering. Her gaze was soft, but her voice was firm. "Get your head in the game, Alex. You wanted this. There is no turning back now. Where are your elemental friends?"

I wiggled back against the chair and sat up straight. Squeezing my trembling hands into fists, I turned toward Kia Lynn. She reached over and gripped my hand. I relaxed my fingers into her hold, then nodded at Wolf and Trinity.

"We will do our part," Kia Lynn said. She closed her eyes and drew in a deep breath. Then she lifted her hands and waved them to the side. The wind blew so loudly I heard its whistle against the ship's exterior.

I settled against my chair and focused, welcoming the darkness behind my eyelids. I connected with the water and drew it toward the anaman vessel, blasting them with hail the size of baseballs. The raging wind brought in more thunder clouds, and even with closed eyes, I could sense the flashes of lightning all around us as Wolf pulled our ship out of the cargo hold and back to freedom.

My heart hammered against my ribs. Why was I so terrified? My eyes fluttered open.

The hail remained centered over the main anaman aircraft. I kept my focus on the growing storm Kia Lynn and I had produced together. We were powerful, but it just did not seem like enough. We were up against an entire fleet of anaman warriors.

Our ship shuddered, and Wolf gripped his controls. "They are firing on us. Can one of you take out their weapons?" His brows furrowed with concentration. "We won't have much time before they regroup and use their undamaged fighter jets to attack us from every angle."

"On it." I watched carefully, waiting for the next shot. I needed to know exactly where they were located.

To our left, there was a brief spark. Wolf moved the ship just in time and they missed. I concentrated on that spot and gathered the surrounding water, then slapped it against the metal and froze it so solid and thick, nothing could break through. At least, that was my hope. It sparked again, and the ice cracked slightly.

Wolf pointed to the right. "They have several weapons

on that ship. Are you ready to ice them all?"

I swallowed back my knot of fear and nodded.

Our ship swung around the top of the major vessel, taunting the anamans who were controlling the firearms. They took the bait, and another shot brightened against the silver exterior. Kia Lynn pressed her wind against the force, and Wolf dodged the slowed laser. I slammed another thick layer of ice against their weapon. It shuddered immediately, and its blasts struck the ice several times. A large crack broke the ice in half.

I gathered more rain and plastered it on the top, icing it so thickly, we could no longer see the sparks of their weapon. My focus turned back to the other one. Its ice was breaking and crumbling to the ground. Their next shot rumbled toward us before Wolf could react.

The ship quivered and then violently shook, followed shortly by another one from the other side.

"We need to take shelter!" Wolf hollered above the noise. He pulled the vessel back and down, hiding under the belly of the larger vessel. He punched the console. "We have mere seconds before they surround us. Our lives are depending on those fancy powers of yours." His furious gaze met mine.

"Our shields are only down to eighty percent," Trinity said, turning in her seat to look at Wolf.

"That's too much," Wolf replied, taking out a handheld screen from a drawer near his knees. "This will help you two." He held it out for me to take, his eyes never leaving mine.

I undid my restraints and took the computer from him. "What is this?" There were X's over several spots on the screen.

"Zoom out." He slid his fingers to pull the photo out. It was the exterior of the anaman vessel we were fighting. "That shows the placement of their firearms."

My eyes widened. "There are over a dozen of them. Maybe two dozen." I was trying to count them, but I was struggling to focus as a fresh bout of fear roared through my nervous system. "I don't have the energy to cover all of these."

"Sure you do." Wolf's gaze softened before turning back toward his screen. "Buckle up, Alex. You wanted a fight; you are going to have to pull on your big girl pants and face the fire."

I hurried to my seat and settled in before focusing on the screen. I showed Kia Lynn, and she blew out a nervous breath.

"Use the hail again. Break the weapons with hail the size of our heads," she said, taking the screen from me and holding it up so I could concentrate. "I will use the wind to direct it at each spot. Let's start with this one." She pointed at the one closest to us. "Are you ready, Wolf?"

"Just waiting on you two," he replied, turning the surveillance camera in a circle to check the entire perimeter. "No other fighter jets yet, but they will be coming."

"Let's go." I focused on the first X, and Wolf guided the ship into the open.

"Just keep those ice boulders away from us," Wolf muttered as his fingers flew across his screen.

The thunder and lightning exploded around us as Kia Lynn built a storm so powerful, it would have sucked us into it if I weren't shielding us in a bubble of water. Wolf glanced out the window and then turned to look at me.

"Brilliant," he said, awestruck by my extra protection.

"Keep us steady." My hail beat against the anaman vessel again, and I focused on the spot Kia Lynn was pointing at.

Her raging winds pushed it all together, striking the weapon with so much force, it exploded, and shrapnel shot in every direction. The water shield around us slowed the pieces as they made their way toward us. Not one hit us, and Wolf threw his arms up in the air.

"Woo-hoo!" he shouted, dancing in his seat and pumping his fist. "That was spectacular. Let's do it again."

Kia Lynn pointed at the next one and I closed my eyes this time, concentrating on the X I could see in my mind. I could hear the hail striking the larger vessel, and the intensity increased until another explosion ripped through the air.

"Two down!" Wolf yelled again.

"Don't celebrate yet," Trinity said, and I opened my eyes to look at her. "We have eighteen more to go and you can bet they are gathering their forces inside for a surprise attack."

I bit my lower lip and turned toward the screen. Kia Lynn tapped the next spot for me to focus on and gave me a reassuring smile.

"We've got this," she whispered so only I could hear. "Just keep focusing and let them do their job."

Wolf steered us closer to the next weapon, and when we neared it, two shots sparked from different firearms. The water shield quivered, and the ship shook from the explosion. Then another weapon shot at us. Wolf dodged that one, but as he did another shot rang out. They were coming too quickly.

I slammed my eyes shut and focused on where Kia Lynn had pointed at, increasing the hail tenfold and ramming it against that weapon. It exploded seconds later, but not before another shot hit us.

Transformed Chaos

The ship shook harder than ever before, and my fingers tightened around the armrests. I pried open my eyes. My water shield had dissipated, and we were being fired upon by not only the larger ship but two smaller aircrafts. The screen had fallen to the floor, and Kia Lynn was white-knuckling her armrests as well.

My stomach heaved, and I suddenly did not feel well. Everything around me spun, so I leaned my head back against the chair to gain my bearings.

Wolf glanced back at me in desperation, just as an explosion rocked us so hard, I was sure they had broken through our shields. Nothing would stop them from ending us now.

CHAPTER SEVENTEEN
Rise Up

KIA LYNN

I screamed as our ship spiraled toward the ground, but in a blink of an eye we were up again and zooming through the sky and around the anaman ship. Trinity shot at the two small ships and struck one. Smoke barreled out of it, but it did not fall to the earth. Instead, it turned back toward the cargo hold and disappeared inside.

"They will send more as soon as they can clean up the mess we created," Wolf said. His lips drew back in a snarl, and he steered us toward the other small ship. "Can you work on the larger ship?"

"Yes, I will do my best," Alex replied. Her words slurred together, but the other two did not seem to notice. Alex's eyes met mine, but hers were slitted as if she were forcing them to stay open.

I leaned over and picked up the screen.

Transformed Chaos

Her trembling fingers found mine. "Just show me the next location. We probably won't be anywhere near it, but I will do whatever it takes to smash it to bits."

I pointed at it, and Alex stared at the space on the screen as if memorizing it. Then she closed her eyes. Her brows drew together in concentration, and I turned back to the fight outside to build my storm once again.

My lightning struck the larger vessel not far ahead of us, and the next strike I pushed toward the firearms but missed. I did it again, but this time, I shattered one of Alex's boulder-size hails. I chewed on my fingernails. It was frustrating feeling helpless while the three others were fighting to keep us alive. I had to bring more power to this fight.

I pressed at my wind and gathered the clouds, darkening them to a sinister black. If anything, I would provide Alex the moisture she would need for her hail.

It fell around us like a rumbling landslide but never once touched our ship, and when Alex could finally focus on one area again, another firearm exploded behind us. The tremor shook our ship, and I nearly dropped the screen again.

I wrapped my hand tighter around the gadget and imagined the lightning hitting the next X on the screen. Another explosion ripped through the air, and that red X disappeared.

"I did it," I cried, grabbing Alex's forearm and squeezing it. "Did you see that? I used the lightning to destroy one of them."

Alex ran her tongue over her lips, and her chin quivered. "Which one is next?"

She did not seem excited about my help. My sudden elation plummeted to the pit of my stomach. I pointed at the next X, and Alex fixated on it, then shut her eyes. I found the next firearm and refocused on the storm. It didn't matter if she supported me or not. I would not die tonight.

I stared out the window and concentrated on my weak lightning, drawing it from the clouds and aiming toward the next firearm. Nothing happened. I slouched forward, feeling defeat wash over me. Another explosion tore my gaze from the ground. The second attacker ship vaporized.

Wolf whooped and jumped from his seat. "You did it, Trinity." He leapt over to her and pulled her into an embrace, crushing her against his chest. "We might get out of this after all."

"Not if you don't stay on task," she muttered, wiggling herself free. "Pay attention, Wolf." She shoved him away from her and dropped back onto her chair.

He scowled at her but returned to his seat and followed

her orders. It was a good thing, too, because three other ships shot out of the cargo hold and circled around to attack us. He groaned and Trinity twisted back to face her screen.

Alex's face scrunched in concentration. Her hail smashed against one of the ships zooming toward us. I snapped my fingers, and three lightning strikes ripped it to pieces. What remained plummeted to the ground and out of our way.

Another explosion tore through the air, and Alex's eyes popped open. "This is exhausting," she whispered, pressing her hands against her forehead and turning toward me. "I don't know if I can keep going. Thank you for helping with that ship." Her voice was so low, I wasn't even sure I heard her correctly.

"Alex, when was the last time you ate?" I asked, pulling off my restraints and holding her head up.

The color had drained from her cheeks. She blinked several times as if she was trying to comprehend what I had said.

"Do you need food?" I asked again, touching her forehead. She was burning up. I whirled around. "Is there a healing station on this ship?"

Trinity glanced my way. "Yes, but why?"

"Alex is not well. I don't think she has had any water

or food since well before I found her." I wrapped my arm underneath Alex's and helped her to her feet. "I know how to use the healing station. Will you be okay until I return?"

"Go," Wolf barked, waving us away. "We have this handled."

I knew he was lying, but Alex needed water and to lie down for a minute. When I had her on the healing station cushion, she grabbed my arm and pulled me close.

"Just get me a drink and food. I will start this," she whispered, her voice hoarse with exhaustion. "I'm sorry I let you down."

"Don't you be sorry," I replied, kissing her forehead. "I should have known better. You needed a meal. Not to be jabbed by a needle and pulled into another fight."

She licked her lips again and tried to smile, but instead, her lips twitched, and her eyes fluttered shut. I raced down the corridor to the place I thought was the eating hall. Sure enough, they had the same machines as Malcolm's ship. A bottle of water and some crackers would have to do for now.

When I returned to Alex, she had stuck herself with a needle, and saline was dripping into her veins.

She shot me a weak smile. "I scanned myself. Once I eat, I will be fine. Go back to help the others."

I handed her the crackers and water, then checked her

restraints and comfort before tearing back down the hallway. I nearly tumbled head over feet when Wolf turned us sharply and barely missed another ship that came out of the cargo hold.

I buckled myself in and picked up the screen. "We have fifteen more to go."

"Use whatever you can to stop them from shooting at us. We are outnumbered, and our shields are down to fifty percent!" Trinity shouted from across the room.

"If they want us in their custody so badly, why are they trying to kill us?" I asked as I situated myself in my seat.

Wolf threw me a startled look. "They aren't trying to kill you. Don't you get it? The senators know you and Alex could survive this, but Trinity and I are expendable."

I shook my head. He wasn't making sense. "How will we possibly survive if the ship explodes?"

"Won't you?" Trinity asked, pausing what she was doing to twist in her seat. "Have you not survived a ship crash before?"

My eyes narrowed. "How did you know that?"

"We accessed your memories, Kia Lynn. Did you forget?" Her hands wrapped over the back of her chair. "We have all of them recorded on our ship, and the senators have access to it. Alex did something to save you when you crashed, didn't she?"

"We are not crashing!" I yelled, returning my focus to the screen in my hand.

A deep fury swelled inside me. I recognized the anger was manifesting from the grief and heartache I had experienced over the past few days, but facing that pain was not something I ever planned on doing. Instead, I used it to build lightning. It crashed down all around us, striking one of the ships attacking us and one of the larger vessel's weapons. Explosions erupted in every direction, and Wolf shot out of the inferno and back under the belly of the ship, hiding our ship in a groove and switching off the machine.

"Remind me to never infuriate the redhead again," Trinity said, pulling her restraints back over her shoulders. "Good job, Kia Lynn."

"You did that on purpose?" I asked, inhaling several deep breaths and squeezing my trembling hands together.

"It worked, didn't it?" Trinity waved a dismissive hand with her back still toward me. "You are not the weak one, Kia Lynn, so stop acting like you cannot fight as well as Alex." She glanced over her shoulder, and I caught the gleam in her eye. "Your wind and the ability to create a storm will bring the world to their knees. Do not play small so others can look big."

"I wasn't—"

"You were," Wolf said, interjecting into our

conversation. "Both of you are amazing, powerful women. The difference is Alex believes it and you don't."

Jax's voice rose in my head. *Don't you realize, Kia Lynn? You command the air. All of it. Never, ever, shrink yourself down to make anyone else comfortable. You do not need anyone's permission to rise in your power.*

I bit down hard on my bottom lip and swallowed back a rising sob. They were right. I was allowing everyone else to shine around me, and not wanting to take away from their victories, I continued to stay in the shadows. Always the supporter. Never the star.

"Are you ready, Kia Lynn?" Wolf asked gently, pulling me back to the world of the living.

I sat up straight, then turned to look at him and nodded. "Yes. Let's do this."

"Come sit up here with me," he said, patting the armrest of the other captain's chair. "We will do this together."

When I was seated next to him and buckled in, I gave him a thumbs-up and smiled. "Thank you, Wolf."

"You are very welcome." He flipped on the screen in front of me and activated the locations of the larger vessel's firearms. "We've got this."

Once again, the storm built above us and as we slid out from underneath the other ship; I traced the ansuz rune on my chest, kissed my fingers, and held them up to the Goddess. We had the divine on our side.

They met us with four anaman attacker ships. They fired together, and Wolf dodged most of them, but the ship quivered when two struck our shields. I clapped my hands together, and lightning shot through the dark clouds, ripping through another ship and tearing it in two. It was like a giant hand had reached down from the sky.

I fist-bumped Wolf, then snapped my fingers, and the winds twisted into a cyclone. They yanked another ship away from the trio and tossed it so far away, I was wondering if it escaped. Seconds later, a faraway explosion burst in the air.

"Looks like you have it under control," Alex said.

I whipped around. Alex was standing behind us, staring at the outside with a small smile twitching on her lips. She wiped her mouth and strolled toward her chair.

"How are you feeling?" I asked, observing her. She had not given herself enough time to heal properly.

"Much better." She drew in a deep breath and collapsed onto her seat. "But I cannot wait until I can curl up in my bed and never think of this day ever again."

I refocused on the fight outside. "Do you have the strength to help us?"

"Already on it," she replied.

Transformed Chaos

Large balls of ice struck the larger vessel, and when the anamans returned fire, Alex's water rose out of nowhere and redirected the laser. The smaller ships were breaking down our shield by circling around us and staying out of sight. Alex turned her hail toward them.

I closed my eyes and held my hands in my lap, palms to the sky, and focused on the wind that was pressing the large anaman ship toward the ground. My lightning continued its aim at their firearms, and I used my mind's eye to concentrate on both tasks.

Another explosion ripped through the air and the intensity of the fire was so powerful it seemed to course through my veins. Shrapnel rippled around us, then plummeted to the ground. I was one with the air, almost as if I were out there amid the commotion.

I twisted my wrists and moved my fingers around, invoking the strength of the wind to fold over the larger anaman ship. Like a giant hand, the air curled its weight against the metal, and I did the same with my own, pulling the ship closer to the earth.

Our ship violently jolted, and my head bounced forward with the motion. I lost my connection to the air. A ringing buzzed in my ears and I squeezed my eyes shut, doing all I could with the commotion to refocus on the iron grip of the wind. I did not want to lose hold of the anaman ship. The next shock made my chair shake underneath me, then a light flashed so bright, I could see it through my eyelids. My eyes fluttered open, and silence enveloped me.

CHAPTER EIGHTEEN
Together

ZOE DAWN

"There they are!" I shouted, tapping my feet against the floor and pointing at the massive vessel ahead of us.

Koleton threw me an amused smile. "Good thing you pointed it out. I would have missed that tiny speck of dust and the lightning storm surrounding it if you hadn't."

"Shut it," I said, falling back against my chair, but I flashed him a grin before he turned back toward his screen.

From the distance, a light flashed brightly, then another, followed by one more. Two small ships were circling around a slightly larger one, shooting at it from every angle. Zeke pointed this time and leaned forward in his seat. My eyes widened at the sight.

"They need our help," Zeke said, his blue light rolling to his fingertips.

"I can see that." Koleton's eyes were glued to his

screen. He pointed at Tatum without looking his way. "Fire, Tatum. Take one of those smaller ships out."

Tatum turned in his seat and centered his target on one of the anaman ships. A nearly silent ray of light burst from our ship and surrounded one of the small ships in a translucent bubble. The ship went dark and fell like a rock to the ground, exploding on impact.

"Next one," Tatum muttered, focusing on his screen again. The target zeroed in on the other small ship, and a few seconds later, it was a ball of fire below us as well.

The giant anaman vessel fired again at the ship Alex was on, but a wave of water burst out of thin air and blocked the attack. Excitement bubbled up inside me. That meant Alex was alive and well. We were not too late.

Balls of ice slammed against the side of the anaman vessel, striking only one spot, but at closer inspection, I realized it was one of the firearms. It exploded moments later. The larger vessel shifted downward and crept away from the smaller one. It was leaving. They knew they were not a match for the water elemental. I beamed with pride, clapping my hands together as I glanced at Zeke.

He returned my smile. "I will go retrieve—"

A light flashed from the retreating anaman ship and shot toward the smaller vessel. A thin layer of water wrapped its way around it, but it was too late. My hands shot up to my mouth when the back of their ship vaporized, and what remained tumbled toward the cliffs below. It smashed into the mountainside, then rolled down the incline and landed with a crack that shook large boulders down on top of it.

"Help them!" I screamed, fumbling with my restraints. "I need to get to them!" My fingers felt like thumbs. I could not unbuckle my safety belts.

A fireball explosion ripped up from the ground and swept over us. Koleton steadied the ship and turned back to face the disaster. Flames nipped at the remains of their ship, showing no signs of life. There was nothing left.

I screamed at the top of my lungs, finally able to yank off the last restraint. I fell to my knees and crawled to the window, then pressed my palms against it. I searched the dark terrain below, but only the light of the fire was visible. They were all gone. Alex and whoever were helping her. I fell to my backside and turned around, leaning against the window for support and weeping into my knees.

A hand touched mine, and I peered up and found two blue eyes staring back at me. It was Beatle.

"I-I am s-s-sorry," she said, rubbing the top of my hand with her thumb.

Alex had said Beatle was innocent, and in this moment,

I could see the childlike manner in her expression. She was not like most people. Her attacks on us were because of her loyalty to Tatum. I knew that now. I leaned toward her, and she wrapped me in her arms, patting my back as I sobbed into the crook of her neck.

Her touch was warm, and I wanted to melt into her. The realization of who she was had me jerking back in response.

"You are a fire bearer?" It was less of a question and more of an acknowledgement.

She nodded and held up her hand to me. I did the same and pressed my palm against hers. The warmth and energy radiated between the two of us.

"I am onl-l-ly heat." Her eyes widened with her smile and she nodded again. "I d-don't have a f-f-flame."

I glanced at Zeke, who was watching our exchange with pursed lips. "This is why Tatum has been given a free pass. He has been her protector."

Zeke nodded and rose from his seat. He stood next to me and looked out the window. "Koleton, we need to land near the wreckage."

"Why?" Koleton asked. He jumped out of his chair and circled around the computer station to look at whatever Zeke was seeing.

I turned on my knees and pressed my forehead against

the glass.

"I saw something." Zeke's fingers traced along the window.

I glanced up at him, but his eyes were closed.

"I feel life down there," he said without opening his eyes. He was reaching out with his mind.

I climbed to my feet and closed my eyes as well, focusing my thoughts on the flickering flames below and then pressing out from that point. I could not feel what Zeke was sensing. The life of the fire was roaring in my mind, and that was when I sensed the lack of death. There were no bodies in the wreckage.

"They aren't dead," I whispered, clenching my hand into fists and tapping against the glass. "There are no bodies in the fire."

"On our way down," Koleton said.

I opened my eyes. Koleton was already back in the captain's seat, and Beatle was sitting next to Tatum. Zeke grabbed my hand and led me to my chair. My heart thumped like a caged wild animal against my chest, and I could not tear my eyes away from the nearing inferno.

Koleton settled the ship as close to the wreck as he could, and once we were down, I leapt from my chair and raced for the exit. For some reason, I knew Beatle was right behind me. The flame connected us, and it made me happy she was one of us now—or I was one of them.

I shot through the exit door and jumped over boulders and pieces of the ship, tearing toward the fire at the bottom of the cliff. The terrain was rocky and steep in some places, but I would not stop until I made it to my sister. There were several other footfalls behind me, and pebbles scattered along the trail as I blazed through the vegetation.

When I broke through to the wreckage, it was all that greeted us. I whirled around in a circle, searching every inch of land I could see.

I cupped my hands around my mouth. "Alex!" I shouted. My voice echoed against the precipice. "Alex, where are you?"

My echoes flitted away, and all that remained was the crackle of the nearby fire. I pushed through more vegetation and nearly tumbled down another steep incline. I caught my footing and scooted to a large boulder sticking out from the dirt, then climbed on top and scanned the terrain.

"Alex!" I screamed at the top of my lungs. She could be hurt—bleeding to death for all we knew.

I scrambled up farther onto the rock and looked out on the other side. Something moved. I squinted through the dark and inched my way closer to the edge. There was definitely somebody or something out there.

Transformed Chaos

Cupping my hands around my mouth again, I drew in a deep breath, then shouted with everything I had. "Alex!"

A head popped up against the darkness. "Zoe Dawn!" Alex cried back, jumping up and down and waving her hand.

Tears of joy burst from my eyes, and I nearly toppled over the edge of the boulder. Zeke was suddenly next to me, and he guided me down with the help of his hand. He slid down beside me, and Beatle joined us next.

"I'm coming, Alex!" I shouted through the thick vegetation.

Branches scratched at my face and snapped back to hit Zeke in his.

"For the love of Theia," he murmured as he lifted his hand over my shoulder. "Let me help you out there." His blue light shot like an arrow, clearing a path through the thick of the brush.

"Thank you," I said, sprinting forward and bouncing on my toes when I saw Alex again.

Another head popped into view. A redheaded woman.

My heart skipped a beat. "Kia Lynn, is that you?" I pushed even harder, leaping over another large rock and landing in the middle of the four survivors.

Kia Lynn threw her arms around me, and then Alex crushed us in her embrace. We held onto one another tightly, crying and laughing at the same time. I did not want to let them go.

When we finally unraveled our arms from one another, I patted both their cheeks. "What mess did you two get yourself into this time?"

Kia Lynn ignored my question and fell against me, holding onto my neck. This time, she sobbed into my shoulder. "I missed you, Zoe Dawn," she cried, sniffling as she turned her head to the side and wiped her nose with the back of her hand. "I'm done being an elemental. Can we all just go back to normal life? Please."

Alex ran her fingers along Kia Lynn's hair and then turned her focus on me. "The anamans need me for something. That was the fight you got pulled into. Thank you, by the way." She turned to finally see Beatle and Zeke. Her eyes widened, and she rushed over to Beatle. "You are okay. I thought after our last encounter that someone had taken you."

Kia Lynn dropped her suffocating grip on my neck, and I hauled her closer to Zeke. "Zeke, this is my sister, Kia Lynn. My best friend."

Zeke's smile lit up his entire face, and he wrapped his hand around her wrist. Kia Lynn did the same to him, following his lead. "It is a pleasure to meet you. I have heard so much about your time with Zoe Dawn."

Transformed Chaos

"I hate to break up the party," a large anaman said from his perch on a rock. "But they will return, and this time they will bring the entire force of their army. If they believe Alex can open the door to the northerners' hideout, they will stop at nothing until it is done."

"Who are you?" I asked, stepping around everyone else and placing my hands on my hips.

The anaman rose to his feet and smirked at my attempt to be intimidating. I would show him. Then a female anaman stepped up beside him, so I held my fire back.

"This is Wolf and Trinity," Alex said, rubbing my shoulder and unknowingly reminding me to keep my cool. "They are the reason we were not taken by the anamans."

"Aren't you two anaman soldiers?" Zeke asked. His tone deepened, catching me off guard.

"We are traitors now," Trinity replied, walking toward us with her arm outstretched. "I'm done living the anaman warrior lifestyle. We are here to start a new life." She glanced back at Wolf. "Together. We will help you end this battle and then all we want is to disappear."

Zeke grasped Trinity's wrist, and she mirrored the gesture. "The more, the merrier. We must return to the ship. Are you all capable of walking there?"

They nodded in unison, and I suddenly realized none of them were injured. "How are you not hurt? Your ship was hit by the anamans, then by the mountain, and finally the fire engulfed it."

"Alex protected us again," Kia Lynn said, playing with the ends of my hair. "She created a water bubble, and not one thing got through to us. When the ship landed, we drifted right through the flames and safely on the other side."

Zeke twisted around, and his gaze traveled up Alex's long legs to her face. "You are the water bearer?"

"Sorceress. Bearer. Elemental. Whichever." Alex shrugged, but her gaze flashed to mine in a silent question. She did not know if she could trust him.

"Interesting," he muttered, tilting his head as a soft smile graced his lips. "So very interesting."

Alex's eyes narrowed at Zeke's comment. She shook her head and turned toward me. "Kia Lynn is being modest. I created the water bubble, but her wind is what carried us to safety. She is the reason we made it out of there alive."

Kia Lynn grinned, and I planted a kiss on her forehead. "She always has been the strongest of us two."

"We need to go." Wolf pointed at the northern sky. "They are already returning."

Zeke's gaze snapped in the direction Wolf was pointing. The rest of us followed suit, and sure enough, five small anaman ships were drifting toward us. They were searching for the remains.

We tore back up the way we came and arrived at Zeke's ship just as the anaman ships spotlighted the wreckage. They could not detect us inside the Theian technology. It was far more advanced than anything the anamans possessed, which was probably what they were really after. But why did they think Alex was the key?

We lifted into the air. Alex and Kia Lynn were watching Tatum with icy contempt. I would explain to them later. For now, we had a war on our doorstep, and if we did not unite our people, I was certain it would be a bloodbath that none of us would survive.

CHAPTER NINETEEN
Theian Blood

ALEX

I did not take my eyes off Tatum the entire flight to Las Vegas. For an unknown reason, he was allowed to be here, and no one else, besides Kia Lynn, was upset about it. As grateful as I was to see Beatle alive and well, I could not understand how a sadistic man could be treated as an ally.

When Kia Lynn nudged me and pointed, I finally pried my eyes away from the man I loathed, and I focused on the rising buildings ahead of us. I was eager to be with Mom and Dax.

"Esta will be thrilled to finally have us back," Koleton said to Zeke, who was sitting closest to him. "We really should wrap up our business and return to Theia."

Zeke's brow furrowed, and he snuck a glance back at me. "Not yet. I believe there is more for us to do here."

Koleton scowled but did not argue. I noticed Dad's

ship parked on the outside of their buildings. It was dark. Malcolm's ship had been brought closer, and there were several people surrounding it.

"They are fixing it," Zeke said. His sapphire eyes had locked onto me.

His ship slipped right through their shield and docked next to the pyramid. I rose slowly, wanting to keep Tatum in front of me, even though I wanted to race for Mom. I did not trust him. He glanced my way but looked away quickly and followed Beatle from the room.

Zeke and Koleton waited for the rest of us to file out, then took up the rear. When I walked into the open, Mom was waiting, and she folded me into her arms.

"We really have to stop doing this," she whispered in my ear, pressing her cheek against mine.

"Mom, how will we do this without him?" I felt lost with Dad gone.

She smoothed down the sides of my hair and cupped my cheeks with her hands. "We just will." A single tear slid down her cheek. "I can't wrap my head around it right now, but when we have returned home, you and I will figure it out as a team."

I pressed my lips together tightly and nodded in response. If I spoke, I was sure I would start crying all over again, and right now there were more important matters to attend to.

Dax stood next to Zoe Dawn and Covyn with his hands jammed in his pockets, eyeing me every time I looked his way.

Mom noticed and pushed me toward him. "He has been a nervous wreck. Go see him."

I squeezed her hand, then turned to face Dax. He was already there with his arms snaking around my waist. I clung to him and the moment my face touched his chest, the tears sprung to my eyes and I wept against his shirt. So much for not crying. He held me tightly, kissing the top of my head and running his hands through my hair. His touch was soothing. I breathed in his mint scent and through the snot and tears, I smiled. We were really in this together.

With the back of my arm, I dried my face, then reached up, grabbed his chin and guided his lips to meet mine. He tasted like mint and berries and I melted into his embrace, pulling him tighter against me. His fingers were in my hair, and his soft kisses became more demanding, parting my lips with a flick of his tongue.

Someone cleared their throat behind me. A crimson flush rose up my neck, and I slowly unraveled myself from Dax's arms and turned to face Uncle Henry.

"I think we all can agree that no one wants to see that," he said with a sly smile, tugging me close and wrapping his arms around me. "I missed your calls. I am so sorry, Alex. I should have been there for you."

"I think my calls were being blocked." I squeezed him, then pulled back. The sorrow in his eyes was not just for me, but I couldn't go there right now.

Confusion furrowed his brow. "How would that happen?"

I pointed at the sky. "The anamans. They have access to our coms. Ask Wolf."

"Who's Wolf?" he asked, turning in a circle. His eyes landed on Wolf, and recognition washed over his features. "I thought he was dead."

"Apparently, that is the trend with anyone who associates with Tallisa," I said loudly enough that Zeke and Zoe Dawn turned to look at us.

Zoe Dawn grabbed Beatle's hand and dragged her toward me as Uncle Henry headed in Wolf's direction. The two women stopped in front of me, and Zoe Dawn held Beatle's hand in the air.

"Place your palm against hers," Zoe Dawn said, grabbing at my hand.

I pulled away at her with a scowl. "Relax, sister. I can do it on my own." I lifted my hand and pressed it against Beatle's palm.

A warmth flowed between our hands, and the girl

smiled widely. I twisted my hand and looked at it, then turned back to look at Beatle.

"What was that?"

Zeke slipped closer to us and stood silently next to Zoe Dawn. His blue eyes sparkled so brightly, I had to force myself to look away.

"She is a flame, an elemental like us." Zoe Dawn placed her hands on both of Beatle's shoulders. "Tatum has been protecting her. And Tallisa"—she glanced over at Kia Lynn, who was in a quiet conversation with Rafael— "is a wind-walker like our sister. There is so much I need to tell you. For now, I need you to trust Zeke and his people."

"Welcome, everyone!" A blonde woman waved from the doors of one of the tall buildings. "Please, come inside. We have food and rooms for all of you."

Zeke waited until everyone passed by, then he fell in step with me. He tucked his hands inside his pockets. "Where are you from, Alex?"

"Excuse me?" Under the circumstances of our meeting, I felt like it was a bold question, or at least a bit out of line.

"I want to show you something," he said, holding out his hand for mine. "I promise, I won't bite. I think you will learn a lot from what I am about to disclose."

Koleton flanked Zeke's other side. "Will you be

joining the rest of us in the banquet hall?"

"First, I would like to show Alex her painting," Zeke replied as I reluctantly took his hand.

Koleton shot me a goofy grin and winked. "Alex, would you like a bodyguard?" he asked, raising his brows at Zeke. "I know a few spider moves from overindulging in the ancient action movies that might slow him down."

I couldn't help but smile. The man was charming, and it was obvious he was looking to calm my nerves. "If the need arrives, I will light up the Bat-Signal."

"Yes, that one!" Koleton exclaimed, jabbing his fingers in my direction. "See, she is already my favorite. She knows the Batman."

Zeke jumped out in front of us, and a blue cape waved materialized behind him. "Superman is better." The cape floated away with the wind.

"No! Never." Koleton was a diehard.

I laughed, and they both turned to face me. Zeke appeared to be examining me, like I was a specimen waiting to be poked and prodded. It was unnerving. My smile melted into a frown.

"Don't mind Koleton. His favorite pastimes on this planet are the food and your old movies." Zeke picked up my hand again and led me toward the pyramid. "We will meet you in the banquet hall."

"Esta will be cross with me," Koleton called after them.

"Work your magic, Koleton. I believe in you." Zeke placed his hand on a square white light next to the door of the pyramid. The door lifted, revealing an art museum.

Like an unseen force was drawing me in, I levitated and breezed through the doorway but then stopped at the first painting. The Mona Lisa.

"How did you find these?" I asked, not daring to touch the ancient art, but standing only centimeters away as I examined the authenticity. "Is this the original?"

Zeke still stood in the doorway, staring wide-eyed at my feet.

I glanced down and realized I was still several inches off the ground. My feet touched the lightly carpeted floor, and I turned back toward Zeke's stunned expression.

"What?" I asked, waving my hand in front of his face. "It is an anaman ability. I forget not everyone knows this about me."

His gaze shot up to my face. "I suspect it is much more than that." He walked by and waved for me to follow. "Come, let's go see your painting."

We zigzagged through statues, photography, and various other paintings until we stopped in front of a large painting of a woman in a red gown. I squinted up at her, and my jaw nearly dropped to the floor. It was me—

exactly me—down to the dimple in my right cheek and my slightly levitated stature.

I did not recognize the dress, but the face was unmistakable. A spitting image of me.

"How?" I asked, unable to find the right words. I peered down at the title of the painting. *Mystic Wonder*.

"You don't remember posing for this painting?" Zeke asked, walking from one corner of the painting to the other. He pointed at the artist's name. "Josh Campbell. Does that ring a bell?"

My eyes widened in disbelief. "Yes." I moved next to Zeke and stared down at the artist's name. Josh. My coworker from 2025. "We worked together back in the time I grew up in."

"And when was that?" Zeke's curious stare made me uneasy once more.

"Maybe we should return to the others." I turned to leave.

"My mother can fly," he said, stopping me in my tracks. "Just like Superman. She can fly like an eagle."

My feet shuffled as I circled back around to face him. "What are you saying?"

"There is something about you I can't put my finger on." He tapped his chin as he walked around the room. "You have nearly mastered a protective shield, yet no one taught you how to do it. Then your levitation, it is not an anaman trait. You know that, right?" He stopped near a small bronze statue and gripped the edge of its stand.

"Just get to the point," I snapped, tired of his roundabout answers.

"Have your parents ever visited another star system, aside from the anamans' home world?" He walked toward me, pressing his palms together in front of his lips.

"I don't think so," I whispered, realizing this man was really not from our world. "I thought you two were joking. You and Koleton really don't belong here."

"It appears neither do you." He pointed at the statue. It was a female anaman with similar markings to mine and the kenaz rune glowing on her wrist. "If I were you, I would be asking your parents some very hard questions."

A deep ache clasped onto my heart, and I felt myself spiraling. "My dad is dead," I snarled before pivoting on my heel and marching out of the pyramid.

Zoe Dawn and I both had the kenaz rune. Mine was an anaman marking, and hers was given to her at birth. What did it mean? Why was there a statue with similar markings? I gritted my teeth. Nothing made sense.

I raced toward the building I had seen the others enter. When the doors opened, an older man stood waiting.

He handed me a lanyard with a key card hanging from

it. "Your group is on the next floor up in the banquet hall. This is your room key for the night." The door opened again, and the man smiled. "Mr. Zeke, it is a pleasure to see you again. Your quarters have been prepped for your arrival."

"Thank you, Tobias." Zeke bowed his head at the man and held out his arm for me to take. "I will escort you to your family. I did not mean any disrespect by mentioning your parents. I only have my mother as well."

"It's fine." I took his arm, and he led me up the flight of stairs. I could smell the food before we reached the landing. I stopped as we turned toward the banquet hall. "I don't know who I am, Zeke. My parents abandoned me in the year two thousand four when I was three years old. I was an orphan until about six months ago when Tallisa popped into my life. From there, I have been tortured, abducted, imprisoned, chased, and somehow healed Mother Gaia in the process. But I don't fit in with anyone. Not my family, not my elemental sisters, and most definitely not the anamans. So tell me, who am I?"

Mom stepped out the shadows wearing a pained expression. "You belong with me, Alex. You fit in with me." Tears streamed down her face, and the glass she was holding in her hand shook so hard, red wine dripped over the sides.

I rushed forward and took the glass from her, then set it on a nearby table. "Mom, why am I different from every other hybrid? You claimed there were other anamans who can levitate, but I have met none. Please, tell me who I am."

She glanced from me to Zeke, and I noticed the weight of her secrets on her sagging shoulders. "We wanted to protect you from the human government, and someone told us of a Theian who would do it for a steep cost." A haunted expression settled across her face. "There was nothing we wouldn't do to keep you safe."

"What did you do, Mom?" My voice shook with emotion, and I had to find a chair before my legs crumbled beneath me. I collapsed into the nearest one.

"We paid for you to be alive, Alex. The warlock came to us. He was already residing on Earth, living out his last days away from Theia." Mom kneeled in front of me and grabbed my hands, resting her arms on my legs. "He is the one who gave Uncle Henry the key to time travel, and he is the one who invoked the blessings of Theia to run through your veins. It wasn't supposed to make you different."

"But I am different, aren't I?" My annoyance was flaring, and I yanked my hands from her grip.

She sat back on her heels, giving me some space. "He

did something we did not ask him to do. I don't know what it was. You hadn't been born yet, and I felt the energy flowing through my womb like tiny lightning bolts. It was painful for several days, but he promised it would keep you safe for the rest of your life."

I threw my arms up. "Tallisa tortured me. How did his magic keep me safe?"

"But she never finished. Uncle Henry found you." She raked her fingers through her hair and then laced her fingers behind her head, looking over at Zeke for help.

He did not give it to her.

"We found you because you have an energy level that is unlike any other person on this planet. It is almost unreadable, like these buildings. It vibrates at a much higher level than a mere human like me."

"Zeke, what am I?" I rose from my seat and stood in front of him. "Who am I?"

"You are only human," he said, tucking his hands into the pockets of his trousers. "Just like the rest of us. But you have the incantations of a Theian warlock flowing through your veins, and it makes you one of the most powerful humans on this planet."

"What did you say?" Koleton asked, interrupting our conversation.

Zeke patted me on the shoulder as he walked by, then

grabbed a cookie from the plate Koleton was holding. "We need to call it a night. In the morning, we will discuss preparations for Alex's transport to Theia."

Koleton's jaw dropped open and crumbs spilled out. He whipped around, but Zeke had already disappeared around the corner. He glanced back at my horrified expression, and without a word, he took after Zeke, leaving a trail of cookies behind him.

CHAPTER TWENTY
Mated

KIA LYNN

I had not stayed in the banquet hall for long. Papa was there, well and safe. We had reconnected briefly, and he caught me up on all the medical attention he received since he had arrived here. They had restored his health, and he was ready to start a brand-new life.

With Rafael and Papa by my side again, I longed for home more than ever and could not wait until morning. There was no firm decision on where we would go from here, with the anaman still seeking our imprisonment, but we were one step closer, and that was what mattered to me.

I crawled into the soft bed and laid my head on the feathery pillow. We each had our own rooms, but I wished Zoe Dawn or Alex were here with me in this large open space. It was too much for my taste.

Someone knocked at the door.

I threw my legs over the bed and tiptoed across the floor, then activated the camera to see who was there. Alex and Adina were on the other side. I opened the door, and they both rushed in.

"They are going to try to take me away," Alex said, pacing the floor between the window and the bed. "Zeke says I have a Theian spell running through my veins, and he wants to take me back to Theia with him."

I clenched my fists. "Over my dead body," I snapped, the pull of sleep disappearing completely.

"This is my fault." Adina paced the floor with Alex as she pulled her hair on top of her head and pinned it in place. She stopped at the edge of my bed and sat down. "We will fight them all."

"Why did Josh paint a portrait of me?" Alex asked, obviously in an entirely other world.

Adina twisted around to look at her daughter. "Who is Josh?"

"He was my coworker in twenty twenty-five," Alex replied. She nibbled on the ends of her fingernails, looking at each of our confused expressions. "He was my friend."

I nodded, finally understanding her. "And he painted you?"

"Yes, but without me knowing." She slapped her

forehead. "He knew I could levitate. How is that possible? I didn't have that ability until after Uncle Henry removed the chip. Mom, none of this makes sense."

"That warlock," Mom muttered, squeezing her eyes shut and rubbing her temples. "Zeke knew as soon as he met you. He knew you were one of them."

"I'm not one of them." Her words sounded hollow, and I knew she did not believe them any more than Adina's troubled expression did. Alex lifted her hands to look at them. "But I can feel the magic pulsating in my body as if they infused it in my very bones." She twisted her wrist, staring at them in wonder.

"Where is Zoe Dawn?" I asked, interrupting her musing. I tugged on the sweater Esta had given me. "We will leave now. Malcolm, Aly, Rafael, my papa... We need to fetch them all and leave."

"They will just come after us," Adina replied, rising back to her feet. "Maybe we could hide in Malcolm's sanctuary. Has anyone reached out to Tiordan to find out what he knows of these people?"

I shook my head. "But we are connected to him." I held out my hands toward Alex. "Let's try to speak to him through our minds."

Alex leapt over the bed and grasped my hands. We shut our eyes, and I relaxed my shoulders, focusing on Tiordan.

The energy between our hands intensified. In my mind, Tiordan's face appeared, but I could not tell if it was him or my imagination. I concentrated harder.

Ladies, you called? Tiordan spoke in my mind.

"Tiordan, is that you?" I asked my question out loud, unsure how this worked.

Yes, he replied. *Are you okay? Is Malcolm safe?*

"We are fine," Alex said, squeezing my hands tighter. "We need to know about the Theians. Do you know anything about these highly evolved humans who live in the north and in the pyramid to the south?"

I have heard of them. Rumors are all. Why do you ask?

"They want to take Alex to their planet." My breath caught in my throat, and my stomach gurgled with nausea. "What have you heard?"

The Theians do not get involved in our world's battles. If they want Alex to accompany them, they have an excellent reason. Find out their why and then negotiate from there. I hate to say it, but if they believe Alex will be a better fit with them, they will take her regardless if she likes it or not.

"We will see about that," Alex muttered, yanking her hands away from mine and breaking our connection with Tiordan. "I am done being told what to do and where to go. Mother Gaia promised us more." She pushed past me, stormed toward the door, and flung it open with so much force, I thought it would crash right through the wall behind it.

Esta stood on the other side, her hand raised to knock. Her brows lifted in question when the door struck the wall with a bang. "Alex, will you please come with me? I think there has been a miscommunication between my brother and your mother."

I slipped past Alex and stood in between them. "Not without me."

"Or me," Adina said behind Alex, waving her hand in the air. "I'm her mother."

The edges of Esta's lips twitched in amusement, and the obsidian irises swirled in a circle. "Of course. You are all invited. It will do my brother good."

She turned on her heel and waved her hand for us to follow. We did without question. The sister seemed to have a better head on her shoulder.

We did not go far before she stopped in front of double doors. She held her hand on the square white light next to them, and the doors swung open.

"Zeke, I have returned," she said, calling out as she approached another set of open double doors.

"She cannot remain here with these people who not only abandoned her but allowed the wolves to see her light and exploit it!" Zeke yelled from another room. "It is just like what happened to Mother. How dare they..." His voice trailed off when we entered.

Koleton rose slowly from the chair he had been lounging on.

"You were saying?" Esta asked, heading straight for the liquor bar and pouring herself a drink.

Zeke glared at Esta. "A warning would have been nice."

"Alex is not your property!" I shouted, stomping toward the beautiful man. His dark wavy hair hung in his eyes, but he swept it out of his face as I drew nearer. "Do you hear me? If you want a war, I will give you one."

I commanded the air to roar, and it listened to my thoughts, raging against Zeke and shaking the drinking glasses behind him. Zeke did not flinch, nor did his hair wave with the wind. He remained calm, waiting for me to finish.

Esta's hand curled over my shoulder. "My brother has something to tell all of you." She stepped in between me and Zeke and stared pointedly at him. "You do not have the right to make demands on a young girl," Esta snapped, holding her glass right below her lips. "Explain to her and her friend why you feel Alex is better off with us." She tipped the glass and took a sip, her eyes never leaving her brother.

"A young girl?" Adina's confused gaze drifted between the three strangers. "Aren't you a young girl yourself?"

Esta's gaze drifted to Adina, then quickly returned to Zeke. "We age differently. Zeke? Explain. Now."

Zeke blew out a long breath and turned to face Adina. "You are not a mother. Parents do not abandon their children." He shook his head as he circled around Alex's mother. The color was draining from her cheeks. "Not voluntarily at least."

Adina opened her mouth to speak, but Esta held up her finger. "Please let him finish."

"I blame you and her father for the battle we are in with the anamans." Zeke laced his hands behind his back as he paced the floor. "By using Theian enchantments, you instead have placed a target on your daughter's back. The painting. Her youth. They believe her supposed eternal life is a direct effect from vibrating at a higher energy, which can only be attained by a secret we refuse to share. *She* is their living proof it exists." He stopped in front of Esta. "Is that what you wanted from me, dear sister?"

Adina sank onto a nearby chair, shaking her head as a guilty expression rose in her eyes. "We did not know. You have to believe me. I was trying to protect her."

"I will not join you," Alex whispered. Her hands clenched into fists, and she raised her gaze to Zeke. "You cannot force me to leave. I refuse."

"If you stay, we cannot protect you." Esta set her glass down and walked toward Alex. Just like her brother, her presence commanded your attention. Her graceful movements made it difficult to turn away from her. She stopped in front of Alex. "My brother offers you a place with us because you will live much longer than your family. The magic was invoked into every cell of your body while you were still developing in the womb. You are more like us than you are them."

"I. Do. Not. Care." Alex set her jaw in a determined showdown with the goddess in front of her. "This is my home."

Esta nodded, and a small smile teased her lips. "Then it is decided." She glanced back at her brother, and her blonde hair swayed against her opposite shoulder. "Zeke, she is not ours to command."

"Phew!" Koleton blurted, running his hand across his forehead. "Now that we have that settled, can we all call it a night? All this proper mumbo jumbo and talk of war has made my eyelids heavy." He set his glass on the table and yawned, stretching his arms up above his head. "What do you say?"

Esta sighed, but I could tell she was trying to smother a smile. It had to be an act. No one was *this* perfect.

"I have one question," Alex said.

Koleton dropped his arms to his side with a loud sigh. "Of course you do," he muttered as he shuffled to a chair and collapsed onto it.

Alex shot him a flat stare and then turned toward Zeke. "Why did Josh paint me? How did he know I could levitate?"

Zeke rubbed the back of his neck, clearly exhausted from the talk. "Levitation is not an anaman trait. I told you this earlier. Your parents suppressed the enhanced anaman abilities, and that is it."

Esta handed him the rest of her drink and he gulped it down, then wiped his lips with the back of his hand.

"Why did he paint you? Because you disappeared into thin air when you traveled through time. Because you must have levitated without knowing it, and he saw it. Because you are magical but thought you were ordinary."

Alex chewed on her bottom lip and slowly nodded as Esta made her way to the exit.

"You look like your mother. A fierce beauty, that woman," she said, turning briefly to look only at me. "Zeke will show you *that* painting in the morning. Goodnight, everyone."

I stood frozen. She knew Mama as well. The secrets that woman carried could likely fill this entire building. Alex took my hand and leaned against my shoulder.

"I will walk you back to your room." She stared at me, waiting for an answer.

I shook my head. "I need to be alone." My feet were moving before she could say another word, and I raced through the hallways until I was standing in front of Rafael's door. I tapped on it, worried he was asleep.

I had barely removed my hand from the door when it slid open. Rafael stood in the doorway, wide awake and half dressed.

"Are you okay?" he asked, pulling me into the room. "You look like you have seen a ghost."

"I did not come here to talk," I murmured, pressing him toward the bed with my fingertips.

His eyes widened as he fell back onto the bed. I climbed on after him and straddled his legs, running my hands over the top of his smooth, bald scalp. I licked my lips and stared down at his.

"What—"

I pressed my finger against his lips. "No talking."

My finger traced across his jawline and around his ear, then all the way to the back of his neck. As I tickled the skin down his spine, a trail of goosebumps rose on his arms and shoulders. He grabbed me around the waist and tossed me to the pillows, leaning over me with the look of a lion ready to devour his prey.

When his lips met mine, I surrendered it all to him. My heart, soul, mind, and most definitely my body.

CHAPTER TWENTY-ONE
Fight Begins

ZOE DAWN

It is time, Zoe Dawn. Come to me.

I jolted upright, my eyes darting around the darkened room. Where was I? I glanced to the side and relaxed when I saw Covyn's spiky black hair poking out from under the bedspread. We were with Zeke. Everything would be fine.

But her voice. It was still echoing in my mind. Mother Gaia must be calling to me.

I scooted to the edge of the bed and tugged on my trousers I had left on the floor the night before. A faint noise from outside was growing louder with every passing moment. I yanked on my shirt and hurried to the window. The sun had not risen yet, but the shield that kept the building safe was sparking. I pressed my forehead against the glass and peered up at the sky. Several anaman ships were hovering above, and they were shooting at the protective barrier.

"Covyn, wake up!" I shouted, just as someone pounded on the door.

I nearly tripped over Covyn's clothes as I bounded to answer it. I threw open the door and found Dax and Malcolm on the other side.

"They have arrived," Malcolm said, tossing me my satchel.

I ripped it open and examined my knives and anaman weapons. "What is our plan?" I pulled out my sheath and wrapped the belt around my waist, securing it just above my hip bones.

"We don't have one," Dax replied, racing to the next door where Alex was staying. "A little luck and fairy dust are the best we can think of this time." He winked and knocked on Alex's door, not showing the least of worry on his face.

"Is he for real?" I asked, turning to look at Malcolm, who had not moved since I opened the door.

"He is a man in love and is surviving on kisses and unicorn wishes. Of course he is for real." Malcolm did not even crack a smile, but I burst into laughter, anyway.

Covyn smoothed down her hair as she stepped through the doorway. "Did they really bring the fight to these people? I thought Zeke and Esta could destroy them with their thoughts alone."

"It appears our secrets are being exposed," Esta said calmly, turning the corner and strolling up the hallway as Alex and Dax emerged from her room. "My mighty thoughts will stop the anaman in their tracks, but why not allow them to play before I do that." She winked at us, clearly amused by the rumors that were spreading in our group. "Those two lovebirds are awake. What about love birds' number two?"

"Who would that be?" I asked, shoving my daggers into the pockets on the sides of my boots. The anaman weapons fit snuggly into their sheaths.

Esta pointed over my shoulder. I turned just as Rafael and Kia Lynn exited her room. My jaw dropped and Covyn reached over and patted my cheek.

"It was bound to happen," she whispered in my ear before kissing it. "Don't you dare ruin it for her."

I glared at Covyn, then turned to do the same to Kia Lynn, but she was not paying attention to me. Despite the war erupting above our heads, she was all smiles, and Covyn was right, I did not have the right to take her moment away from her.

"Listen up!" Esta shouted, clapping her hands.

Everyone stopped talking and turned to look at her.

"They will not break through our shield, but," — she

held her finger up in the air — "we would prefer to keep the development of our project out of the center of the incoming battle. Goal number one, redirect the ships away from us." She held up another finger. "And goal number two, discover a way to end this battle and keep your planet safe from those who wish to harm Her."

Alex raised her hand. "They want me. We end this peacefully by my surrender. If not, they will keep coming."

Dax grabbed Alex's hand and shook his head. "No. Not an option."

The edges of Esta's lips quirked up. "There is always another way. Dig deeper for the solution."

"Where is Zeke and Koleton?" Kia Lynn asked, walking closer to us with her arm snaked around Rafael's waist. "You said I could see that painting today."

"My brother is outside." She pointed at the lift. "Which is where we should all be. You are free to take a stroll through the pyramid. You will know which painting I speak of, when you see it." She pushed through our small crowd, and one by one, we trailed after her.

When we reached the outdoors, I craned my neck over the throngs of people and spotted Koleton up ahead, speaking to a group of people. I waved, and he hurried toward us, but he stopped in front of Esta.

"More are coming," he said, jabbing his finger at the barrier. "They have the hoverbikes."

"How many?" Esta asked, her brow furrowing as she shielded her eyes with her hand. She surveyed the seeable terrain.

"Dozens." He rubbed his hands together and actually smiled. "Possibly a couple hundred."

"What?" Esta whipped around to face him. "How did they get their hands on that many hoverbikes? Those are ours."

Tatum moved in closer to Koleton, and I did the same, trying hard to ignore the fear clawing at me like a wild animal. I was not going to miss this conversation.

"Lindon's father. It was him." Tatum pointed at screen he held in his hands. "Zeke asked me to monitor that family. This is the footage from the camera I installed just outside their shop back up north. This happened yesterday after we left."

I circled around Tatum and squeezed in next to Koleton and Esta. Lindon and his father were loading a ship with hoverbikes.

Koleton grabbed the screen and squinted at it. "That crooked little—"

"I will deal with them," Zeke said, pressing his way into the middle of the cozy group. "Our people must move on, with or without those who deceive us. I hope Jamila and Enoch had nothing to do with their betrayal."

My parents. In the excitement, I had forgotten all about the life I could have lived. I drew in a sharp breath. Gratitude filled my chest for the Doyen who had abducted me as a baby and gave me to Mum. The kenaz rune did not define me, nor did it have any say in who I chose as my family. It was a symbol of my connection to Goddess, and that was it. All claims of it being anything else would fall on deaf ears.

"Are all your people leaving Earth?" Alex asked. There was an odd glimmer in her eyes I did not understand. Excitement or fear, I could not tell.

Zeke shook his head. "No. Just moving on—something I hope you will understand soon enough." His fingers combed through his curls and he winked at me. He was not worried like the rest of us.

What did he know that he was choosing not to reveal? The hoverbikes only seemed to concern Esta and Koleton. I focused on the blonde woman.

"Why are you worried about the hoverbikes?" There was a piece to this puzzle I was missing, and something told me it was right in front of my face.

"Worried?" Esta turned toward me. Her brow furrowed. "No, you are mistaken. They do not worry us.

Frustrated that so much of our technology was just thrown out to a world that is not ready for its advancements. They would have been useful once peace settled across these lands once more." The wind picked up around us, and Esta gathered her hair and wrapped it near the bottom of her neck. "These people will use these bikes to slow us down."

"Where are we going?" I asked. She still was not making sense.

She shook her head. "Not we." Her gaze shot past me and she gave someone a curt nod before refocusing her attention on me. "At least, not yet."

"Here they come." Tatum pointed, and we all turned in unison.

Large machines, maybe the size of the bed Covyn and I had slept in last night, were barreling toward us. They did not touch the ground, which would explain the hover part of their name. I watched in amazement. I wanted one.

"That's what I used to get me to the ocean," Alex said, linking her arm with mine. "If I wasn't running for my life, I would have really enjoyed the drive. Those people are probably the same ones who took me captive and attempted to torture me."

I jerked back to see her better. "Say what? They tortured you?"

She shrugged. "I feel like it was just A Day in the Life

of Alex. Every turn I take, someone is trying to take me apart, piece by piece."

I threw my arms in the air. "That is ridiculous." Whirling in a circle, I strained my neck to see over everyone's heads. "Where is Kia Lynn? We need to end this today. You, me, and her. Forget this nonsense."

The wind was picking up, and Kia Lynn had vanished. Rafael and Dax were all the way on the other side of the large pyramid, with Malcolm's and Adina's ships. At least those had been brought inside the protective barrier before the anamans had arrived.

"Do you see her?" I asked, squeezing Alex's forearm.

She shook her head, and her hair blew in her face. She spit out a strand from her mouth and combed the rest back. "I will ask Rafael if he has seen her."

I nodded as she sprinted away. Even my tight curls were whipping me in the face and around my neck. The dust kicked up, and several people ducked back inside the buildings to avoid it.

The wind gusted in a circle, creating small tornadoes between the buildings and near the groups of people who remained outside. I scanned over each face, searching for Kia Lynn, but she was nowhere in sight. I looked up at the ships still hovering above. They rocked back and forth to the point they almost hit one another. Finally, they shot off in separate directions to avoid colliding as the storm raged uncontrollably above.

But was it a natural storm?

It is time, Zoe Dawn. Come to me.

I whipped around, searching for the source of the voice, but everyone else was wrapped up in their own conversations and tasks. This time, I knew it was not Mother Gaia. I could feel a new energy flowing between me and whoever was speaking to me, but I did not understand what she wanted. What was it time for?

My focus returned to Kia Lynn. I would worry about the voice in my head later. I cupped my hands around my mouth. "Kia Lynn!" I shouted. A few people turned my way, but none of them were her. "Kia Lynn!" I raced toward the pyramid and through the open doors.

An eerie silence greeted me, and I came to a screeching halt. It was almost too calm within these walls. I tiptoed forward and circled around a stone statue of a horse and a bronze statue of a woman with a child. I rose onto my toes and peered between the other objects. Standing in the center of the pyramid was Kia Lynn, staring up at a painting of her mother.

As I drew closer to her, I could see the details. Tallisa was walking in a windstorm, her hair flowing down to her waist like a waterfall of fire, but not a hair on her head was out of place. Kia Lynn did not know. I'd never had the chance to tell her. Underneath the painting, there was a plaque with the words: WIND WITCH.

"Kia Lynn," I whispered, taking her hand and bringing it up to my chest.

Tears flowed down her cheeks. "She is a wind walker, like me." Kia Lynn turned toward me, her resolve crumbling right before my eyes. "She knew who I was. She knew the confusion I would face. And instead of showing me the way, protecting me, loving me through it, she threw me into the storm alone." She covered her eyes with her hands, shaking her head repeatedly. "No. This is not my life. My mother is not a heartless monster."

"Kia Lynn, there has to be an explanation for this." I tugged on her elbow so she would look at me. "We will find out together. Your mother must have a reason."

"No!" she screamed in my face.

I took several steps backward, surprised by her tone. She had never spoken to me this way.

"Do not defend that demon!" The flush on Kia Lynn's face and neck had deepened to a deep scarlet. She squeezed her hands into fists, and more tears welled in her eyes. The wind was now blowing inside the room. "She is nothing to me. In fact, she is dead to me. If I ever see her again, I will strangle her with my own hands."

I grabbed her arm, but she yanked it free. "Please, sister."

"I have been alone with this," she hissed. Her nostrils flared as she leaned in closer to me. "You have your new family and Alex has the water elementals. Me? I have had no one to talk to about commanding the air. She had every chance to be there for me and help me navigate through this, but as usual, she chose herself." She squeezed her eyes shut and her voice was barely a whisper. "She has always chosen herself above everyone else." Her eyes flashed open, and they narrowed. "Especially me."

She blew past me so quickly, several smaller paintings shot off their stands in her wake and crashed against the floor. My hair settled back around my face like a big puffball. I gulped as I pressed several strands away from my eyes. I had never seen Kia Lynn in so much pain. I tore from the building after her and came face-to-face with dozens of stunned expressions.

My gaze shot upward just as lightning struck the shield, and the entire protective barrier fizzled and cracked, then melted away like ice on a hot summer day.

CHAPTER TWENTY-TWO
Vanished

ALEX

I whirled around when something flashed by me, and I nearly knocked over Rafael in the process. Somehow, he held his ground and pointed at the sky.

The barrier that separated us and the anaman fleet crackled as if a hundred firecrackers had been set off at once. I twirled in a circle, watching with dread as our protection disappeared completely. Every muscle in my body locked up as my blood ran cold. I gasped, struggling to inhale a full breath.

Our enemies surrounded us from every side. I clasped onto Rafael and he did not budge, even when my fingernails dug into his skin.

They were coming, and we no longer had a barrier to hold them back.

Screams filled the surrounding air, and the rogue riders

on the hoverbikes lifted their weapons in response, shouting at one another to take aim. It was chaos beyond the buildings, and those were the worst kinds of enemies. No control.

Zeke's team and several of our warriors pointed their weapons at the masses surrounding us, pushing those who could not protect themselves behind the nearest blockade. The crowd was growing, and a line was forming. These people were putting their lives on the line to keep me out of the enemy's grasp.

I knew what I had to do. I lifted my hands high in the air and walked toward the rogue riders. They wanted me. Their key.

The throngs of people on either side of me grew quiet as I stepped into view. Rafael scrambled to grab me, but I shoved him back with a splash of water. There were too many of them, and I would not allow another person to place their lives on the line for me. I had come to this world uninvited. I was only reaping the consequences of my actions.

Uncle Henry darted through the masses, pushing his way toward me. I held my hand at him, and he skidded to a halt, shaking his head.

"Alex, no," he hissed so quietly, I barely heard him.

I lifted my head higher and pressed my lips together in

response. I was doing this. No one else was going to get hurt because of a greedy desire for eternal life. I wanted to be in their ship, the one that held their senators. I yearned to stand before them and be judged; then when it was all said and done, my waters would fill their lungs and freeze them from the inside out. It would be over, and my loved ones would be safe.

The vision kept one foot moving in front of the other. I had a plan to end this for good. They would never be able to hurt my family and friends again.

Be bold in your quest, Alex. Come to me.

I paused mid-stride and glanced around. I could hear a pin drop. It was that quiet. No one had spoken, but I know I had heard a voice.

Mom's face appeared in the crowd. "Stop, Alex," she cried, holding her hand out between two men. They moved to the side, and she stepped forward. "Please. Don't do this."

"I have to. I love you, Mom." My eyes blurred with tears, and I turned away from her, wiping at my eyes as I took another bold step.

The line broke as I neared the warriors, giving me an unobstructed view of my enemies.

The old man, with his cowboy hat and a dusty face, sauntered into the open and pointed his weapon at me.

"Keep coming, little lady. Your surrender will make this much easier."

All other weapons were raised, pointing at the surrounding people. I was their only chance. The Theians were not jumping to our aid. It was true what they had said; they do not interfere in our affairs.

I glanced back one last time. Surprisingly, Zeke strolled through the crowd, and they parted to let him through. I turned my head to see him better. A tiny glint of hope rose in my chest. A blue light haloed around Zeke's entire body, and when our eyes met, the light snapped forward and encased us all inside.

"Engage!" the old man shouted, throwing his hat to the ground in frustration. Shots rang out and struck the light, but none broke through.

I wet my parched lips and blew out a bated breath, grateful I had a moment longer to think of a more solid plan. Zeke continued toward me, and when he reached me, his fingers curled around my arm. He pulled me in close to him and hugged me tight. A mild scent of cinnamon and spice swept into my nose, and I relaxed against his chest.

"You do not need to sacrifice yourself. This battle can be won, but only when you are fully bonded," he whispered in my ear. He pulled back slightly to look me in the eye. "They will not break through my light, and they cannot destroy yours. Just wait."

"Kia Lynn left the barrier," Zoe Dawn cried.

My ears perked up at the sound of her voice and both Zeke and I turned to see her barreling toward us, with her arms flailing about her. Her eyes darted between the two of us.

"What do you mean, she left?" I asked, tucking my hair behind my ears and adjusting the sheath around my waist, finally able to inhale a full breath again. Zeke had calmed me with his touch and the lingering effects swirled around in my skull.

Rafael was suddenly beside me, waiting for Zoe Dawn to answer.

She jabbed her thumb up to the sky. "The barrier." Then she waved her hands around wide. "She did that. Kia Lynn. She found out her mother holds the powers of the air elementals, and she lost her mind. Literally. Lost. Her. Mind. I have never seen her so angry before."

Zeke did not look surprised, and his attention returned to the advancing warfare. His light was holding them back, but I could not imagine he would have the endurance to keep them out for long, despite his confidence otherwise.

Rafael rubbed his eyes. "Let me get this—"

The shield lifted from the ground and surrounded the buildings once again. Cries of relief swept through the crowd. Everyone jumped into action, preparing their ships and hoverbikes for battle.

"Zeke." I suddenly had an idea—a reckless one, but an idea nonetheless. "You want this battle away from here, right?"

One side of his lips quirked up. "We want all that we have built to be protected from those who do not want to evolve."

I stared at Zeke, calculating my next response but unable to find the words. He talked in riddles. Instead, I turned toward Rafael. "And we need to find Kia Lynn."

"Yes, please," he replied, wiping away the perspiration beading on his forehead.

I focused on Zoe Dawn. "Can you control your fire enough to push the riders on the hoverbikes away from the buildings?"

"Of course. Zeke has been teaching me." She puffed out her chest with pride. Drawing in a long breath, she turned her attention to the outer ruckus of the anamans and rogue riders.

"What is your plan?" Zeke asked, his fingers trailing over a marking on his right arm. It looked like the same symbol I had—his kenaz rune in the exact spot as mine.

I stared at it, unable to tear my eyes away until he covered it. My gaze drifted to his face. "Zoe Dawn uses her fire as a shield on one side, and my waters on the other. We move the battle away from this valley, just her and me. All others stay inside the walls of your barrier until we are ready for you to attack from the air."

Zoe Dawn's breath came out as a loud sigh, and she glanced Zeke's way. "I will do my best." She held her fist toward me, and I bumped it. "If only I could find the woman who keeps whispering in my ear. She wants me to come to her."

I froze. "What did you say?"

"I am probably losing my mind." She waved her hand to dismiss what she had said.

"Then I am too," I whispered, not missing the way Zeke's eyes brightened from our exchange. I wish he would disclose everything he knew instead of being so cryptic. I looked his way. "Do you really know the true motive behind their fight with you? Is it really about me, or am I just a symbol of something they can't have?"

"In all my travels, eternal life is the most sought after gift." Zeke waved at his sister and Koleton, and they started toward us. "You have given them proof, as you were painted in a portrait nearly fifteen hundred years ago. Now you are here. Do they want you?" He shook his head. "Not necessarily for anything pleasant."

"That is an obvious conclusion." I sighed and twisted

to view the scene unfolding beyond the barrier. "I do not understand why it is so difficult for you to disclose what you know."

Zeke's fingers wrapped around my forearm, and I turned back to face him. "From what I understand, the anaman from your time, who have been stuck here, wanted to return to their home, and the senators knew this," he said, folding his arms over his chest. "If those anaman produced proof of eternal life, they would be allowed to take a ship back to your time, using the time machine everyone seems so interested in. No one expected the void invading one of them and hijacking the mission."

"What do you know of the void?" Zoe Dawn asked. The coloring in her cheeks had faded to an ashy gray.

Zeke undid his belt that held his sheaths and folded it in his arms. "You cannot have light with dark. We all know that, right?"

We both nodded. I had one ear on him and the other on the shouts behind me.

"The void can infiltrate worlds and people who have not ascended to a higher density." His gaze drifted to me, still unfazed by any of the commotion erupting just outside the barrier. "The void wanted you, but your energy resonates too high for it to invade. You must all achieve that status to meet us where we are going." He winked as

Transformed Chaos

Koleton drew nearer.

He stopped next to Zeke. "Yes, boss?"

Zeke held up a finger at Koleton and kept his eyes on me. "Returning to your questions, the anamans do not have a fight with me, nor with my people. We remain neutral, despite their desire to learn our secrets. I believe in you—all three of you—and the offer will always stand. You have a place with us, if you so choose to join us." He turned toward Koleton. "The elementals are ready to rise in their power, and they have a mission ahead of them we will unfortunately have to miss." He handed Koleton a shiny object. "I think Kia Lynn, through her deep pain, has fully connected and will return once she realizes she cannot outrun her destiny."

Zoe Dawn threw me a confused look. My eyes narrowed.

"What?" I shook my head and grabbed Zeke's arm with the kenaz marking. It shocked me, and I jumped back in surprise.

"It will come. You are almost there." Zeke did not seem to notice the sting but gave me a reassuring smile. "You are both right at the brink of accessing it all." He reached over and planted a kiss on Zoe Dawn's forehead. "I am honored to be a witness to this moment in Earth's history. I will be your silent supporter. You have to complete this transformation without me."

"What in Goddess's name are you saying?" Zoe Dawn asked, snorting at the same time she laughed.

Koleton covered his mouth and turned away. The man did not have a serious bone in his body and seemed to find the worst times to respond in humor. I stared at Zeke, completely lost as to what had just happened.

He moved in close to me, his breath hot on my face. "You already know what you must do if they capture you. I sense what you have decided. If that time comes, you will discover your greatness on a level you never thought possible." He smiled and stepped backward. "You have a plan, Alex," Zeke said loud enough for others to hear, waving me toward the barrier. "Do it." He pulled Zoe Dawn forward as well. "Do it together. We will be here when you have made it to the other side. The world is waiting for your guiding hand." He pivoted on his heel and nodded at Koleton. "Now."

Koleton cupped his hands around his mouth. "To your stations!" he yelled and his voice echoed against the barrier as if he had used a megaphone. Then he lifted one hand and the object Zeke had given him sparkled against the sun.

Their people raced by us, either climbing into their ships or disappearing into the buildings, ignoring anyone else in their path.

Be bold in your quest, Alex. Come to me.

I wiggled my finger in my ear and turned in every direction, looking for the source of the voice. It did not sound like Mother Gaia, and it definitely was not Tiordan, but Zoe Dawn was hearing her as well. It had to mean something.

The ground rumbled, and my eyes flashed back toward Koleton, who now wore a wicked smile on his face. From the corner of my eye, I noticed the rogue riders slowing to a crawl. The old man had not moved, and his eyes were still locked on me. I looked back and forth between him and Koleton, holding onto Zoe Dawn's shoulder as the dirt shook under my feet.

"We do not get involved in the Earth's affairs," Koleton said, shrugging before he pressed down on whatever he was holding. "This is your home. Save it."

The buildings quivered and then flashed like bright lights. I covered my head and eyes until the shaking stopped. My arms slowly fell to my sides, and I stared wide-eyed at the surrounding emptiness. They had vanished. The buildings, the pyramid, Koleton, Zeke, and the rest of his people. Even Tatum and Beatle. They had just disappeared.

Zoe Dawn screamed, grabbing at her hair as she

whirled around. Dax was running toward us, frantically pointing over our shoulders. The rest of our people were scrambling for the two ships, Mom included. She didn't even look back at me before disappearing inside.

My breath caught in my throat, and the world slowed as I turned in a dazed circle. They had abandoned us. My gaze fell on the old man, whose firearms were pointed at me, and beyond him were the anaman ships and hundreds of rogue riders, ready and waiting for me.

CHAPTER TWENTY-THREE

Release

KIA LYNN

I rode the waves of my wind toward the north. Mama was there, and we had unfinished business to face together. I felt her presence growing nearer, and I knew it was time to release her hold on me. She would no longer have this control over my mind, but in order to accomplish that, she had to go. Be eliminated. It sounded dreadful, but the thought was freeing.

I remembered the door she had taken me to when I was young. That was where I would find her.

Her betrayal bit at my heart, nibbling away at my pain and turning it into a bitterness I no longer sought to fight. She had wanted me to die with this world so she could escape to a better life, even when she could have done it herself all along. The loathing swirling in my gut was ready to explode, but I needed to save it for her. Only her.

When I passed the red mountains, I slowed slightly. An unseen force was calling me to turn in that direction. The wind calmed around me until my feet touched the ground again. I stared at the passageway that led to Mother Gaia's sparkling waters and the rock we had gathered around not too long ago, even though it felt like eons had passed at this point. It was the place I had felt completely loved and protected.

I sighed, then turned back to the north.

Be true to you, Kia Lynn. Come to me.

I swung around, searching high and low for the source of the voice, but no one was there. The fury I had felt earlier inside the pyramid was no longer beating as hard against my head, but I still yearned to end the sorrow building in my chest. I sighed and closed my eyes, enjoying the warmth of the sun on my cheeks.

The thought of ending Mama's life had seemed like the right move, but as I remembered Mother Gaia and connecting with my sisters, the desire was slowly flitting away with the calm breeze. So what if she was an elemental? She really had zero control over me unless I chose to give it to her. Releasing whatever hold I thought she had on me required something much deeper, much grander than death.

Jax had reminded me of that right before he sacrificed

himself. I owed it to him and everyone else I loved to pull myself from this dark abyss.

I sank to the ground and dug my fingers into the dirt. The energy of Mother Gaia instantly filled my heart, and I smiled at the sensation as it swept through me like my wind was carrying it to each cell in my body. Knowing she was always there with us as the constant ground beneath our feet made it easier to face what I had to do.

The ground quivered. I looked around, but there was nothing but the red mountains, the vegetation, and dirt in every direction. I rose to my feet and strained my neck to see farther. A silver object to the north glistened in the sunlight as it moved closer. I squinted. Was that what I thought it was? It looked like Zeke's ship. Accept this one did not blend in with the terrain and sky.

As it grew closer, my eyes widened. It really was one of the northerners' ships. I turned back the way I had come. Anguish bit at my heart. I had left my loved ones to fight without me, while I pursued the woman who only loved herself. Zeke must have called in reinforcements. The fight must be worse than I thought it would be. I cringed as guilt slid over me like a vice.

The ship zoomed over me, headed toward the way I had come. I glanced at the passageway to Zion, then back north to Mama, and I sighed when I turned back to face the battle I had left. I built up the wind to push me after their vessel, but froze at the sight of the rolling clouds my force had not caused. My feet bounced lightly on the dirt again, and I stared in shock as the clouds parted, roaring to the side to guide in another anaman ship.

My breath caught in my throat. I waved my arms back and tore into the air, then threw myself forward with each gust of wind. I had to reach my loved ones before the anamans did.

Moments later, I flew over the hill and tore down toward the old, buried city, expecting to see the three buildings towering high in the air. Except they were not anywhere to be seen. Instead, several small anaman ships, the large vessel that had held me prisoner, hundreds of hoverbikes, and the northerners' ship were surrounding Malcolm's and Jax's ships that remained grounded.

In front stood Zoe Dawn and Alex, holding them back with their fire and ice. They needed me.

I pushed the wind with everything I had, aiming at the nearest hoard of hoverbikes. The gusts of wind smashed into their rear ends, sweeping them forward and colliding with the others in front of them. Then I blew toward them, clearing a pathway to my sisters. More hoverbikes crashed to the side, and a tunnel of wind and dust gave me safe passage through them.

Transformed Chaos

Alex's water rose around us, and with my wind distraction, Malcolm and Henry were able to slip their ships through the masses and rise above the other vessels, aside from the largest one. They still did not know that another anaman vessel was moving toward us.

I skimmed over the water as Alex pressed it out, building a wall of ice between us and the hoverbikes. Zoe Dawn was at her back, sending waves of fire at the ships, whenever they drew too close and any hoverbike that circled around the back way. I took my stance next to them.

Alex glanced my way. "Welcome back."

"I see I missed the best part!" I yelled over the noise. "What happened to the buildings? Zeke?"

"They deserted us!" Zoe Dawn shouted, turning her angry eyes my way. "The cowards abandoned us."

"How? Did he say anything beforehand?" I flicked my wrist, and two hoverbikes smashed into one another, their occupants flying past us.

"They basically told us this was not their problem," Zoe Dawn replied, clenching her jaw at the memory. "'We need to clean up our own mess' is the message I received. Then poof, they were all gone. Vanished right before our eyes."

"They expect us to rise to our potential," Alex retorted,

elbowing Zoe Dawn in the side. We turned together so Alex could keep building her ice wall around us. "I have no idea what Zeke knows, but I suspect we are about to find out." She glanced my way. "Or die. One or the other."

"There is something more we have to do," I muttered, remembering the voice and the pull to return to Zion. "This is not the end for us."

A sudden euphoric sensation slid from my fingers and exploded in my core as I connected with a power much deeper and stronger than anything I had sensed before. With only the thought of lightning, several struck the surrounding land. Dirt and debris shattered and spread in waves.

The world seemed to slow as I finally realized what had been right in front of my face this entire time. There was another. Not just Mother Gaia, but a physical being who would stand by our side in this ultimate battle. It was what Mother Gaia had wanted all along. Heal the Earth, cleanse the skies, awaken our missing piece, and complete Her transformation. We had not completed our mission.

I grabbed Zoe Dawn's arm. "She is in Zion. That is where we must go." I turned toward Alex to make sure she had heard me.

"Who are you talking about?" she asked, holding her hands high in the air as if keeping the ice wall from falling.

Transformed Chaos

It all made sense to me now. "The missing elemental. Have you not heard her? In here." I pointed at my head.

The ice wall cracked, and we all jumped as it shattered around us. The hoverbikes were closing in, and the smaller anaman ships were engaged in battle with our two ships. I pointed at the northerners' ship.

"Are they not on our side?" I asked as they fired on Malcolm's ship.

"That one is not friendly," Zoe Dawn replied, tossing a ball of fire at a hoverbike. She smirked when it exploded. "Whoever is in there, they are against us."

"Whatever happens…" I turned to face them both and grabbed their hands. "We must meet at the pool of water in the red mountains."

I whipped around and flew with the air, waving my hands in a circle and building a tornado in the middle of the hoverbikes. It grew and spread, creating lightning that struck the ground as it pushed against the riders. They broke away from their small groups and raced away from my cyclone, but not before it sucked a few into the eye of the storm and shredded them to pieces.

It was unpleasant to end their lives, but it was us or them, and with our destiny not fulfilled, it had to be them who perished. With each life, I traced the ansuz rune on my chest and blessed their passage into the afterlife. They had not known better.

As I finished the last one and twisted with my storm, something smashed into my side, sending searing pain ripping up my side. My hand pressed against it, and I lifted my fingers to see. Blood stained my palm and fingertips. I grimaced when another one struck me in the shoulder. I tumbled forward, biting back a scream.

My focus remained on my wind. Despite the agonizing pain ripping through me, I was able to keep my tornado tearing over the land and over all those in its way.

I lowered slowly to the ground, my inhalations shaky and short with each pained breath. My feet slid against the dirt, and I gulped back the tears threatening to spill out. The throbbing was unbearable.

Be true to you, Kia Lynn. Come to me.

I cried out, screaming as the agony tore through my insides. I pushed my storm toward the northerners' ship, but it dodged the cyclone and flew out of sight as I fell to my back. They were the ones attacking me, and Mama was one of them. Had she asked them to target me?

The clouds were darkening above, but they were also shifting as the massive anaman ship drew closer. In all the excitement, I had forgotten to tell Alex and Zoe Dawn we were expecting company. I could only stare while I concentrated on strengthening the tempest, working with

Transformed Chaos

Alex to bring in a thunderstorm so ravenous, our enemies would never return.

But my eyelids were heavy. I blinked away my exhaustion and forced my eyes to stay open. Rolling to my side, I swung my knees under me and then lifted myself back to my feet. The pain was excruciating, and I cringed when I took a step, but I kept going, shoving the wind against every hoverbike that was nearby. They toppled like leaves, flying into one another and crunching together before falling to a broken heap to the ground.

I tripped and stumbled forward, but caught myself before I fell flat on my face. Something else bit into my calf, and I screamed at the sky but held myself up with what little energy remained.

A wall of ice circled me completely, and I leaned against the cold barrier, weeping in agony. Alex was protecting me, and I was grateful for the reprieve. I wiped away my tears and refocused on the battle beyond the ice. Through the blurry barrier, I watched in horror as the northerners' ship circled around until it was right above Zoe Dawn. A light shot out of the bottom, and her eyes widened to saucers before she shot into the air, flailing her arms and legs. She had vanished.

I beat my fists against the ice wall, screaming at Alex to free me.

"Let me out!" I cried, pointing frantically at the vessel turning away from us.

The ship shot straight up and then over, disappearing just as I shattered through the barrier and crawled to the other side. I lifted my head and held my hand out, screaming for the ship to return.

CHAPTER TWENTY-FOUR

Connection

ZOE DAWN

Lindon's light-colored eyes stared down at me. The pale elf. What would Koleton say if he were here now?

"You won't be holding me for long." I rolled away, but someone kicked me from the side. I glanced back. His father stood with his arms folded across his chest and a condescending smirk on his lips. I would wipe that from his face before the day ended.

"Don't be so sure about that. Get up," Lindon ordered, pressing his boot into my calf.

I yanked my knee toward myself and glared at him. "My pleasure." I bounded to my feet and elbowed him in the nose.

Lindon stumbled backward, his hand against his face. Blood dripped between his fingers, so he wiped it away, splattering some of it on the floor and walls. He gave his dad a curt nod.

I whipped around, but it was too late. Shockwaves shot through my nervous system, bringing me back to my knees. I threw out my hand in one last desperate attempt to escape, but Lindon's father shoved it away, then grabbed me by my hair and dragged me down the corridor.

My body went limp, and I could not open my mouth. The only thing I could do was watch Lindon's lips twitch with amusement as he strolled behind us.

Moments later, I was tossed into a dark room, and they shut the door behind me.

It is time, Zoe Dawn. Your powers will guide you. Come to me.

I cried out as best I could, but my lips barely moved, and my tongue seemed glued to the top of my mouth. I turned to my flame, and a small fire burst from my motionless fingertips. My focus turned inward, pulling the fire energy to my core and building it from within just as Zeke had instructed. As it grew in strength, my nerves sparked to life, and I could finally wiggle my fingers and toes again.

A warmth filled my chest, drowning out the terror I had felt at seeing Lindon and his father. They really would do anything to control my flame. This time, they would understand without a shadow of a doubt—I was not theirs for the taking.

I envisioned light radiating throughout my entire body, and slowly, my limbs unraveled from the hold Lindon's poison had on them. I rolled over and pulled myself to my feet. The room was dark, but my eyes were adjusting. It was empty, and metal walls surrounded me.

They obviously were confident in their weapon holding me prisoner or they underestimated my heat. Even metal could not hold me.

Waves of flames spread along my skin, covering me from head to toe in the protective shield Zeke had shown me. I smiled when the metal melted underneath my feet, and I solidified my defensive fire wall between my skin and the outside world, allowing me to sink through to the other side.

"Good riddance!" I screamed loudly, hoping Lindon and his father would hear me.

Before I sank all the way through the nearly open hole in their ship, I heard the door slide open. Lindon's gaze darted around the room until it finally landed on my delighted expression. I smiled and waved my fingers, relishing in the surprise rising on his face. I slipped down farther and looked up to see him peering down at me. He knew he had lost.

The wind caught me, and I flew backward, nearly

yanking my arms out of their sockets and tumbling like a rock, fast approaching the ground. I had not thought this far ahead. The only thing I could do was spread out my arms like a bird. I slowly steadied, then ignited my flame again and burst into a bright fireball.

"Mother Goddess," I cried against the wind. "I am in your hands."

My body spiraled toward the ground. I traced the kenaz rune on my chest and squeezed my eyes shut, convinced this was it. There was no way I would survive a landing from this height. The earth was coming at me too fast.

The wind came to an abrupt stop, and an eerie silence filled my ears. I pried open one eye, only to be greeted by utter blackness. I opened my other eye, just as I burst into the sunshine. My legs flailed out, and I tumbled forward, skidding on my knees along the mossy ground.

I whirled around, dragging my bruised and beaten knees with me. The entrance to Zion was only up the hill from me, and a chasm the size of my body was slowly filling back up with dirt as if an unseen force was shoveling it back together. I watched in amazement.

"Zoe Dawn, is that really you?" Tiordan's voice brought me back to reality.

I jumped to my feet, only slightly wincing from the ache in my knees and legs, and faced Tiordan and several others from Zion. "Did you see that?" I waved my hands at the sky, bouncing on my toes as excitement exploded within my chest. "That. Was. Extraordinary!" I whooped and bounded in the air, then landed like a feline when my feet met the earth again. I held my hand toward the sky and waggled my fingers. Even if Lindon could not see me, the disrespectful gesture brought me so much joy.

Tiordan's gaze was glued to me, his eyes as wide as saucers. I was sure I was a sight to see. I glanced down at my torn clothes and smoothed them over as best I could. Tiordan stopped in front of me and pointed at my head.

"We will need to do something about those curls," he said, with a soft smile teasing the edges of his lips.

I reached up and stuck my fingers into my hair. The snarls immediately stopped me. I yanked at them and tore out a strand from the root.

"All that is holy," I muttered, cringing as I dropped my hand in front of my face and stared at the hair. I shook my head. "It will take ages to comb through this mess."

"How are you even here?" he asked, taking my hand and pulling me toward the entrance.

The solitary door came into view not too far up ahead. His companions followed us quietly.

"Beats me," I replied, running my filthy palms down the sides of my shirt. "What did you see?"

"An orange light falling to the ground and then the dirt flying so high from the ground, we were convinced it was a meteor or debris from the ship that had flown overhead." He pressed the door open and waved me inside. "We were coming to inspect when you burst out of the ground."

"I just went for it. Those heathens took me away from—" I clasped my hand over my mouth and ran for the other door. When I stepped outside again, I tilted my head toward the sky, then looked back at Tiordan. "We need to go back. I left them there. Kia Lynn, and Alex, and all the others."

"Slow down. Come with me, and we will contact Malcolm. The only ship we have remaining here is small and unprotected. We do not want to put more of our people in danger." Tiordan adjusted his dark-blue robe around his waist and swept past me. "Malcolm will know the best course of action."

You must come to me, Zoe Dawn.

I glanced over my shoulder, but no one was there. "Did you hear that?"

Tiordan turned, but the others continued without us. "Hear what?"

"That woman's voice? She sounds so close." I turned in a circle, inspecting every nook and cranny I could see.

"You must have hit your head." He cupped my face

with both hands and turned my head back and forth, inspecting it for injuries. He pursed his lips when he found nothing. His fingers wrapped around my arm. "We should have our medical team do a thorough examination."

I walked alongside him, still amazed at what had happened. Did the earth just fold into me, or did it open so it could cushion my fall? I had no idea, but it was fascinating to feel the energy of that moment still pulsating through my veins.

We reached the small city but stopped when a few others were looking at the sky. My gaze shot upward. Lindon's ship was hovering near the mountainside with a gaping hole in the bottom.

I pointed at it with a wide grin. "That was me."

Tiordan turned toward me. "And they know you are here. How is that?"

"Can they see us?" I asked, suddenly realizing the weight of his question.

"They should not be able to view inside our barrier," Tiordan replied, storming toward the nearest building. As he neared the doors, he came to a sudden halt. "There is another." He whirled around and ran back toward me, his robes flapping in the wind. "This is not over. Come with me."

"I know it is not over." We barged through the doors

and I yanked my arm away. "What has gotten into you, Tiordan? Are we going to speak to Malcolm or not?"

"You cannot leave." Tiordan ran his fingers over his clean-shaven chin, and he blinked as if he could not see me. "She is waiting for you, all three of you. The healing of Mother Gaia was only the beginning. I knew it!" His eyes finally focused, and he stepped so close, I could smell the mint on his breath. "Don't you see, Zoe Dawn? This all had to happen to show you attachments are unnecessary. The heartache, the trauma, the fighting... All of it was brought into your space for a reason."

I groaned and circled around him. "Stop lecturing me. Can we please reach out to Malcolm?" I had to know they were safe.

"You do not need me for that," Tiordan replied, his voice suddenly calm once again. "You always had the power to connect with your sisters. Do it now."

I eyed him with careful thought, then nodded. "How do I start?"

"Those attachments. They are heavy." He led me to a chair in the front area of the building. "You must first release all that is holding you down."

I sank onto the chair, and Tiordan strolled to another and did the same. What was heavy on my heart? I released a long breath, leaned back against the cushion, and closed my eyes.

Mum. Her life had ended, and the thought tore me apart inside.

Kia Lynn. I had to know she was safe. She was my best friend and my anchor to reality.

I smiled at the memory of Covyn's spiky black hair and her sassy attitude. She was strong but relied on me to feel whole.

My newest sister, Alex. The moment our eyes met, everything had shifted, yet despite the pain, I would not change anything.

Zeke and Koleton. I had connected with them instantaneously, but they were not here to keep me grounded. They had interrupted my life to show me I could fly. This was what Zeke had wanted me to discover. I had to allow the light in, to navigate through the fury I had been holding onto for so long, and then let it go. It *was* like a weight on my heart.

My emotions ebbed and flowed like the ocean's tides, and I dragged them to my core and held them there. Tears tumbled down my cheeks, and I felt every moment of agony and pain release as I wept uncontrollably. When was the last time I had really cried? Letting all the pain go was clearing the clutter from my mind and creating space for something better.

I wiped at my face and nose several times, thinking of the hurt Mum had caused. I was never good enough for her, at least from such a limited viewpoint. She had loved me the best way she had known how, and in the end, she had fought for me—given her life for me. Her love had been boundless.

When all the ugly and hateful emotions fluttered away from me, what remained was a bright energy of swirling yellow light. A channel opened up within me and I sensed my sisters. Kia Lynn's thoughts entered my mind as if she were standing over me and whispering in my ear.

There is another. The fourth. We must return to Zion.

My eyes snapped open. "Kia Lynn already knew we had to return. She said so during the fight." I leaned forward and clasped my hands together on my lap. "How did *you* know?"

Tiordan's shoulders relaxed as if he had been anxiously waiting for this moment to arrive. "I was never fully content with how things had ended with the healing of Mother Gaia. It did not feel complete, but I could not understand why. There was a continuous nag at the edge of my mind, begging me to bring you back, but I could not rationalize its meaning." Tiordan crossed one leg over another and closed his eyes. "Now, I am seeing clearly again. You need to finish your inner journey. When you are done, you will know the same truth as Kia Lynn. I will wait here for you."

I settled back against the seat, regarding the seer for several silent moments. For the first time in my life, my anger did not rule my emotions, and in its place was focus and awareness. Tiordan's words rang in my skull. I was missing the ultimate piece.

My eyes closed, and I quieted my mind. It was easier this time. A blurred vision flitted across my thoughts, and as it became clearer, I noticed I was picking up on Alex's fear as she stared down at Kia Lynn. There was blood everywhere, and I knew they injured my sister. Zeke's advice helped me remain calm and in control.

As the vision of Kia Lynn flitted away, another woman appeared in her place. Dark skin. Green markings. A brightness pulsated around her. My flame spread like a glass encasing my body, and my eyes flashed open. I glanced down at my kenaz marking, feeling the heat before I saw its orange glow.

I see you, Zoe Dawn. It is time. Come to me.

CHAPTER TWENTY-FIVE
Greatness

ALEX

I held Kia Lynn's trembling body in my lap. My growing terror wormed its way through my gut and inhaling each breath became more difficult as the seconds ticked by. We were in the middle of a war zone, and my sister was bleeding out right before my eyes. I pressed down hard on her most severe wound that spread from her side to her belly button.

Dust and ash swirled around me, mixing with all the blood and my sweat. With my free hand, I wiped the back of my arm underneath my nose and then rubbed my burning eyes to clear them. The fires Zoe Dawn had lit were keeping the remaining few rogue riders busy, but the billowing gray smoke was making it difficult for us to find our ships.

"Mom," I called on my com, my voice scratchy from

the ash. I coughed and wheezed before I could continue. "You have to land and pickup Kia Lynn. They have shot her three times, and I cannot stop the bleeding." I leaned closer to Kia Lynn. "You stay with me. Do you hear me? I will keep you safe."

Kia Lynn grabbed my arm and squeezed so tightly, her nails dug into my skin. "We have to meet back at the red mountains. Please listen to her, Alex. The fourth is calling to us." Her voice trailed off, but she opened her eyes fully and gave me a pointed look.

I could not find my voice, so I nodded in response. Was she hearing the same voice?

"We are on our way. I have your location pinpointed," Mom replied. She sounded so far away. "We cannot land, but I will open the bay door so we can pull you on board."

The lights from the ship landed on us as they lowered toward the ground. Malcolm was covering them and drawing the other anaman ships away from us. When the dust kicked up, I coughed again and covered my mouth with my arm. I pulled up my hood from my jacket and shielded my head and cheeks as best as possible, then I climbed to my feet and awkwardly lifted Kia Lynn to hers. We hobbled to the hovering ship.

Dax and Rafael were waiting with outstretched arms, with the ship hovering a few feet from the terrain. I boosted up Kia Lynn, and they hauled her inside but fell backward when the large anaman ship shot at Dad's vessel. It swayed back and forth and nearly struck me. I ducked and rolled out of the way, then bounded to my feet and used the remnants of Kia Lynn's storm to pelt the enemy with hail.

I shuddered when I noticed the parting clouds near the larger anaman ship. My feet slipped on the wet rocks, and I stumbled backward, never taking my eyes off the sky. It couldn't be another one. How would we ever fight both?

"Alex, let's go!" Dax yelled, waving his arm to get my attention.

My gaze darted between him and the incoming vessel as it broke through the atmosphere and slowed to a crawl just above us. Terror overtook every muscle in my body. I leapt forward and took off running toward Dad's ship.

Out of nowhere Aly barreled toward me, ramming against me with so much force, I flew backward and into the throng of what remained of the bike gang. I rolled away from one hoverbike and bounded to my feet. My gaze landed on Aly, who stood defiantly in my path to the ship. She had found her moment to separate me from my allies, and now the hoverbikes and anaman surrounded me.

I looked back at the approaching anaman ship, then

Transformed Chaos

faced Aly again. Her eyes narrowed, and she raised her hand high and waggled her fingers at me. Throwing one last look at Dax, she whirled around and sprinted into the dust and fire. My gaze drifted to Dax as Uncle Henry was forced to move the ship farther away. Dax yelled and held out his hand to me, but it was impossible to reach him from where I crouched.

I leapt to one side to avoid one hoverbike, then circled around another and levitated toward Dax's outstretched hand, narrowly missing being torn away by one of the riders. My pulse thundered in my chest as I swerved around another hoverbike, never taking my eyes off the love of my life.

A burst of light surrounded me, and the world around me grew silent. I flailed my arms, reaching for Dax as his eyes widened and he screamed my name. I rose higher in the air, thrashing against the pull that was forcing me backward. My arms ached as I strained my hand toward Dax, pleading to the goddess to free me from the light's hold on me. An invisible force closed around me, yanking me backward and away from him, right through the battle in the sky.

My heart barely had a moment to beat again, before I found myself in a brightly lit room, surrounded by anaman troops. My legs shook, and they did not give me a chance to take in my surroundings before they threw a bag over my head. They dragged me, kicking and screaming, from the room.

When my feet found solid ground again, I heard the whispers of dozens of people around me. My heart thrashed inside my chest, and a chill swept down my spine in anticipation of what was to come. All the fighting to keep them from taking me had been pointless.

The bag lifted, revealing a brightly lit room. I squinted and blinked as I focused on those who had abducted me.

I bit down on my lower lip to hide the trembling in my chin. I stood in the middle of a large room with towering ceilings. The seating circled the entire room and, in each chair, an anaman sat staring at me with curious or guarded looks. They each wore black clothing with the same two-headed snake emblem Freydis had stitched on her uniform.

I tugged at my arms, but the binding held fast. I felt the cool material of the iron gloves fold over my hands once again. The guard flinched as he touched me, and when they were secure, he scurried away like a rat. They obviously were less educated about my powers than I had once believed.

"Is this really the girl? A filth and putrid stench covers her," a woman asked, her tone laced with disgust.

I whirled around to see who spoke, but no one had stood, and they all continued to stare in silence. I sniffed. Did I really smell that awful?

"Yes, Majest," an anaman soldier replied, bowing toward a woman to my left. "Freydis inserted a tracking device when they infiltrated the impoverished village."

I flinched at his words.

The elderly female anaman nodded in response. Her silver eyes pierced through me and she leaned forward in her chair as she thoughtfully examined me. "She is a scrawny one and not much to see right now. We have journeyed a long way and cannot afford any further mistakes."

It finally made sense. That was why Freydis said it was not their problem. The ones who were really after me had been on their way to Earth, and she had led them right to me. I glared at the silver-eyed woman.

"I am surprised the Theians allowed her to be out in the open," a male anaman said. He was sitting a few seats away from the silver-eyed female who had asked the earlier question.

Several others nodded in agreement, and a few spoke quietly to another while pointing excitedly at me.

"They are fools!" another male anaman with sleek black hair shouted, rising from his chair and banging his staff against the floor. He sat at the end of the long room, surrounded by guards. A lock of his hair fell in his face, and he pressed it back with his thumb. "Their confidence in their technology and its ability to hide their worlds from us will be their downfall. The Theian magic coursing through this woman's veins is all we need. The passageway will be opened, and our fleets will overwhelm them."

Zeke was wrong. The battle *was* with his people.

"Are you sure?" I asked, raising my brows. I sighed with exasperation to mock their ignorance. "Do you really believe they would make it that easy? Are you positive my blood will open a passageway to their worlds?"

He glared, but several others nodded, and the whispers grew louder.

"Silence!" he yelled, banging his staff against the floor again.

"I am anaman. Just like all of you," I shouted, ripping my arms loose from the binding, surprising myself from my sudden strength.

Several of the anamans jumped to their feet, while others cowered against their seats.

I had no idea how I had broken through them so easily. My lips twitched with delight. I ripped off the iron gloves and tossed them to the ground. They clanged against the hard surface and more anamans rose in panic. I held out my arms toward their startled faces. The light-blue lines glowed against my pasty-white skin, and the kenaz symbol on my wrist, which matched Zeke's, sparkled orange and white.

"You have played right into their hands. My blood may have Theian magic, but my anaman DNA ties me to you. They already knew your next move."

"Shut her up!" the male anaman screamed at the guards.

I laughed. Water gurgled out of his mouth and he choked on any other words he might have had as ice formed around his lips.

A sting in my shoulder snapped my focus away from the man. I whirled around and threw an ice dart at the guard's face that had shot me. It sank deep into his eye socket. He screamed, thrashing his hands around and then trying to pull it out, but it kept slipping through his fingers as it melted down his cheek, mixing with his blood.

My knee buckled underneath me when another shot sliced through my calf. I tumbled to the floor. My skull struck the hard ground, and everything around me blurred. I rolled to one side, but another shot nicked my abdomen. I screamed, grabbing at the wound. My fingers slipped against it as the blood trickled out, and I knew it was flowing too quickly for me to survive if I did not stop it soon.

I reached upward and spread my fingers wide, summoning the moisture from the air. A wall of ice separated me from the others. The guards shot at it, then dropped their weapons, kicking and punching until the ice cracked. I whimpered. I could not fight them off if they broke through. My fingers shook from the pain searing through my gut, and I blinked away the black haze threatening to push me into a dark abyss.

"Do not kill her!" a male anaman senator screamed. "She will be of no use to us if she perishes."

Alex.

That voice. There it was again. I sat up straight. The melodic sound had me twirling around on my knees in the middle of my ice shelter, searching for the source.

Be bold in your quest, Alex. Come to me.

Ice shattered to the floor, and the guards advanced toward me. There were too many of them. I staggered to my feet, then with what little energy I had left, I rose a few feet off the ground and surrounded myself with an icy blue light. That was unexpected as well, but I could feel an endless supply of power coursing through my veins, creating the unbreakable shield.

The guards tumbled backward, scrambling to escape.

Transformed Chaos

My focus drifted away from them and landed on the male anaman at the head of the room. His staff quivered, but he held his ground. Our eyes met, and fear shattered across his expression.

I spread my fingers at a snail's pace. When I used my hands and body, my commands on the water were far more powerful. Using my thoughts alone was enough, but connecting motions with my thoughts was the key I had not understood until this very moment.

An ice storm circled the anaman leader. He tried to break through and escape, but the ice thickened as it formed into a block around his body. He thrashed against its hold but froze when he noticed my approach. His eyes widened to saucers and the color in his face drained to ashen white. I sauntered around him, then faced the others. Those who remained in the room cowered in fear. It would have been amusing if I were not in a hurry.

"Greed has no place on Earth," I said, stopping in front of him and running my fingers along the ice. It crackled from my touch. "I bet you wish you had remained in outer space. I know I do. It did not have to be this way."

"I will make sure you regret this," he hissed. His gaze flitted from me to the ones leaving him behind, desperation suffusing his features.

I glanced over my shoulder. "I doubt that. There are

those of you who will not move on with the rest of us." I turned back to face him, tapping the ice with my fingertips as I circled to his side. "It is a shame. We could have done this together. Maybe those who are tired of your rule will have the opportunity to continue on with the rest of us."

He whipped his head back and forth, trying to break free and screaming at the top of his lungs. My gaze turned to the windows to my left, and I winced from the pain in my side. I had no more time to waste.

"Mother Goddess, please keep me safe," I whispered, closing my eyes for a brief moment. "Sisters, I am on my way."

My eyes flashed open. I formed a ball of ice that hovered just above my hands and built it gradually while listening to the murmuring and cries of the others as they scrambled over one another, trying to break through the exit before it sucked them out into the open sky. My ball of ice grew as big as a bowling ball, and I lifted it higher into the air.

I turned to look at the majest one last time. I met his terrified expression with a smile, then twisted and hurled the ice ball like a rocket. It tore clean through the largest window, sucking debris and seating through the hole. Those who remained inside the room slid across the floor toward the aperture, flailing their arms in desperation.

Transformed Chaos

I sprinted toward the gaping hole and burst through the opening, spreading my arms out and ignoring the searing agony gripping my side. My sister's wind cradled me in its embrace as it steered me toward solid ground.

Zeke's words, before he had vanished, echoed in my skull. I understood my abilities more than ever now. My greatness came from a place deep inside me that could not be explained, only experienced. My past did not define me and neither did anything or anyone who had influenced my life. All that had been given to me, was meant to be mine. Always.

I grinned like a buffoon with the wind at my back. No one could separate me from my sisters again. We were connected by more power, energy, and sheer desire than anything the anamans could throw at us. The fighting ended today.

Kia Lynn's words echoed in my mind as I landed gracefully on the earth, bouncing on the dirt as if it were a soft cushion. The fourth was ready and waiting for us to unite again. This time, Mother Gaia's transformation would end the bloodshed for good.

I limped through the trees and smiled through my pain when the tips of the red mountains popped into my view. Tucked away behind the vegetation was the door that led to Zion.

CHAPTER TWENTY-SIX
Transcendence

KIA LYNN

It was quiet once again. Elation fluttered within me as the ending task returned to my thoughts.

I opened my eyes and saw the white walls where the healing station was located, then turned my attention to the woman beside me. Her ice-blue eyes met mine. I pressed my hand against the glass of the healing station, then reached back like Alex had taught me and released the lock that held me within.

Adina shook her head with a sigh as the glass lifted away from me. She reached up to pull it back down.

I grabbed her hand. "You have to take me to Her waters."

Adina shook her head again, wiping her forehead with the back of her free hand. "You have barely started healing, Kia Lynn. We cannot risk an infection." Her eyes wore grief like a badge.

I knew she was distraught for leaving Alex behind and losing Jax. Her regret was written all over her face. It was also obvious she believed she was failing her daughter by not caring for me, but I was not negotiating. We needed to leave all our attachments in this room. It was my responsibility to show her the way.

Rolling to my side, I pressed myself to my feet and stood on my shaky legs.

"Stop, please." Adina tried to push me back onto the bed.

"Either I crawl there, or someone helps me," I said, wrapping my fingers over her shoulder and gripping it tight to hold me steady. "I am making it to my sisters one way or another."

"Sisters? As in both Zoe Dawn and Alex?" Her eyes brightened with hope.

My lips twitched with a smile. "Of course. Who else would be waiting for me?"

"But she's gone. They took her." Her shoulders sagged again. She turned toward the door with a sigh, all of her fight gone. "Rafael, we need your help."

Rafael stuck his head through the doorway. "Lie down, Kia Lynn."

"Have we landed?" I asked, ignoring his demands. I

loved him more than I ever thought possible. I wanted him as my mate, but I did not need him—except to help me to the cave waters.

"Yes, we are unloading now, but you need to finish healing." Rafael stepped into the room.

I pinched the bridge of my nose while shaking my head. "Take me to Mother Gaia's waters." I shrugged off my torn sweater and tossed it to the ground. The pain in my side was throbbing, but I knew it would not matter soon. "Please. I will make it there faster with your help." I held my hand toward him and waved him closer.

He looked to Adina for help, but she just nodded. His gaze shot back toward me. "Fine, but this is one of your worst ideas." He circled around to my side and wrapped his arm around my back.

"We will see about that," I whispered, feeling the others so near. We were almost to the end. These people did not understand, but they would soon. The entire world would see. I did not know where we were going, but I knew it would be a journey we would not forget.

Rafael led me down the bay door and onto the landing platform, looking surprised when he noticed Zoe Dawn waiting. She held out her arms for me.

"We will go together," she said, wrapping me in her embrace.

Transformed Chaos

"You disappeared into the northerner's ship," Rafael said, stepping out of the way. "How are you even here?"

"They were no match for me." Zoe Dawn chuckled.

We meandered toward the butterfly sanctuary and stopped amid them. My body ached, but there was something magical about being surrounded by the mystical insects. As if sensing the same from me, they landed in swarms across my body, appearing like the dancing petals of blossoms in the wind. I closed my eyes and inhaled the power they fed me, healing me from the inside out. The chaos of the world faded away, and I surrendered my grief and pain to them.

Zoe Dawn tugged me forward. My eyes fluttered open, and I continued with her. My gaze wandered around the vegetation and red rocks, with the blue sky as their backdrop. I was completely enthralled with the vastness of our lives. We were unfolding from our cocoons and spreading our wings, just like the butterflies had done.

The cave entrance came into view, and a trail of warm steam nipped at our feet as we approached the cavity.

"What about Alex?" Dax asked, yelling behind us.

I sensed his anguish for leaving her behind. I paused mid-stride and turned to look at him over my shoulder. "She will be here."

His eyes widened, but he did not respond.

We continued with a growing crowd of people trailing us. The air warmed when we stepped inside the cave and the steam filled the surrounding space. The scent of fresh, warm water was a promise for what was ahead. When we reached it, we stopped at the edge of the pool and looked at one another.

"Are you ready?" Zoe Dawn asked, clicking her tongue in her old familiar way.

I smiled. "The better question is, are *they* ready?" I jabbed my thumb over my shoulder.

"We are about to find out." She took my hand in hers and held them up by our shoulders.

My free hand drifted behind me, and I waited. A hush fell over the crowd while they pushed to squeeze into the cave with us.

"Alex. You're okay," Adina whispered, releasing a sigh of relief.

A hand wrapped within mine, and I lifted Alex's fingers to touch my shoulder. I glanced her way with a smile, then the three of us stepped into the pool together.

A bright white light filled the cavern, and the water rippled against my wounds, soothing away my pain and sealing them shut. A burst of energy shot through every inch of my body, and I held it steady against my skin, watching in amazement as Alex and Zoe Dawn did the same.

Alex's light-blue light radiated from her anaman markings, flowing like the rivers of the world. The one on her wrist glowed orange, and it shone against Zoe Dawn's kenaz rune, which had brightened to a deep crimson. Tiny orange-and-yellow flames kissed every inch of Zoe Dawn's skin, illuminating the speckles of green in her eyes I had never noticed before.

I glanced at my arms and stared in wonder at the fluorescent glow of the white light illuminating like the fireflies that swarmed our village during the harvest season. From behind me, I noticed a crimson light warming my calf. I lifted my leg. My birthmark radiated a white light that flowed out and around, swirling like a tornado in front of us.

The intense energy pulsated around us and all chatter from the group behind us faded away. Once the room brightened more, a woman materialized between Zoe Dawn and Alex. My pulse quickened from the sight of her and like a lightning bolt, my white light shot over her shoulder and collided with the kenaz marking on her forehead. It shone like an emerald, bold and breathtaking. Her deep-brown skin sparkled with green flecks, and her long black locks cascaded down to her waist. The emerald light from her forehead marking flowed down to Alex's wrist, and when it connected, a burst of energy exploded through my body.

The woman's eyes fluttered open, and she lifted her chin to meet my gaze. The edges of her lips curled into a bright smile.

"I am awake," she said, her melodic tone echoing around me, familiar as if I had known her for eons. "It is time." The sparkles embedded in her flesh brightened, and a green hue flowed just above her skin.

Together we turned to face the surprised crowd. They parted as we walked toward them. Once we were out in the sunshine, a force lifted us into the sky and through Malcolm's barrier. The northerners and anamans waited as if they knew something was about to take place, or perhaps they really believed they would once again capture those who had escaped.

Our light detonated as one, weaving in and out of each other as it flowed like an avalanche across the land. The ships were pushed from our energy, and both anaman ships struck the earth with so much force, the ground rippled outward in every direction, spewing dirt, rocks, and vegetation into the air and across the terrain. The northerners' ship somersaulted through the air and exploded in a ball of fire against one of the anaman vessels.

Transformed Chaos

As the shift of the earth continued, our light spread as if a wildfire had overtaken the world. It grew so bright, I had to turn away from it and focus on the three before me.

I knew what was happening. The thoughts came to me as if they were my own. This would cleanse the control over Mother Gaia. Her wait was over. I sensed her ascension, and only those who chose the path of oneness and unity would remain. Tyranny, greed, and corrupt rule over these lands would be eliminated today.

The bright light, just like the one from the cave, folded over us like a warm blanket, and Mother Gaia's voice encircled us.

Fire.

Zoe Dawn's face brightened at the sound of the word, and her flames rippled as she straightened her posture.

Your free spirit and love of adventure called to me from a young age, and your wild heart was the only one of the flames who was raised by pure love. I placed your mum in your path to lead you to this moment, a spark to awaken the world's inhabitants to the next step in evolution.

Air. Your compassion is wide and fierce. You are loyal, challenging, and a breath of fresh air to all those who are welcomed into your circle of trust. I brought your mother here to fulfill one mission, and that was to bring you into this world. All the heartache you endured at her hands was a pathway to the divine. You have broken that glass ceiling she built above you.

A smile burst across my face. Everything I had faced had made me better, leading me to this amazing moment right here. My heartache had disappeared. *Mama, I forgive you.*

Water.

Alex's grip tightened around my hand. She reached for our new sister, the earth elemental. Their fingers intertwined.

Just like Tallisa, I knew you would join us here. Your connection to the Theian magic and the strength of the anamans was always meant to be, and so was your journey to your new home. The pull to us was no mistake, a destiny written in the stars.

The earth elemental closed her eyes.

We are one. Her melodic voice carried with Mother Gaia's. *And we are separate. The earth spirits have awakened, and we will continue to connect until the ascension is complete.*

She reached for Zoe Dawn, and when their hands touched, another wave of light flashed outward. I melted into the energy as I sensed it flow downward to the core of the earth and out to the other side. It was healing the land from the inside out and expunging those who could not move on. We were really leaving them behind and for the first time in my life, I was at peace.

I closed my eyes, released every emotion and pain that remained heavy within my heart, and allowed all that I truly was to pour into the celestial body.

My eyes fluttered open. The stars twinkled above, and a soft haze of lavender and blue flowed between their lights. I stretched my arms above my head and yawned. What a wild dream.

I rolled to my side and nearly jumped out of my skin. It had not been a dream. I crawled to my hands and knees. Alex and Zoe Dawn were lying on the dirt next to me. I shook Alex, then leaned over to Zoe Dawn and did the same.

"Zoe Dawn, wake up," I whispered loudly as I searched for a familiar landmark. Nothing looked recognizable. The trees and vegetation crackled and snapped beside me as if they were growing right before my eyes. I followed the roots of one tree as it reached across the earth, then its branches stretched toward the sky. I fell back on my knees in astonishment. "Woah! Alex, come on. Wake up, you two. You will not believe your eyes."

Zoe Dawn murmured in her sleep and then rolled to her side and snored.

Alex stared up at me, a confused expression sliding down her face. "What happened?" she asked, scooting to her knees and pressing her palms into her temples.

I shook my head. "No clue." I blinked several times, sorting through the fuzzy memory of the earth elemental. She had really been with us. "Wait. Did we—" I stopped talking and scratched my head as I squinted into the darkness, searching for the rest of our people.

"Did we what?" Zoe Dawn rolled to her stomach and pressed up to her hands and knees. "Did we save the world?"

"Um, yes?" My memories were blurry, but I remember the euphoria. It was still swirling in my stomach.

A light flickered against the nearby tree branches.

"I think they are over here!" Dax shouted.

Alex whirled around as thundering footsteps neared us. Dax burst through the bushes and skidded to a halt in front of us. His gaze landed on Alex just as she raced into his arms. Papa, Adina, Henry, Rafael, and Covyn rushed through next, nearly barreling right into the hugging couple.

"Kia Lynn!" Rafael shouted, folding me into a bone-crushing embrace. "Did you see what you did? Did you see how brilliant you were?" He was trying to wipe away tears from his cheeks as he squeezed me tighter.

"Air," I said through a gasp, pushing his arms away from my sides. "I need air. Still human, Rafael."

He burst into laughter and picked me up into his arms, then twirled us around in circles. When he set me down, Papa pulled me in close and planted a kiss on my forehead.

"I am so proud, my love," he whispered in my ear.

I laughed and burst into tears at the same time. We had left Mama behind. I no longer sensed her presence like I had before the ascension. So many had not made it, but their absence brought a wave of peace. We all had a journey, and theirs was to remain in a place that would serve them best.

Papa squeezed me tightly one more time. He pointed at one of the anaman ships. "I suspect there are few who joined us."

"They have to have been left behind," Covyn said to Zoe Dawn. They stood forehead to forehead, while Covyn tried to smooth down Zoe Dawn's wild curls. "Their ships crashed, and once we could climb out of Zion, it looked impossible to escape their ruins. We won. You literally beat the entire anaman fleet."

Adina's arms wrapped protectively around Alex and Dax. Henry had not said a word but stood in the middle of everyone, smiling like a buffoon. He glanced my way.

"Better yet." Henry took my hand. "You have to come see this to understand our meaning. We are no longer in Kansas, my friends."

My brows ruffled with confusion, but Alex laughed as if it were an inside joke.

"Come on." Alex waved for the rest to follow. "Let's go see."

I took Rafael's hand, who took Zoe Dawn's, and one by one, we filed out of the thickening forest of trees. They were really growing right before our eyes.

When we reached an opening from the tree canopy, I noticed the peaks of Zion just up ahead, but green vegetation now covered even the red rocks. The earth elemental was finishing her job. She was completing the rise to our next step in evolution. I lifted Rafael's arm and pointed at it with a nod of my head.

He glanced down at the lines in his skin. They were illuminating against the starlight, and when we looked at everyone else, they were all glowing as well. Henry pointed at the sky, and I turned to look. The moon was bright above us, but just behind it was another, much larger, celestial body. Farther out were several more, glowing from the light of our new sun.

"We have moved," I whispered as Rafael folded me in

his arms. I felt drunk with happiness. "We really did it. How is this even possible?"

Alex bounced on her toes and pointed to the side. "Mom, our ships! They are here with us."

I turned to follow where she was pointing. There were several ships entering the atmosphere and landing nearby. Adina's hands covered her mouth, and several tears ran down her cheeks, creating rivulets through the dust and ash. Alex threw her arms around her mom's shoulders and squeezed her close.

"Dad would be so proud," Adina said, kissing Alex on the cheek and then glancing at me and Zoe Dawn. "He is with your mum, Zoe Dawn. They are both shining up there for all of you and beaming with pride. Our world has transcended because of you."

Shouts filled the night sky and several lights shone from the valley below where the anaman ships had settled into the earth. There were hundreds of anamans waving their hands at us, trekking through the growing vegetation as it overtook the terrain. They had actually survived.

Zoe Dawn bounced on her toes and pointed at them. "They did make it." She glanced back at me.

All those people had finally found a new home, and it was away from the rule of their tyrannical leaders. I hoped Wolf and Trinity were still alive. If anyone deserved a new start, it was those two.

I held out my arms and twirled in a circle, taking in every detail, even as it transformed. It really was an entirely different world. Mother Gaia had shifted into a higher state of being, and she had brought us with Her. Our mission had been accomplished, and we were well on our way to creating heaven on Earth.

EPILOGUE

ZOE DAWN

Tiordan and Malcolm waited outside on the landing pad, while I stood just inside the doors. When they told me Zeke had contacted them, I had been wanting nothing more than to see my friends again. But now that the time was drawing near, I was not sure I wanted them to interrupt my content new life.

Alex squeezed my hand. She had expressed the same thoughts earlier.

We had made Zion our home. A few smaller buildings were being constructed to house our people. It seemed pointless to live away from one another while we continued to feed our love into our planet. Once we had assimilated to our new world, we had traveled across the globe, assisting those who had taken this journey with us. Witnessing other's desire to create a better world was by far the best part of this entire voyage.

Zeke's ship lowered onto the landing pad and my pulse

beat faster in anticipation of seeing him again. Moments later, the door opened and Koleton poked his head out, followed by Zeke and Esta.

As soon as I saw them, I dropped Alex's hand and raced through the doors. I flew into Zeke's embrace and pressed my face against his chest, inhaling his sweet cinnamon scent.

"I missed you too," he whispered, running his fingers down my hair. He leaned back and tilted his head slightly. "You sure know how to put on a show." His gaze drifted over my shoulder. "All of you. That was like nothing I had seen before."

I moved to the side and glanced at Kia Lynn and Alex. We understood our powers and our role as the protectors of Mother Gaia.

"Our mother protects Theia and her moons, so we understand the demands on your time and energy," Esta said as if she were reading my mind.

I scrunched up my nose. I did not like that she could read me so easily.

"Relax." She patted my shoulder as she strolled by. "Mother Gaia has found her guardians, just like Theia has hers. All is in its proper order, once again."

Alex smiled as she approached the blonde woman. "It is good to see you again, Esta."

Transformed Chaos

Esta grabbed Alex's hand and pulled her along beside her. "We were always meant to be in this moment with you, Alex. You have my gratitude for all that you and your sisters have done."

Tiordan joined the two women as they strolled toward the gardens.

Koleton nudged me with his shoulder. "Don't mind the princess. She keeps her walls high and strong until she feels comfortable. Underneath all that high and mighty is a sweet young girl who used to ride on my shoulders and squeal with laughter."

I smiled at the thought. It was hard to envision Esta as young and innocent, but the woman obviously enamored Koleton.

I wrapped my arm around his waist. "I missed you, friend. I was a little hurt you abandoned me."

He patted my shoulder, and we followed the others, who had already left. "We knew you had it handled. It just took the final revelation of Tallisa's betrayal to shatter the resolve around Kia Lynn's tightly knit fantasy world. Yours and Alex's attachments were far easier to release then hers. She only needed a little shove forward, and Esta knew exactly how to make that happen."

"The painting of her mother." I nodded. It had been Esta's plan all along to have Kia Lynn see it. "But how did

Esta know that Kia Lynn was still in the dark about Tallisa's elemental gifts?" I pushed a tree branch out of my way and ducked underneath another.

"She has visions," he whispered, stopping beneath a large oak tree and turning to look at me. "She is also telepathic, but not here—only on Theia and her moons. The visions have plagued her mind our entire visit this time around, and she has barely slept a wink to avoid the more intense ones. They were invading her mind every time she closed her eyes." He folded his arms over his chest and glanced toward Esta, who was petting Chester.

That sweet horse. I smiled at my memory of my first encounter with the beautiful beast. It had been a disaster trying to mount him, but despite that, he had been my instant friend. My eyes narrowed when I noticed Chester's immense contentment at Esta's touch. *Traitor.*

"Will she have to return home?" I asked, returning my attention to Koleton.

He shook his head with a smile. "You aren't that lucky." He winked. "Ever since you moved the Earth across the stars, the visions have dissipated, and she has slept again. She needed this to happen, or else we would have had to leave Earth for good."

I glanced her way again. I did not really want her to go, and I definitely had no desire to see Koleton and Zeke leave. "Is that why you are here?" I asked, watching the blonde woman as if I was seeing her for the first time. Her obsidian eyes glistened with joy.

"She is grateful, and yes, this is her way of thanking you." He drew in a long breath and held out his hand for me to take. "By the time we leave, you will love her just like I do."

I turned to face Koleton and grabbed his arm. "Why didn't you just tell us what needed to be done? Why the secrecy? I really could have done without the disappearing act."

He snorted and laughed at the same time. "That was a necessary evil. And I personally"—he pointed at his chest—" did not want to miss out on the moment you three figured it out on your own. But if we had stayed, it would have taken you much longer and your strength would be far less than it is today. You never help a butterfly break out of its cocoon."

I raised my brows in question.

"Same goes with people." He ran his fingers through his beard, and he winked at me. "If we had given you the answers and did all the heavy lifting, do you really think the result would be the same?"

My teeth grazed over my bottom lip and I ran my fingers over my kenaz rune, thinking back at all that occurred over a short period. As much as I did not want to admit it, he was right. The Earth's transcendence needed its guardians to pave the way, not the strangers from another world. Their guidance had been enough.

"Point taken." I clicked my tongue as my gaze swept over the crowd of my family and friends, pausing again at the blonde woman and horse. Chester nuzzled against Esta's neck, and her burst of laughter echoed against the red mountains. "I think Esta will grow on me. Chester loves her already, which has to mean something."

Zeke glanced our way and a knowing smile brushed across his lips as if he sensed what we had been discussing. He adored his sister, for far more reasons than I would ever understand. She had known they would have to move their buildings, which was why she made sure we were all outside. Her visions had told her that Kia Lynn had to release her grievances, even if it meant her heart would shatter first, and Esta had known Alex belonged here, and only here, long before the others realized.

I was not angry anymore. My fury had remained with the old Earth, and now as I stared at Esta, I realized I owed it to the Theian woman who had guided us to our ultimate steps of transformation. She lifted her gaze to meet mine. A knowing smile, similar to Zeke's, twitched on her lips. They were a team, a force to be reckoned with, and now I could call them my allies.

Want to understand the connection between Earth and the Theians?

Download the Theia's Moons series today.

Theia's Moons Series

Perfect for fans of The 100 and The Divergent Series. This Epic Fantasy series begins with one woman's haunted dreams of a forgotten past, which then spirals into a gripping story of courage, perseverance, and unconditional love.

A broken past. And a propaganda so dark, it could shatter a person's soul.

Years after the sky people's destruction upon the Esaki moon, Malkia's people are now facing a new threat and mysterious enemy. Except this time the savages are gliding toward them by land, with strength, speed, and powers unknown to them, creating a mayhem of panic among her friends and family.

Deciding to abandon their home, Malkia and her people travel across their deserted world, racing away from the barbarians. They collide with the mystical creatures from ancient tales, dance along the path of uncertain death, and receive a startling reminder that they were never alone in the universe.

ACKNOWLEDGMENTS

This was by far my most exhaustive write. Between the world affairs, my busy job, and trying to live a normal life within a pandemic, not to mention the fast-approaching holidays, I was in a bit of a state. But here we are. I made it and I am delighted to finally share the end of this story with all my readers. Thank you for showing up for me, being a part of my journey, and supporting me to the best of your abilities. I cannot express how grateful I am to have you all in my life.

Thank you to my patient and brilliant editor, Angie Wade from Novel Nurse Editing. She was an angel through all my frustrations, and I appreciate her perspective and guidance. Her witty humor and direct constructive criticism are the reasons this story flowed so well all the way to the end. She kept my head on straight and pushed me to rise back up to my potential.

To the super talented Lorraine from Niki Ellis's Book Cover, thank you for the perfect book cover to showcase the final story of this series. Even through all her grief and heartache from a year that changed her life, she continued to construct this book cover until it was complete. I appreciate all her hard work and dedication.

My family and close friends were my rocks this past

year. I am sure so many of you feel the same as I do. Without their love and support, this story would never have been completed. I owe my partner a big, fat kiss for his unwavering dedication to my goals and dreams. He is the mountain that holds me steady and I am grateful he chose me to be his best friend.

It was a rough year, but we have come so far. I am thankful to be here today so I can continue to bring my imagination to the world. Until next time, my friends, I am sending you all peace, love, laughter, and high vibes.

ABOUT THE AUTHOR

 International Bestselling Author Niki Livingston writes tales of fantasy worlds filled with magic, mysticism, and mystery.

When she's not busy writing enchanting stories of diverse women rising in their power and strength, she spends her time walking her rescue puppy, quieting her mind with meditation and yoga, diving into the newest books of Veronica Roth and Anne Bishop, and binge-watching Game of Thrones, The Mandalorian, and The 100.

For all her latest releases and updates, subscribe to Niki Livingston's newsletter!

www.NikiLivingston.com